Violent Crimes

ALSO BY PHILLIP MARGOLIN

Lost Lake
Sleeping Beauty
The Associate
The Undertaker's Widow
The Burning Man
After Dark
Gone, but Not Forgotten
The Last Innocent Man
Heartstone
Worthy Brown's Daughter

Amanda Jaffe Novels

Wild Justice
Ties That Bind
Proof Positive
Fugitive

Dana Cutler Novels

Executive Privilege
Supreme Justice
Capitol Murder
Sleight of Hand
Vanishing Acts (with Ami Margolin Rome)

Violent Crimes

An Amanda Jaffe Novel

Phillip Margolin

HARPER LUXE

An Imprint of HarperCollins*Publishers*

HarperCollins books may be purchased for educational, business, or sales promotional use. For information, please email the Special Markets Department at SPsales@harpercollins.com.

FIRST HARPERLUXE EDITION

ISBN: 978-0-06-241691-9

HarperLuxe™ is a trademark of HarperCollins Publishers.

Library of Congress Cataloging-in-Publication Data is available upon request.

16 17 18 19 20 ID / RRD 10 9 8 7 6 5 4 3 2 1

For Randee Gerson, who left us way too soon,
and Amanda Margolin, my new daughter-in-law

Violent Crimes

Chapter 1

Amanda Jaffe had no court appearances or client meetings scheduled for June 7, so she set aside the whole day to work on a brief that was due in the Oregon Court of Appeals, but something told her that she was going to have to put her plans on hold when she walked into the reception area of Jaffe, Katz, Lehane and Brindisi and saw Christine Larson sitting next to a worried-looking man she did not recognize.

Amanda was tall and athletic, with broad shoulders that were the end product of years of competitive swimming. She didn't have the slender figure of a magazine model, but her grace, high cheekbones, and clear blue eyes attracted male attention whenever she entered a room. Since Amanda had not expected to meet anyone professionally, her long black hair was tied in a ponytail and she was dressed in jeans and a T-shirt.

Christine presented a sharp contrast to Amanda. She was five four, slightly overweight, wore her dirty blond hair short, and was dressed in a severe black Armani suit and white silk blouse. Christine practiced business and tax law at Masterson, Hamilton, Rickman and Thomas, a large firm in Portland, Oregon, and her no-nonsense, analytical personality fit her specialty.

The man sitting next to Christine looked uncomfortable in the suit he was wearing, which most likely came off the rack. He was a shade under six feet, with muscular shoulders and a narrow waist, and he wore his brown hair in a military cut. He was clasping and unclasping his hands nervously, and Amanda noticed dark circles under his tired brown eyes.

Christine stood up when Amanda walked in.

"Hi," Amanda said. "Are you here to see me?"

"Yes. Do you have some time to meet with us?"

"Sure," Amanda answered with a smile.

Christine didn't return the smile, and Amanda could see that she was worried.

"Amanda, this is Tom Beatty. He's a paralegal at my firm."

The man stood up slowly. He seemed unsure of himself.

"Pleased to meet you," Amanda said as she held out her hand. Beatty paused for a moment, then shook it. His palm was sweaty and he withdrew his hand quickly.

"Hold my calls," Amanda told the receptionist as she led the way down the hall to a corner office with a view of the hills that towered over downtown Portland. The walls were decorated with her law school and college diplomas, certificates proving her admission to Oregon State and federal bars, two abstract paintings she'd purchased from an art gallery near her condo in the Pearl District, and a photograph of downtown Portland in the years just before World War I.

"So, what's up?" Amanda asked when they were seated and the door was closed.

"Tom was arrested last night on an assault charge stemming from a fight in a bar," Christine said. "I bailed him out this morning and suggested that he hire you to represent him."

Amanda turned her attention to Beatty. He was staring at the floor and looked embarrassed. Amanda decided that they needed to have privacy if she was going to gain his confidence.

"Tom," Amanda said, "I'm going to ask Christine to step outside while we talk."

"I'd rather have her here," Beatty said. He spoke so quietly that Amanda had to strain to hear him.

"I've known Christine since law school, and I trust her completely," Amanda assured Beatty, "but I have to protect your attorney-client privilege. Christine is a lawyer, but she's not representing you. If she's present when we talk, she could be subpoenaed by the DA and forced to tell a jury everything we say in private."

Christine stood up and touched Beatty on the shoulder.

"It's okay. I'd do the same thing if Amanda brought you to my office and asked me to represent you. Amanda is an ace—she'll take good care of you. I'll be in the waiting room."

Christine handed Amanda a copy of the complaint and left the room. Amanda studied it. Beatty was charged with causing a man named Harold Roux serious bodily harm by striking him with his fists and feet.

"Before we discuss the facts of your case, I want to go over the attorney-client privilege. Anything you tell me is confidential, with a few exceptions. That means I can't be compelled to reveal anything you tell me, even if you confessed to being a serial killer. It also means you can be completely honest with me without having to worry that I'll run to the DA the minute you leave.

"Now I need you to be honest with me because a lot of what I'll do for you will depend on the facts of the case, but you need to be aware that in addition to being your attorney I'm also an officer of the court and I'm bound by the ethics of my profession. So I can't condone perjury. If you're charged with bank robbery and you tell me you robbed the bank, I can't let you testify in court that you were in Idaho and don't know anything about the crime. I wouldn't tell on you, because we have the attorney-client privilege, but I would ask the judge to let me resign from your case and I *will* keep your retainer."

Beatty looked Amanda in the eye, and the look was intense. "I do not lie and I did not start this fight," he said forcefully.

"Okay. Why don't you tell me what happened."

"There's a bar, the Lookout. I go there sometimes to watch a game—I don't have a TV. I got to the tavern early, around five. The game had started already and it was the second inning. I got a beer just as the Yankees loaded the bases. There was one out and the Yankee batter hit into a double play. The guy on the stool next to me jumped up and jostled me and I spilled some beer on him. That's all there was to it. But he had to . . ."

Beatty's breathing accelerated, his face darkened, and his fists clenched.

"Are you okay?" Amanda asked.

"I shouldn't have done it. I should have walked away."

Her client was in so much distress that Amanda grew concerned.

"Do you want some water? Should I have Christine come back?"

Beatty squeezed his eyes together and took some deep breaths. His shoulders sagged as he put his head in his hands.

"I'm sorry," he whispered.

"It's okay. You're under a lot of stress. I'm going to get you some water. That will give you a minute to pull yourself together."

Amanda left her office and walked into the reception area. Christine stood up.

"Your friend just had a meltdown in my office. What gives?"

"Oh, shit," Christine muttered to herself, then said to Amanda, "Tom's got a background."

"What kind of background?'

"He was in the military in combat. He won't say what he did but I think it was bad. I'm guessing Delta Force, Navy Seal stuff. He's seeing a psychiatrist at the VA for post-traumatic stress disorder. I know that makes him sound dangerous but he's really a decent person. And he's a hard worker, very conscientious. When he got back to the States he put himself through community college and learned to be a paralegal. And he's good. In fact, he's probably brighter than half the attorneys in my firm. I've suggested that he go to law school but he doesn't want to do it. He says it would be too stressful."

"What do you think happened in the bar?"

"I think someone who had no idea what they were getting into picked on Tom. I can't imagine he'd start a fight but someone with his training . . . He might have reacted on reflex."

"Okay. I'm going back in, but you wait. I'll probably want to talk to you after I'm done."

Amanda went to the break room and filled a tall glass with cold water. When she reentered her office Beatty seemed calmer.

"I'm sorry," he said when she handed him the glass.

"No need to apologize. People who have been charged with a crime are under a lot of pressure, especially if they're not guilty. Now, why don't you take a drink of that water, then take a deep breath and tell me what happened at the Lookout."

Chapter 2

Tom Beatty didn't say a word during the walk from Amanda's office, and Christine didn't break the silence until they were ready to pass through the revolving doors that opened into the lobby of the forty-story, glass and steel building that housed the Masterson, Hamilton law offices.

"Look, I know you probably don't want to do this, Tom, but I think we should tell Dale Masterson you were arrested."

Beatty tensed, and Christine laid a comforting hand on his forearm.

"Amanda is going to have her investigator talk to the witnesses at the bar. If they back up your version of the facts, she thinks she'll have a good chance of getting the DA to drop the case. In the worst-case scenario, she thinks she'll have an excellent chance of winning at trial on a theory of self-defense. I'll tell Dale what Amanda said."

Beatty looked sick. "I really need this job, Christine. I feel very comfortable here."

"If you hide the arrest and someone finds out it will look bad. You know the old saw about honesty being the best policy? I think you'll be much better off if we tell Dale what happened."

Fifteen minutes later, Christine and Tom were ushered into Dale Masterson's large corner office, where floor-to-ceiling windows gave them a view of the river and the snow-covered slopes of Mount Hood. The firm's founding partner was tall and patrician-looking, with a Roman nose, clear blue eyes, and styled gray hair.

"What's up?" he asked Christine when she and Tom were seated in the client chairs across from his desk. Christine sat up straight, looking confident and poised. Tom's shoulders hunched and he looked down at the desktop.

"Tom was arrested last night," Christine said.

Masterson frowned.

"I brought him to see Amanda Jaffe this morning," Christine added quickly. "We just came from her office. Tom was watching a ball game in a neighborhood bar when one of the patrons started a fight with him.

Amanda told me that there is a good chance the DA won't bring charges if witnesses support Tom's version of what happened. But he thought you should know about the arrest."

Masterson nodded. "I'm glad you told me, Tom. I can see you're worried, but you needn't be. I'm not going to do a thing until your case is resolved."

Masterson smiled. "The first thing they drummed into our heads in Criminal Procedure was the rule that every citizen who is arrested for a crime is presumed innocent. I'd be a pretty poor lawyer if I prejudged your case. So don't worry."

Tom exhaled and sat up straight. "Thank you, sir. I really appreciate this. My job means a lot to me."

"Christine has had very good things to say about how you're doing. Take care of this matter and fill me in when the case is over."

"Thank you, sir," Tom said again as he and Christine stood up.

"Christine, stay a minute. I have something I want you to do."

Christine sat down as Tom left. When the door closed behind him, Masterson focused on his junior partner.

"What I'm going to tell you is extremely confidential. We can't afford to let one word leak about it."

"I understand," Christine said, suddenly nervous.

"Global Mining is dissatisfied with its legal representation. A few weeks ago, we were approached by a representative of the company, and we are currently involved in secret discussions with them."

Masterson paused to give Christine a moment to take in what he had just said. Global Mining was one of the largest coal mining enterprises in America, and the firm would earn millions in legal fees if it became the corporation's legal representative.

"You are aware that we had a rough go of it a few years back when the recession hit, and Francis and Striker decided to drop our firm and go with in-house counsel?" Masterson continued.

Christine nodded. The high-tech company had been one of the firm's largest clients, and Masterson, Hamilton had lost a large chunk of revenue when Francis and Striker walked away after a dispute over legal fees.

"Global has heard rumors about our financial situation, and these concerns are the only thing standing in the way of their hiring our firm. We've had an independent auditor go over our books and he's written a report that accurately states our financial position. I'd like you to review the report and present the findings when we meet with Global's people in a few weeks."

"I appreciate your confidence, but why do you want me to give the report? Surely you or Mr. Hamilton could do that."

Masterson smiled. "I'm glad you think so, but Mark and I are litigators and negotiators. We don't have your knowledge of tax and financial matters."

Christine sat up straighter. She was being let in on a major negotiation, and she knew that carrying out her task to the firm's benefit would advance her career.

"Thanks for having confidence in me," she said.

"You've earned our confidence. I'll have the auditor's report and anything else you need sent over to you. Oh, and you were right to bring Beatty to me. He's got great legal counsel in Jaffe, and I'm sure she'll ease him through his problems."

Chapter 3

As soon as Amanda had seen Christine and Tom Beatty out, she walked down the hall toward the office of Kate Ross, the firm's in-house investigator. As she walked, she thought about what Tom Beatty was going through. Amanda was no stranger to post-traumatic stress disorder. Several years ago, she had been taken prisoner by "The Surgeon," a serial killer. Amanda had escaped unharmed physically, but the trauma had left psychic scars. PTSD was terrible and crippling. For the most part, Amanda was okay now, but what she had endured at the hands of The Surgeon had lasted only a few minutes. She could not imagine what it would be like to face the horrors of war, over and over.

Kate Ross was five seven, and her dark complexion, large brown eyes, and curly black hair made her look vaguely Middle Eastern. Today, she was wearing tight jeans, a man-tailored white shirt, and a navy blue blazer. Kate had been a Portland cop before she had gone to work as a private investigator for Reed, Briggs, Stephens, Stottlemeyer and Compton, Portland's largest law firm. While at Reed, Briggs, Kate had asked Amanda to represent Daniel Ames, a young associate at the firm who was charged with murder. After Kate and Amanda cleared Daniel's name, Kate and Daniel had become lovers and had joined Amanda's firm.

"We have a new client," Amanda said as she took a seat.

"What's the case?"

"A simple assault. Our guy goes into a bar . . ."

"This sounds like an old joke."

"That's a rabbi, a priest, and a Buddhist monk. And get serious."

Kate held up her hands. "My bad. Continue, Bwana."

"Tom Beatty—our client—was seated on a stool watching a baseball game at the Lookout . . ."

"I know where that is."

"I figured you might. Anyway, Tom says that everyone was jammed together. There was a big play. Harold Roux, who was seated next to our client, jumped up and threw out his arms, knocking over Tom's beer.

Roux got sopping wet and blamed our client. Tom apologized, but that wasn't enough for Mr. Roux and he threw a punch."

"So our guy is saying it was self-defense?"

Amanda nodded. "But we may have a problem. Our client was a Navy Seal and he saw combat in Afghanistan and Iraq. He won't talk about what he did but I have the impression it was heavy-duty stuff. The problem for Harold Roux is that Mr. Beatty knows how to defend himself and, he grudgingly admitted, he's very good at it."

"What happened to Roux?"

"He's in the hospital."

"Whoa."

"Yeah, whoa."

"How bad are the injuries?" Kate asked.

"That's for you to find out. Get the police reports and go to the Lookout and see if you can find someone who saw the fight."

The Lookout was an old neighborhood hangout on the far corner of a three-block strip of quaint, trendy boutiques, art galleries, and restaurants running through a middle-class residential neighborhood in Southeast Portland. Kate walked into the dark interior at four, when she figured the bar would be less crowded.

A trio of young men were sipping beers and eating burgers at a table. Near the back, a young couple snuggled in a booth, laughing and talking in the low tones used by new lovers. Two locals sat at the bar, eyes glued to a baseball game that was showing on a TV that hung from the ceiling.

The bartender was fortyish, bald, and potbellied. He was mopping up a spill at the end of the bar near the door when Kate sat down in front of him.

"What can I get you?" he asked.

"A Black Butte Porter would be nice," Kate said.

When the bartender returned with an ice-cold bottle and a glass, Kate flashed her credentials.

"My name is Kate Ross and I'm an investigator."

The bartender smiled. "I thought you guys couldn't drink on duty."

Kate smiled back. "That's cops. I'm private, Mr. . . ."

"Bob—Bob Reynolds. So what can I do for you?"

"I'm working for the attorney who's representing Tom Beatty. He was involved in a fight here last night."

"They charged him?"

"You sound surprised."

"Well, yeah. That asshole Harold Roux started it, and he threw the first punch."

"So you saw the whole thing?"

"Most of it, and I'm not likely to forget it."

"Why is that?"

"Outside of one of those kung fu movies, I never saw anything like it." The bartender shook his head. "Tom's been in here a couple of times. He keeps to himself, watches the game, then leaves. Never causes any trouble. So I didn't figure him for a guy who could fight like that."

"Can you walk me through the fight from the beginning?"

"Harold and Tom were next to each other on stools at the bar."

"What's Harold like?"

"He's a loudmouth, one of those guys who peaked in high school. I think he was an all-district lineman or something because he knows *everything* about football, if you know what I mean."

Kate nodded. "If he played on the line, he must be much bigger than Tom."

"Oh, yeah, but the weight's mostly fat."

"What does he do for a living?"

"He delivers beer to supermarkets, drives a truck."

"Okay, so what happened?" Kate asked.

"I was at one end of the bar when I heard Harold yell. He sounded angry, so I turned around. Harold stepped back from the bar and glared at Tom while he wiped beer off his shirt. I walked over because I know Harold and I thought there might be trouble.

"Anyway, everyone backs away and Tom tells Harold he's sorry. Harold said, 'Sorry won't cut it,' so Tom offered to buy him a beer. Harold says, 'What about my shirt? You gonna buy me a new one?' Tom just stared at him. I could see his face close up. When Tom didn't answer, Harold said something like, 'Well, asshole? I'm talking to you,' and when Tom still didn't say anything Harold hauled off and started to throw this big roundhouse punch. A second later he's flat on his back, screaming. His nose was broke but Tom did something to his leg too, only it was so fast I couldn't be sure what he did."

"You're certain Harold was the aggressor and threw the first punch?"

"Definitely!"

"Would you be willing to sign an affidavit that sets out what you just told me?" Kate asked.

"They arrested Tom?"

Kate nodded. "He spent the night in jail."

"That's ridiculous. I'll definitely sign an affidavit. And the beer is on me."

Chapter 4

The Veterans Administration hospital was located off Southwest Terwilliger Boulevard high up on one of the hills that overlooked downtown Portland. A week after taking on Tom Beatty's case Amanda Jaffe entered the office of Dr. Martin Fisher armed with a waiver signed by her client that authorized the psychiatrist to talk openly with Amanda about Tom Beatty's medical problems.

Dr. Fisher was a tall, angular African-American with high cheekbones, a wide forehead, and dark brown eyes that appraised Amanda through thick tortoiseshell glasses. His office was typical government issue: a gray, gunmetal filing cabinet, cheap wooden bookshelves stuffed with medical tomes, and an old scarred desk that had probably been doing duty since World War II. The dull green walls were decorated with university and medical school diplomas as well as photographs of the doctor in uniform nestled among other soldiers in some tropical setting. From the doctor's salt–and–pepper hair, Amanda guessed the photo might have been taken in Vietnam.

"Thanks for seeing me, Dr. Fisher," Amanda said. "I'm representing Tom Beatty, one of your patients. He's been charged with assault growing out of a bar fight. My investigator interviewed several witnesses and they all say that Mr. Beatty did not start the fight and was defending himself against a man named Harold Roux, who is much bigger than Tom."

"Then why do you need to talk to me?" Dr. Fisher asked.

"Roux is in the hospital with some pretty bad injuries. I'm afraid that the district attorney may take the position that regardless of who started the fight, Tom used way more force than was necessary under the circumstances. Tom says you've been treating him for post-traumatic stress disorder, and I thought it might have some bearing on the way he reacted."

"It might," Dr. Fisher said.

"Can you tell me about Tom's military service and how he developed PTSD?"

"I can tell you that he was a Navy Seal, but I'm not authorized to tell you the details of Tom's missions even with a release, except to say that he was involved in serious combat operations."

"Okay, I'll accept that. But he has developed PTSD as a result of his military service?"

"Yes."

"Under Oregon law a person acting in self-defense can use a degree of force he reasonably believes is necessary for the purpose," Amanda said. "Roux's knee was shattered, his nose was broken, and his shoulder was dislocated in a matter of seconds. I need to know if you think Tom's response was overkill or the reasonable use of force, given the circumstances, Tom's training, and his PTSD."

"Tell me the facts surrounding the fight."

Dr. Fisher listened closely while Amanda laid out the story that Kate Ross had pieced together. When she was finished, he stared into space for a while. Then he refocused on the attorney.

"Roux is much bigger than Tom?" he asked.

"He's several inches taller and outweighs him by fifty pounds or more."

"And they were in very close quarters?"

"Yes. Could his condition have influenced the way he reacted to Roux's provocation?"

"That's a definite possibility," Dr. Fisher said. "People suffering from PTSD can be more irritable and impulsive than someone without the problem. It would be reasonable to assume that Tom might not take as long to think about how to react to a punch as a person without PTSD. Then you factor in that Tom was not just in the military—he was in an elite fighting unit. This could have a bearing."

"How so?" Amanda asked.

"Elite forces like the Navy Seals, Green Berets, and Delta Force work mostly in secret and they are front-line troops sent time and again into the most danger-ous and violent sections of war zones. Elite forces are trained to take care of problems with overwhelming force. In combat, you kill. There is no mercy because, in addition to defending yourself, you have to look out for the people in your unit and eliminate any threats to your comrades. From what you've told me, Tom kept striking Roux until he was convinced that no threat existed. This would fit with his training. Civilians who are not used to being in fights would be hesitant to strike someone, and loath to hurt someone they've struck. Tom would have none of those restraints. Given his background and the circumstances of the attack, I would say that it was entirely reasonable for someone with Tom's condition and training to act as he did."

Chapter 5

The Multnomah County Courthouse is a brutish, eight-story gray concrete building that takes up the entire block between Fourth and Fifth and Main and Salmon in the heart of downtown Portland. When Amanda stepped out of the elevator on the sixth floor, she almost ran into Mike Greene. Amanda and Mike had been dating steadily for a year, and they flashed wide smiles the minute they saw each other.

Mike had curly black hair, pale blue eyes, and a shaggy mustache. People always assumed that he had played football or basketball because of his massive, six-five body, but Mike, who didn't even watch sports on TV, was a jazz musician and an expert-rated chess player.

"What are you doing in my domain?" the chief criminal deputy of the Multnomah County District Attorney's Office asked.

"I'm here to try to convince Larry Frederick to dismiss a case," Amanda answered.

"If your client is innocent, I'll instruct Larry to resist your entreaties," Mike answered sternly. "Anyone can convict the guilty. Convicting the innocent presents a challenge."

"Have I ever told you that you are a fascist pig?"

"Frequently."

"What are you up to?" Amanda asked.

"A short appearance in Judge Embry's court. I should be finished in a half hour if you're up for coffee."

"I can't. I'm interviewing a new client at the office. But you can take me out for sushi tonight."

"Deal. I'll pick you up at your office around five," Mike said before heading to Judge Embry's courtroom.

Larry Frederick was a mild-mannered Georgetown Law grad, whose wire-rimmed glasses were always slipping down his nose and who constantly brushed back the long brown locks that fell across his brow. Amanda got the impression that Frederick wore his hair long not for style but because he forgot to get it cut. The deputy DA took an intellectual approach to his cases, and Amanda appreciated Frederick's reasonable attitude. She could not say the same for Detective Alan Hotchkiss, a stocky ex-wrestler who dealt with defendants in the same overly aggressive way he'd dealt with his opponents when he'd been racking up pins for Oregon State.

"What have you got for me?" Frederick asked with an easy smile once Amanda had seated herself across from him. Amanda could see a section of the West Hills through the window behind the DA. The fact that Frederick's office had a view was a tip-off that he was a senior deputy.

"It's Tom Beatty's assault case. My investigator has interviewed four witnesses to the fight, and they all say that the complainant started it and threw the first punch."

"Did they also tell you that Beatty broke the victim's nose, dislocated his shoulder, and smashed up his knee so bad he needs surgery?" Detective Hotchkiss said.

Frederick held up his hand to silence the detective. "This wasn't your average barroom brawl, Amanda. Mr. Roux is in terrible shape. When Alan talked to him at the hospital, he was in a lot of pain."

"I feel sorry for Mr. Roux and so does Mr. Beatty, but Mr. Roux is much bigger than my client and he was the aggressor."

Amanda handed Frederick a stack of investigative reports. "Every witness says that Mr. Roux is a bully. This isn't the first time he's picked on someone smaller. What he didn't know is that Tom is a hero, a decorated Navy Seal. He can't tell me about his missions except to say he was in Iraq and Afghanistan, but he did say that he's skilled at hand-to-hand combat. When Roux started the fight, Tom got scared, and he acted on reflex."

"If he's so good why couldn't he just deflect the punches?" Hotchkiss asked. "There's defending yourself and there's beating the piss out of someone. He could have killed Roux."

"You're right, Alan," Amanda agreed. "Tom could have killed Roux easily, but he didn't. Tom feels terrible about Roux's injuries, but Roux is so much bigger Tom couldn't take a chance. He told me he had no idea how good a fighter Roux was and the fact that Roux was so aggressive made him keep fighting until he felt safe."

"I hope you're not buying this John Wayne crap, Larry," the detective said.

"I'm not going to form any opinion until I've read these reports and you do a follow-up," the DA answered. "Then I'll get back to you, Amanda, okay?"

"Sure. And why don't you hold off on an indictment."

"Don't worry. I won't go to a grand jury unless I'm convinced your client wasn't acting in self-defense."

Chapter 6

Something was definitely wrong. The figures didn't make sense. Take Dale Masterson's income. In order to meet the conditions of bank loans that had helped Masterson, Hamilton weather the recession, the partners had agreed to take less when income was distributed, and the auditor reported that Dale's draw was substantially lower than it had been. But Dale's credit card statements had been included in the mounds of material she'd been given, and Christine had noticed that Masterson was spending a lot more money than he was being paid by the firm.

And the taxes. She'd asked for the firm's books but Masterson kept putting her off, so she'd pulled the actual invoices from cases to see how much the firm made. The taxes the firm were paying were far in excess of what they should have been paying. Why would that be? One explanation that had occurred to Christine was that the income in the books that had been shown to the auditor was inflated to make the firm's financial situation look healthier than it really was; the reported income would require the firm to pay more taxes than it should have been paying. Christine had rejected that explanation early on, but now she was beginning to wonder if it might be true.

Christine wanted to ask Mark Hamilton or Dale Masterson about these and other discrepancies, but they had been meeting with the Global representatives at an undisclosed location and had been out of the office for two days, with no indication of when they would return. She looked at her phone. It was seven thirty. She blinked. She had been so wrapped up in the dilemma posed by the firm's figures that she'd lost all track of time.

When Christine stood up and stretched, she noticed that the normal hum of conversation and machinery had disappeared from the office. She walked into the hall. Somewhere in the distance she heard voices, but most of the floor was silent. Dale Masterson's office was at the end of the hall. She turned toward it. A member of the cleaning crew was vacuuming the floor after having emptied the trash can. An idea occurred to her. A few months back, Dale had needed some information from his computer during a negotiation and had given her his password so she could locate an e-mail that was essential to settling a term in a contract. She remembered the password, which would give her access to Masterson's computer and, she hoped, the answers to some or all of her questions. But that would mean intruding on the privacy of one of the firm's senior partners without his permission. If Masterson found out . . . Well, she didn't want to think of what would happen to her.

Christine went back to her desk and stared at the figures again. The auditor had found nothing wrong. All Dale had asked her to do was explain the condition of the firm as set forth in the auditor's report. The auditor didn't have any doubts about the firm's financial position, so why should she? The easy thing to do would be to go with the flow, but her conscience wouldn't let her tell the people at Global that everything was just great when her gut told her that it wasn't.

Christine went into the hall again. The voices she'd heard earlier had gone quiet and she saw two associates heading for the elevators. She looked around and listened. Nothing. She was alone. She looked at Dale's office again. She knew she shouldn't, but she had to. Christine headed down the hall. She hesitated at the entrance to Masterson's office, then took a deep breath, walked behind his desk, and sat down in front of Masterson's computer. She booted it up, then paused, her fingers floating above the keyboard. One more deep breath and she was typing in Dale's password. Moments later, she was in.

The first thing she did was try to locate the books, but they weren't in any file she could find. Maybe, she thought, they were forwarded to Masterson in an attachment to an e-mail. She logged on to Masterson's e-mail account and thought for a moment. Then she typed in "Kenneth Jennings," the name of the auditor. A large number of e-mails came up. Some were from Jennings, some were to Jennings, and one of the more recent e-mails was from Mark Hamilton to Dale Masterson concerning Jennings. Christine read it, and grew light-headed.

"Jennings taken care of," it said. "He's playing along—the report will provide smooth sailing and everything is going as planned."

Christine leaned back and squeezed her eyes shut. She felt like she might throw up. When she had regained her composure she reread the e-mail and tried to put a different spin on it, but there was no interpretation she could think of that would do that.

Christine went through the other e-mails that mentioned Jennings but found no more incriminating texts.

She turned off the computer and the lights in Masterson's office. She walked back to her office in a daze. She loved her job and she was definitely on track to move up in the firm, but she had evidence that her bosses were committing fraud. If she exposed the fraud, her career would be destroyed. If she didn't, she would be abetting a crime. Christine slumped in her seat and put her head in her hands. An hour later, after she had pored over the records again, she turned off the lights and went home, with no idea of what she should do.

Chapter 7

Amanda had been having a terrible week. On Monday, July 7, she'd lost a motion to suppress that she thought she was going to win. On Tuesday, the Court of Appeals had affirmed the conviction of another client. An old superstition held that things happened in threes, so she feared the worst when Larry Frederick called her on Wednesday morning.

"What's up, Larry?" Amanda asked.

"I've got an early Christmas present for you," the DA said. "I'm not prosecuting Tom Beatty."

"Thank you," Amanda said after exhaling with relief.

"I'm just doing what I think is right. Alan disagrees with my decision, but after talking to the bartender and the other witnesses to the fight, I'm convinced

Mr. Beatty acted in self-defense. Considering the sacrifices your client has made for his country, I'm relieved that I won't have to go after him."

A few minutes later, Amanda hung up and smiled. Her original motivations for practicing criminal defense had not been philosophical. Her mother had died giving birth to Amanda and she had been raised by her father, Frank Jaffe, and one of Oregon's leading defense attorneys. As soon as Amanda was old enough to understand what her father did for a living, she wanted to follow in his footsteps. In junior high, Amanda's girlfriends fantasized about boys and shopping while Amanda read legal thrillers, watched *Perry Mason* reruns, and daydreamed about trying murder cases.

When Amanda was old enough to understand that Frank's clients were usually guilty, she had asked him why he was so passionate about his job. Frank had explained that making sure that the American System of Justice was working the way it was supposed to was more important than any particular case. Frank believed that giving the worst defendants a fair trial assured others that they would be treated fairly if they were ever arrested for a crime. When people lost faith in their government, the result was revolution. He also told Amanda that she would represent innocent clients from time to time and that helping an innocent person stay out of prison was the most important thing she would ever do. Tom Beatty's case reinforced her belief that she had chosen the right profession.

Not long after they made junior partner at one of the older established Portland law firms, Dale Masterson and Mark Hamilton grew impatient with their slow climb up the firm's ladder and formed their own firm. Masterson, Hamilton had grown swiftly by bonding with the young entrepreneurs who were turning high-tech start-ups into multimillion-dollar enterprises. But Masterson and Hamilton had been unwilling to put all of their eggs into one basket, and had used their contacts to pull in a number of coal mining and oil companies. Now Masterson, Hamilton, Rickman and Thomas leased three floors in a modern glass-and-steel, forty-story building in downtown Portland.

Tom Beatty was in his cubicle on the twenty-first floor working up a witness list for one of the litigation partners when his phone rang.

"I've got great news," Amanda Jaffe said. "The district attorney isn't going to pursue your case."

"What do you mean?" Tom asked.

"I gave him our investigative reports and an affidavit from Dr. Fisher and he's decided that you acted in self-defense. So you're free and clear. The charges have been dropped."

"That's . . . that's great. Thank you, so much."

"Every once in a while the system gets it right. I'm just sorry you were arrested and spent a night in jail."

"That wasn't so hard. And I do feel bad about hurting Roux but I—"

"There's no need to say anything more. You can put this incident behind you."

"You did a great job, Miss Jaffe. What do I owe you?"

"Your retainer covered my work so we're square. It was a pleasure meeting you. I appreciate your service to our country."

Tom hung up. Then he leaned back in his chair and took some deep breaths. He still felt bad about what he'd done to Harold Roux, but he was relieved that his ordeal was over. When he was calm again, Tom got up and walked down the hall and up the stairs. He wanted to tell Christine the good news in person.

The partners' offices were two floors above his cubicle. Tom climbed the stairs, opened the door, and entered the twenty-third floor hallway. Christine's office was halfway between the stairwell and Dale Masterson's huge corner office. Tom had taken several steps when the door to Masterson's office opened and he saw Christine come out. Her head was down and she was walking swiftly. Her gait and the set of her shoulders made Tom think that his friend was upset.

Christine flung open the door to her office, then slammed it shut seconds before Tom reached it. Tom debated whether he should disturb her. Brittney Vandervelden, Christine's secretary, occupied a cubicle across the hall from Christine's office. She was in her early thirties, a well-dressed redhead with a nice figure and a sharp mind. Tom did a lot of work with Christine, so he also saw a lot of Brittney. He'd thought about asking her out, but dating a coworker was usually a bad idea. And he had so much baggage that he hesitated anytime the idea of getting close to someone became a possibility.

"Hey, Brit, I wanted to tell Christine something but she looked upset. Do you think I should wait?"

"I would."

"What's up?"

"I don't know, but it has something to do with Mr. Masterson. And don't ask me what because I don't know."

"Okay. When you get a chance, can you tell her my case was dismissed . . . ?"

"That's so great!" Brittney said, flashing a wide smile.

"Yeah, I'm really relieved."

"Christine was pretty confident her friend would handle it."

"Miss Jaffe did a terrific job. She convinced the DA I acted in self-defense so he's dropping the matter. I guess Christine can get her bail money back. You should tell her that too."

"I will. And I'm sure she'll want to talk to you when she has some time."

Tom left Brittney's cubicle, and frowned. Christine was normally intense, but she'd looked unusually upset. Tom wondered what was bothering her. Then he decided that it was none of his business.

Brittney knew better than to interrupt her boss when she was in one of her moods, and she also knew how long it normally took for Christine to calm down. After a reasonable amount of time, she walked across the hall and tapped on the door to Christine's office.

"Yes," Christine barked.

Brittney walked in even though Christine's tone told her that she was still seething over whatever had upset her.

"I just thought you'd want to know: Tom's case was dismissed."

Christine's scowl morphed into a grin and she straightened up.

"That's fabulous. How did you find out?"

"Tom came up to tell you but you'd just come back from your meeting with Mr. Masterson and it didn't look like you wanted to be disturbed."

Christine's smile disappeared, and she looked lost in thought.

"Please ask Tom to come up," she said.

"Sure thing," Brittney said as she backed out of the office and closed the door.

"Boss wants to see you," Brittney told Tom over the intercom.

Four minutes later, Brittney looked up and saw Tom walk into Christine's office and shut the door behind him.

Twenty minutes later, Brittney heard loud voices coming from Christine's office. She couldn't make out the words, but Tom and her boss were definitely arguing. Ten minutes after that the door to Christine's office swung open and Tom walked rapidly down the hall and disappeared into the stairwell.

Chapter 8

Two days after Tom Beatty's case was dismissed, Alan Hotchkiss was writing a police report when Greg Nowicki walked up. Nowicki, a fitness freak, had a massive chest and a ridiculously thick neck. He worked narcotics cases, and in his younger days he'd gone undercover in the Desperado biker gang. The tight black T-shirts he liked to wear displayed bulging biceps covered by angry, threatening tattoos. Hotchkiss handled violent crimes, so they'd worked together on cases involving drug-related homicides.

"I got something that might interest you," Nowicki said. "You were bitching and moaning when Larry Frederick was thinking about dropping charges against some guy who was in a bar fight, right?"

Hotchkiss looked up from his report.

"Was his name Tom Beatty?" Nowicki asked.

"Yeah, why?"

"I've got a longtime informant who's trying to work off a beef by feeding me information. She says Beatty sells heroin and keeps his stash in his house. It's on a cul-de-sac and backs on forest, so it's private. She says she bought from him on four occasions. A few days ago, she went to his house, so I have golden info for a search warrant."

Hotchkiss pumped his fist. "I knew that asshole's John Wayne shit was too good to be true. Who are his contacts? Can we use him to bust his suppliers?"

"This is where it gets real good. Beatty told my informant he gets his stuff from guys who served with him in Afghanistan and made contacts with drug lords while they were there. So this could be the start of a bigger investigation."

"What's the plan?"

"I'm going to Judge Rodriguez for the warrant. Then we go in tonight. Wanna come along?"

"You bet."

Hotchkiss rode shotgun in Nowicki's unmarked car. A van with a SWAT team followed the detectives. Hotchkiss had briefed everyone on Beatty's military background and they weren't taking any chances. On the way to the bust, Hotchkiss read over the search warrant and the affidavit. Carol White claimed to have met Beatty for the first time near the Lookout on May 9 after another addict had pointed him out. She swore that she bought from Beatty after dark on the evenings of May 9, May 17, June 6, and three days ago, on July 5. On the last occasion, White said, she had seen Beatty on the street and approached him. Beatty did not have any drugs on him so he'd taken Carol to his house and had her wait outside while he went in and got her heroin. White swore that Beatty assured her that he always had a store of heroin in his home and asked her to tell her friends about him.

Hotchkiss frowned. That didn't sound right. Why would Beatty show a strung-out addict where he lived and kept his stash? Then again, if all criminals were geniuses the police would never make an arrest.

Nowicki parked at the entrance to the cul-de-sac where they would not be visible from Beatty's house.

Just before they got out of the car, Hotchkiss looked at the affidavit again. Something was bothering him. He reread the dates when White claimed she'd made the buys, and frowned. Something was definitely wrong but he couldn't figure out what it was.

"I scoped this out earlier," Nowicki told Hotchkiss. "There's a front door and a back door that opens into a big backyard. I'm gonna send a team around the back. They go through the woods and enter through the back door. We'll come in through the front."

"Sounds good," Hotchkiss said as he checked his gun.

Nowicki conferred with the head of the SWAT team. Then several men headed toward the woods. Nowicki gave them time to make the circular journey before leading the rest of the men toward the front of the house. Hotchkiss couldn't see any lights. There was no garage and no car was parked out front. If they were lucky, Beatty would be out and they could search without incident, then bag him when he came home.

Nowicki signaled everyone to stay back while he crab-walked toward the front porch, keeping below the windowsills in the front rooms. When he was alongside the front door, he signaled and Hotchkiss and the SWAT team members spread out along the wall on either side of the door. That's when Hotchkiss figured out what was bothering him.

"Greg," he whispered. "There might be a problem with the affidavit for the search warrant. One of the dates—"

"Not now," Nowicki said as he leaned forward and knocked loudly.

Hotchkiss realized that Nowicki was right. He had to concentrate, because he might be fighting for his life in the next few seconds.

"Police—open up!" Nowicki shouted.

There was no response. Nowicki nodded and two officers used a battering ram to smash the flimsy lock on the front door. Two other SWAT members moved inside.

"It doesn't look like anyone's home," one of them shouted after a few minutes.

Nowicki walked inside and flipped on a light switch. The front room was neat. The only thing out of place was a newspaper that had been dumped onto a coffee table.

Hotchkiss heard a door open, and the members of the SWAT team who had approached the house through the woods announced their presence.

"All right, guys," Nowicki said, "I want a lookout to alert us when Beatty comes home. The rest of you spread out and search."

The house was small. Nowicki started in the kitchen while Hotchkiss walked down a short hall to the back of the house. The door to a small bathroom was open and the detective took a brief look inside before stopping in front of a closed door he assumed opened into Beatty's bedroom. Hotchkiss wasn't going to take any chances—Beatty could be lying in ambush in the dark. He gave a hand signal to one of the other officers while he waited beside the door. The officer turned the knob slowly before shoving the door into the bedroom. They waited. Nothing happened. Hotchkiss ducked inside and felt for a switch. The light came on. One of the men behind him whispered "Holy shit" at the same time the detective's jaw dropped.

"Until I've completed the autopsy I won't draw an official conclusion about the cause of death, but I'd be shocked if she didn't die from trauma as a result of a severe beating," Dr. Sally Grace said. The assistant medical examiner was a slender woman with frizzy black hair. Hotchkiss liked her because she had a dry sense of humor and a keen intelligence, and made a dynamite witness.

"Time of death?" Hotchkiss asked Grace. They were standing around Tom Beatty's bed, staring down at a blond female in her early thirties who was dressed in a black business suit and a white silk blouse. She had been so badly battered that it was hard to look at her face.

"She's been dead for a while," Grace said. "Not more than a day but not recently. And I don't think she was killed here. There's some blood on the covers but no spatter that's consistent with her being pummeled in this room. Did you find any blood anywhere else in the house?"

"No," Nowicki answered.

"Then I'd say she was probably killed elsewhere and brought here."

Before Nowicki could say anything else his phone vibrated.

"Someone's headed this way," he said when he disconnected.

The lights in the front part of the house had been turned off. Hotchkiss switched off the light in the bedroom and moved into the living room. Moments later, a car parked out front. As soon as Tom Beatty got out, he was surrounded by police officers. Hotchkiss walked out the front door, with Nowicki close behind him.

"What's going on?" Beatty asked.

Hotchkiss held up the search warrant. "We have a warrant to search your house, Mr. Beatty."

"For what?"

"Heroin, sir."

"Heroin! You're serious?"

"I'm very serious. We found your stash in the basement."

"What?!"

"And we found something else that I'd like to show you. Can you follow me into your bedroom," Hotchkiss said.

Beatty followed the detective. When they reached the bedroom, Hotchkiss stepped aside. Beatty took one step into the room. Then his knees buckled.

"Oh, God," he moaned. "It's Christine."

Chapter 9

"If you keep this up, I'm gonna have to have a cardiologist on speed dial," Mike Greene gasped when he caught his breath.

He and Amanda were lying side by side in Amanda's bed. They'd been so busy lately that they hadn't been able to see each other, but one of Amanda's trials had been set over and crime had taken a holiday for a few days so they were finally spending a night together.

"Listen, old man," Amanda said, "if you can't keep up I'll have to look elsewhere for sexual satisfaction."

"Who would you find who'd put up with you?" Mike answered.

Amanda laughed. "Point taken," she said. Then she rolled on top of Mike and started playing with his chest hair.

"God, woman. You're insatiable."

Before Amanda could reply, her phone rang.

"Don't answer it," Mike whispered as he ran a hand down her back.

"I've got to," Amanda said as she sat up. "That's my business phone, and that means a client is calling."

Mike sighed.

"Amanda Jaffe," Amanda said when she had the phone.

"Miss Jaffe, this is Tom Beatty. I'm in jail. They're saying I murdered Christine."

Prior to 1983, the Multnomah County jail looked the way a prison was supposed to look. Constructed of huge granite blocks, the foreboding fortress perched on Rocky Butte and shouted, "Abandon all hope, ye who enter here." Then the Rocky Butte jail was torn down to make way for the I-205 freeway and the detention center was moved to the fourth through tenth floors of the Justice Center, a sixteen-story, state-of-the-art facility in the heart of downtown Portland that was across a park from the courthouse.

Amanda barely noticed her surroundings as she walked through the Justice Center's vaulted lobby and pushed past the glass doors that opened into the jail reception area. She'd been upset when the phone rang, interrupting her evening with Mike, but she'd lost any interest in sex the moment she learned that Christine Larson had been murdered.

After showing her ID to the guard at the reception desk and going through a metal detector, Amanda entered the elevator that took her to a floor in the jail with contact visiting rooms. When the elevator door opened, Amanda found herself in a narrow hall with a thick metal door on one end. Next to the door, affixed to a pastel-yellow concrete wall, was an intercom. Amanda pressed a black button and announced her presence. Moments later, electronic locks snapped open and a uniformed guard ushered her into another narrow corridor that ran in front of three soundproofed visiting rooms. The upper half of the corridor wall of each contact visiting room was made of thick, shatterproof glass that let the guards monitor the activity in the room. Each room was outfitted with two molded plastic chairs that stood on either side of a round table secured to the floor by metal bolts.

The door to the contact visiting room was solid steel. The guard spoke into a radio and the locks on the door snapped open. Amanda took one of the chairs and placed a pad and pen on the table. Moments later, a second metal door at the back of the room opened and a guard led Tom Beatty inside.

Amanda's client looked terrible. He was dressed in an ill-fitting orange jumpsuit. His face was blank, his hair was uncombed, and there were deep circles under his eyes.

"What happened?" Amanda asked as soon as the guard left.

A good defense attorney never asked that question because of the limitations it put on the defense if a client confessed guilt. But the news of Christine's death had stunned Amanda and she had forgotten to act professionally.

Tom shook his head. He looked exhausted.

"I don't know. The police were all over my house when I came home. They took me to my bedroom. Christine . . ."

Tom paused and wet his lips. "She was lying on my bed. Her face . . ."

Tom shook his head again, and that gesture convinced Amanda that her client was innocent. She guessed that Tom had seen horrible sights as a soldier and would be this moved only by the unexpected, violent death of someone he knew and cared for.

"Why was Christine at your house?" Amanda asked.

"I don't know."

"And she was murdered?"

When Tom looked up, anger animated his expression.

"She was beaten to death. Her face was pulp. When I get out of here, I will find the person responsible and make them wish they had never been born."

"Tom, do not say anything like that to anyone but me. Do you understand?"

Tom's features hardened, and he did not respond. Amanda understood his anger and didn't press the point.

"Where were you before you came home?" she asked to change the subject.

Confusion replaced anger and Tom lost focus.

"Tom?"

"It was a setup."

"What was a setup?"

Tom looked at Amanda. "Everything. It was around seven, I was reading, and the phone rang. The caller said he was Albert Roth. He said he was an associate at the firm and Randall Spaulding wanted me to come back to the office."

"Who is Randall Spaulding?"

"He's a junior partner."

"Do you know him?"

"I know who he is but I've never done any work for him."

"What about Roth? Do you know him?"

"No, I'd never heard of him, but there are so many attorneys in the firm that I wasn't concerned."

"What did they want you to do?"

"That's the thing. When I got to the office, Mr. Spaulding wasn't there. I used the office directory and got his home number. He said he had no idea who Albert Roth was and denied he'd asked anyone to call me. Then I looked for Roth in the directory. No one by that name is listed."

"So, whoever murdered Christine lured you downtown so they could put the body in your bedroom."

"And plant heroin in my basement."

"The police found heroin in your house?"

"I have never used or sold heroin, Miss Jaffe."

Amanda had occasionally been conned by clients, but she was pretty good at spotting a lie. If she had to bet, she would bet that Beatty was telling the truth.

"Do you have any idea why someone would murder Christine and frame you?"

"No . . ." Tom paused. "Well, there was one thing. When you called me to tell me that my case had been dismissed, I went to Christine's office to tell her the good news. I walked up. The door to the stairwell is at one end of a long corridor and Christine's office is about midway. When I walked into the hall I saw Christine leaving Dale Masterson's office. She looked upset. Before I could get to her she shut her office door, so I didn't go in. Instead, I asked Brittney, Christine's secretary, to call me when she thought it would be a good time to talk to Christine.

"Later, Brittney called and told me to come up. Christine was happy that the case had been thrown out, but I could see something was worrying her. I asked her why she was upset. She told me that the firm was trying to get Global Mining as a client. She thought something funny was going on with the firm's books and she wanted me to help her look into it. She said she thought someone high up in the firm was juggling figures to make the firm's bottom line look better than it was."

Tom looked down. "I . . ."

"Yes."

Tom reddened. "I told her I wouldn't help her."

His eyes pleaded with Amanda for understanding. "I was afraid. I really needed my job, and I needed peace and quiet. I didn't want to get involved. I'd just been arrested; if you hadn't cleared everything up I could have been fired. So I said I wouldn't help and we had an argument. I felt awful, after she'd stood by me, but I . . . I just couldn't take the risk of losing my job."

Tom looked down, ashamed. "Maybe if I'd been there for her like she was for me . . ."

"Do not beat yourself up," Amanda said firmly. "Whoever killed Christine had a well-thought-out plan. I doubt there was anything you could have done to save her. What you have to concentrate on now is saving yourself, because the police won't look for Christine's killer as long as they're convinced that you murdered her."

"Okay, but I don't know anything."

"You said that Christine thought someone high up in the firm was doing something with the books. Did she tell you who she suspected?"

"No."

"She was upset when she left Dale Masterson's office. Did she suspect him?"

"I cut her off before she gave me a name; I told her I didn't want to know. Mr. Masterson is one of the most powerful partners, so it could have been him.

"Tom, I'm going to ask you a question, and I need a completely truthful answer. And remember, anything you tell me is confidential; your answer stays between us."

Beatty looked directly at Amanda. "What do you want to know?"

"A prosecutor doesn't have to prove what motivated a criminal to commit a crime, but the first thought that will pop into the mind of a juror when a woman is found murdered in a man's bedroom is that a lovers' quarrel was the motive. What was your relationship with Christine?"

"Christine was my boss," Tom stated emphatically. "She was also my friend, but there was never anything romantic between us."

"Will the police be able to find witnesses who can make a case to a jury that you were romantically involved?"

"How would they do that?"

"If I was prosecuting you, I'd show the jury that Christine bailed you out when you were arrested. Why did you call her?"

Tom looked down at the tabletop. "I don't have friends here. I get up in the morning and go to work. Then I come home. Every once in a while I go to a movie or the Lookout to watch a game. The only people I know well are the people I work with and Christine is . . . *was* the partner I worked with the most.

"When I was arrested for the fight, they told me I could call a lawyer. I didn't want anyone at the firm to know I'd been arrested for fighting in a bar—I was scared I'd lose my job. But Christine . . . I thought she wouldn't judge me, that she'd listen to my side, and she's a lawyer. I knew she didn't practice criminal law, but I hoped she'd know a lawyer who could help me."

"So that's all there was to it. You never went out socially, say to dinner or a movie, with Christine?"

"Never." Beatty paused. "We did have breakfast after she bailed me out. But all we did was talk about what happened, and that's the only time we ever ate together. We never dated."

"Did you ever argue?"

"Just when I said I didn't want to get involved in her investigation of the firm's finances."

"Could anyone have heard you argue? This is important, because she was killed soon after."

"Brittney could have heard us."

"That's Christine's secretary?"

Beatty nodded. "And there are other secretaries and para-legals who sit near her." Beatty shrugged. "The walls aren't that thick. The partners on either side could have heard us."

"Okay. I think that's enough for now. But we do have to discuss my fee. Defending a murder case is expensive . . ."

"I can cover it. My folks died in a car accident. Between the insurance and my inheritance . . . I have some money."

"I'll need two hundred and fifty thousand to start."

"I can do that."

"All right. I'll get a better idea of what we'll need for experts and investigation when I have a better handle on the case."

Beatty gave Amanda the name of the person who was managing his finances.

"Am I going to get out?" he asked while she was writing down the information.

"There's no automatic bail in a murder case. I'll set up a bail hearing when I've gone over the discovery, but you'll have to sit tight for a while. Will that be a problem?"

"I'll be okay. I trust you to do your best."

"Thanks, Tom. Be assured that your case is my top priority."

Chapter 10

Carol White's apartment was a real shithole. Peeling wallpaper, mold growing on a pee-colored carpet encrusted with food she'd dropped and never bothered to pick up, all topped off by a terrific view of a brick wall and Dumpsters. Carol lay on her side on her bed. Its mattress sagged and the stained and sweat-soaked sheets stank, but she was hurting and she didn't have the energy to think about her apartment, her bottom-feeder life, or anything beyond how she was going to get a fix.

Carol needed a fix bad, and she'd already burned through the money she'd been paid to lie about this Beatty guy. She had to think, but thinking was hard when the craving was on her.

The TV was on. It was her only companion and she kept it running every minute of the day whether she was awake or asleep. The programs distracted her and the sound was comforting. Carol rolled onto her side and stared at the screen. A lacquer-haired broadcaster was talking about a lawyer at a big law firm who had been beaten to death. A man named Tom Beatty was under arrest.

Carol started to hyperventilate. She had not signed on for this. This was fucked. Carol sat up and gulped down air until she was calmer. Then she forced herself to think. The adrenaline generated by the news story had sharpened her senses, and a plan flashed into her suddenly alert brain. These people were not people you fucked with, but she was desperate, and it occurred to Carol that this could be the opportunity of a lifetime if she played her cards right.

Carol made a decision. She found her phone and punched in a number. Moments later, she heard a familiar voice.

"What are you doing calling me?" the man asked. Carol could tell he was furious. She willed herself to stay businesslike.

"It was on TV. You never told me someone was going to be killed."

"I'm not going to get into this on the phone."

"Then we should meet, and when we do you're going to give me ten thousand dollars."

There was silence on the other end. Then the man said, "Tonight. We'll meet, we'll talk."

"There's nothing to talk about. Give me what I asked for and you'll never see me again. I'll move far away. Otherwise, I'm sure the DA would love to hear about your little plan."

When the man spoke again he sounded contrite. "Okay, you hold all the cards. Pick a place. It should be private—we don't want to be seen."

Carol had started to say something when warning bells went off. A lot of things could happen to her in a private place.

"We meet downtown in Pioneer Courthouse Square."

"Someone could see us there."

"So wear a disguise. We won't be together very long anyway. We walk past each other and you hand me the bag with the money. After that, I'm gone."

"Okay. What time?"

"Five o'clock," she said, picking an hour when there would be plenty of people around.

Carol hung up. She was scared but she also felt proud of herself. She'd been in control, in charge. And she'd soon be rich. Ten thousand fucking dollars. She'd never possessed anything near that sum. Carol paused. Maybe she should have asked for more. Then she shook her head. No, that was a lot of money, and there was no need to be greedy.

Carol left her apartment at four thirty. She was wearing jeans and a sweatshirt with a hoodie, and she was carrying her worldly possessions in a backpack. Pioneer Courthouse Square was on the other side of the river and too far to walk, so she headed for the bus stop. The thought that she was going to be rich energized her. She was so pumped that she didn't pay attention to what was going on around her until a black van pulled to the curb. Its side door slid open and the man who had been following her shoved her into the opening. Carol started to scream but a cloth was pressed over her mouth. Seconds later, Carol and her dreams died.

Chapter 11

Two days after Tom Beatty's arrest, Kate Ross told her boss that the scuttlebutt around the courthouse was that Larry Frederick had begged for Tom's case. When his wish was granted, he quickly convened a grand jury that returned a true bill charging aggravated murder. One of the potential penalties for aggravated murder was death.

That afternoon a messenger delivered a thick manila envelope with a copy of the indictment and several hundred pages of police, forensic, and autopsy reports. After receiving the discovery, Amanda placed a call to Larry Frederick. His secretary told Amanda that the DA was unavailable, and he remained unavailable every time Amanda called. That was odd, because Larry Frederick was one of the most accessible prosecutors in the Multnomah County District Attorney's Office.

The day after she received the discovery package, Amanda went to the courthouse for Tom Beatty's arraignment. The case had been assigned to the Honorable David Chang, a former prosecutor who had shown no favoritism to the prosecution or the defense since taking the bench five years before. Cathy Prieto-Smith was the only lawyer seated at the prosecution table. She was tall and slim, had auburn hair cut in a pixie style, and was wearing a severe black business suit and an open-neck, cream-colored blouse. Amanda wondered if Larry Frederick was going to skip the arraignment.

Amanda took her seat at counsel table and set up her laptop while she waited for the deputies to bring in her client. Moments later, the courtroom door opened and Frederick entered. He did not look at Amanda when he walked to his seat or after he sat down, so Amanda took the initiative.

"Hi, Larry," she said when she was standing next to the DA. When he turned toward her, she was shocked. Frederick had the washed-out appearance of a man who was having trouble sleeping.

"Amanda," Frederick answered tersely.

"You know I've been calling since I heard you got Tom's case."

"I do. And I haven't returned the calls because we have nothing to talk about. I blame myself for Christine Larson's death, and I'm going to set things right by putting your client on death row."

"You're not serious? You have a duty to see that justice is done in every case you handle. Tom acted in self-defense—your own investigation showed that. If you hadn't dropped the case, you would have been violating your oath."

"I'm in no mood to discuss legal philosophy and ethics. Christine Larson is dead because I didn't prosecute Beatty and I'm not making the same mistake twice. So let me make myself clear: There will be no plea-bargaining in this case; no life without parole, no plea to manslaughter. Your client is going to die for what he's done."

"Jesus, Larry."

"I assume you received the discovery."

"Yes. Thank you for being so prompt."

"I intend to follow the letter of the law in this case. You will receive everything you are entitled to when you are entitled to receive it. If you have any problem with the way I'm conducting this case let me know. I am going to cross every *t* and dot every *i*, and when you go through the transcript during your preparation for your client's appeal of his sentence of death, you will discover no errors. Your client will go from our jail to death row and stay there, thinking about what he did to Miss Larson until his miserable life ends in the death chamber."

Neither Amanda nor Mike was a decent cook and their jobs often kept them in their offices well past five o'clock, so they ate out a lot. On the day of Tom Beatty's arraignment, the couple met for dinner at an Italian restaurant on Morrison. Amanda was a hearty eater, so Mike knew something was up when she spent the first ten minutes picking at her food and staring at the table.

"What's wrong?" Mike asked when he couldn't stand it anymore.

"Off limits," she answered.

"I want to help."

Amanda looked up, and Mike could see she was in distress. "I can't, Mike. When we started dating we agreed that we would never discuss our cases if the discussion might create an ethical conflict. If I told you what's bothering me it would put you in a bind. You could be accused of helping me."

"Let me guess. It's the Beatty case."

"I told you, I can't discuss it."

"Larry is stonewalling you. No plea bargaining, right?"

"Goddamn it, Mike."

Mike didn't let Amanda's anger faze him. "Larry has a hard-on about this case. It's a vendetta. I didn't want him to prosecute it because he's too involved personally but I was overruled. You are going to have to live with the fact that this one is to the death, literally. So stop worrying about how unfair Larry's attitude is and fight for your client."

Amanda stayed angry for a few seconds more. Then she looked embarrassed.

"You're right, Mike. Thanks for giving me a stiff kick in the butt."

"Well, it's a very nice butt so it's my pleasure."

Amanda laughed. "You know what I like best about you? You've always been there for me, even when I treated you like shit."

Mike smiled. "It's worth the abuse. You're very special."

Then Mike stopped smiling and looked uncomfortable.

"There's something we need to discuss," he said. Amanda heard a slight tremor in Mike's voice, which surprised her. If there was one thing she knew for certain about her boyfriend, it was that he was always self-confident.

"What's on your mind?" Amanda asked.

"You know I went through a bad divorce."

Amanda nodded.

"That's the reason I moved to Oregon from California."

Amanda nodded again, not sure where this was going.

"So trusting someone—a woman—isn't easy for me."

Mike paused and took a deep breath. "Look, I'll just say it. I love you and I want to be with you and having two apartments, well, it doesn't make sense because we each have clothes in the other person's place and we're one place or the other almost every weekend."

Mike paused again and took another breath. "We should move in together. You can choose the place; I don't care as long as we're together."

Amanda hesitated. Her romance with Mike had been rocky at times, especially when she had been traumatized by the events in the Cardoni case, but any of their problems had always been her fault. Despite that and a lot of other things, he was always in her corner and never judged her. Amanda's problem was that she valued her independence, and moving in together was a big step.

"This is sudden," she said to stall for time.

"Not for me. I've been thinking about it for a while. I just had to work up the courage to talk about it. If you don't want to I'll understand," he added quickly.

"No, it's not that. It's just . . . Well, it's a big move and . . . Can you give me some time to think?"

"Sure, take all the time you want," Mike said with a smile, but Amanda could see that the smile was forced, and that he was hurt that she hadn't accepted immediately.

Amanda reached across the table and squeezed his hand. "I really care about you, Mike, you know that."

"I shouldn't have just dropped this on you," he said, backtracking.

Amanda squeezed his hand again. "No, don't think that way. You are the best thing in my life. You've been my rock through good times and bad. This is just a lot to get my head around. So give me some time, okay?"

"Okay."

Amanda leaned back. The moment was awkward, and she could see that Mike was struggling to think of something to say. So she smiled and asked, "So, how about those Blazers?"

Mike burst out laughing, and Amanda joined him.

Now it was Mike's turn to squeeze Amanda's hand. "You're the best," he said.

Chapter 12

The morning after the arraignment, Amanda walked across town to meet Kate Ross at Dale Masterson's law office. Thinking about her conversation with Mike had kept her up most of the night and she was exhausted. Did she love him? If she did, moving in would be the right thing to do. She tried to analyze his proposal the way she worked through a problem on one of her cases, but lawyers were trained to be unemotional and objective when analyzing the issues in a case, and love was all emotion.

Amanda kept thinking about the move during her crosstown walk, and she was still conflicted when she saw Kate in Masterson, Hamilton's waiting room.

"We may have caught a break," Kate said as soon as Amanda was seated next to her.

"What makes you say that?" Amanda asked, grateful for a chance to think about something other than her personal situation.

"I went through the discovery. Have you read the affidavit for the search warrant carefully?"

"I skimmed it, but I was too busy to give it a hard read."

"Okay. Well, two things stand out. First, Carol White told Nowicki that Beatty took her to his house. No drug dealer with an ounce of brains would take a junkie to his house. And then there are the dates when Carol White claims that she bought heroin from our client."

"What about the dates?" Amanda asked.

Before Kate could answer her question, an attractive woman entered the waiting room.

"Ms. Jaffe?"

"Yes?"

"I'm Julie Birnbaum, Mr. Masterson's legal assistant. He can see you now."

Amanda and Kate followed Birnbaum down a long hall to a corner office. When his assistant opened the door, Dale Masterson walked around his desk and crossed the room.

"Thank you for seeing me and my investigator, Mr. Masterson," Amanda said.

"Dale, please. This has been terrible. Christine was a valued member of our firm and a very decent person. And Tom . . . I don't know him that well but . . . Well I know about his assault charge. Still, that was self-defense."

Masterson shook his head, and Amanda noticed that every one of his silver gray hairs stayed perfectly in place. The law firm's managing partner was a little over six feet tall and looked fit and muscular. Amanda had researched his background and knew he'd played football and wrestled at Arizona before going to law school at the University of Washington. Masterson sported a perfect tan and was wearing a suit that Amanda guessed had been hand-tailored. If she didn't know what the lawyer did for a living, Amanda would have guessed that he was an actor or a TV news anchor.

Masterson indicated two client chairs and returned to his seat behind the desk.

"How can I help you?" Masterson asked after they were all seated.

"I've read the police reports. Several witnesses said that Christine and Tom Beatty had an argument a few days before Christine was murdered. There are other witnesses who told the police that shortly before Tom and Christine argued, Christine had left your office and appeared to be upset. Can you tell me what upset her?"

"Yes, I can. How well do you know Christine?"

"We were classmates in law school. She was in my study group."

Masterson flashed a sad smile. "Then you know your friend was strong-minded."

Amanda nodded.

Masterson sighed. "Christine was assisting me with a case. I can't go into details—the case involves a negotiation we were conducting for a client, so the details are privileged. I can tell you that we had diametrically opposed views on how a certain matter should be handled and she argued very strongly that I should adopt her approach. When I declined to do so, she became upset." Masterson shrugged. "That's all there was to it."

"Do you have anyone named Albert Roth working at your firm in any capacity: contract work, a security guard?"

"Not that I know of. I can ask HR to check our records. Is there anything else I can do for you?"

"I'd like Kate to talk to the people who told the police about the argument between Christine and Tom and other people at the firm who might be character or fact witnesses. Would that be okay?"

"Certainly, with the proviso that there be no discussion about specific cases."

"Naturally," Amanda agreed. "I'd especially like to talk to Brittney Vandervelden, Christine's secretary. Can we see her now?"

"I'll have my secretary ask Brittney to go to one of our conference rooms. And, if there's nothing else, I have a meeting for which I need to prepare."

"What did you think?" Amanda asked Kate as they walked to the conference room where Brittney Vandervelden was waiting.

"He's very smooth," Kate said, "and, to be honest, I couldn't get a read on him."

"Me either. If he was lying about why Christine was upset, I couldn't tell."

They arrived at the conference room to find an attractive, very nervous redhead waiting for them.

"Thanks for meeting with us," Amanda said after she'd introduced Kate and they'd taken seats at one end of a long conference table. "How are you holding up?"

"I'm not great," Brittney answered quietly. "I really liked Christine and Tom. I . . . It's hard to believe he could . . ."

"If it helps any, Tom vehemently denies hurting Christine, and I believe him."

Brittney nodded.

"Have you ever seen anything that would lead you to believe that Tom would do something like this?" Amanda asked.

"No, never. They really got along, and Christine helped him when he got arrested. Tom was very grateful."

"In the police reports, several people said they'd heard an argument between Tom and Christine. Do you know what that was about?"

Suddenly Brittney looked nervous. The conference room had a glass wall through which she could see the hall. Brittney took a quick look through the glass before shaking her head.

"I heard them talking in loud voices but I couldn't hear what they said."

"So you don't know why they argued?"

Brittney broke eye contact with Amanda and shook her head.

"Shortly before the argument, I understand Christine came back from a meeting with Mr. Masterson and was upset. Do you know why?"

"No."

Amanda studied Brittney for a moment. She was certain that Christine's secretary was holding something back but decided not to press her. She could always have Kate contact Brittney later.

"The police are going to say that Tom killed Christine in a lovers' quarrel. Have you ever seen anything that would make you believe Tom and Christine were romantically involved?"

This time Brittney looked directly at Amanda. "Absolutely not! A detective came to the firm. He interviewed me and several other people. He knew about the argument Tom had with Christine. Someone else heard them. Probably one of the people in the cubicles on either side of mine. He wanted me to say it was a lovers' quarrel but I told him I was certain that Tom and Christine only had a working relationship." She paused. "I don't think he believed me. I don't think he wanted to believe me. He kept asking me why Christine would be in Tom's bedroom if they weren't romantically involved."

"Tom assures me that he and Christine were co-workers and nothing more," Amanda said.

"You should believe him, and if anyone says they were lovers, well, that would be a lie."

Kate and Amanda spent another twenty minutes talking to Brittney before excusing her so they could interview some of the others who had heard the quarrel.

"What do you think?" Amanda asked Kate.

"There's something she's not telling us," Kate said. "I'd like to give her a day or two to think, then take another shot at her."

"I agree."

Chapter 13

"There's a call for you on line two," Amanda's receptionist said.

"Who is it?"

"She won't say, but she did say that she had information about Mr. Beatty's case."

Amanda thanked her, then took the call.

"This is Amanda Jaffe."

"Miss Jaffe, I know something that could be important about Tom Beatty's case," Brittney Vandervelden said.

"I'm listening."

"I don't want to talk over the phone. Can you meet me on the second floor of the parking garage at the Lloyd Center Mall in one hour?"

"I could, but—"

"I have to be certain that no one will see us."

"Okay, I'll be there."

"Stand by your car. I'll drive by and pick you up."

Amanda had been standing by her car for less than a minute when a red Miata stopped in front of her. Amanda bent low and peered into the car. Brittney was behind the wheel. She looked anxious. Amanda got in and Brittney took off down the ramp, pulled into traffic, then drove into the middle of the large parking lot for a multiplex theater across the street from the mall. No one said a word until the car was concealed between a van and a pickup truck in a part of the lot where they were not likely to be seen.

"Before I say anything, you have to promise me you won't tell anyone about this meeting," Brittney said.

"Are you worried about your job?"

"After what happened to Christine, I'm worried about my life."

"Why did you want to meet me if you feel you might be in danger?"

"It's Tom. There's no way he would have hurt Christine, let alone beaten her to death. And this heroin thing . . . I just don't believe it. If I kept what I know to myself and Tom was convicted . . . I couldn't live with that."

"Do you know something that might help Tom?"

Brittney nodded. "I'm not sure. You'll have to decide."

"Okay."

"I think I know why Christine was upset when she left Mr. Masterson's office."

"Go ahead," Amanda urged.

"About two years ago, the firm had some business reversals. One of our biggest clients had a dispute about fees and decided to drop us in favor of using in-house counsel. After that happened, we heard rumors that the firm was having trouble generating sufficient revenue to pay the contracts of the name partners and cover the payments on loans that had been incurred during the recession. There was a lot of talk about layoffs; it was all gloom and doom.

"Then the firm started secret talks with Global Mining; I knew about them because Christine was involved. I also knew that Global had heard the rumors about the firm's financial troubles and was concerned. So the partners let Global examine the books. And they looked great—only Christine thought they shouldn't have. She was worried that the big partners were making fraudulent accounting entries that showed increased revenue and decreased expenses and appeared to rein in distribution payments to partners. I think that's what she was talking about to Mr. Masterson on the day Tom learned his case was dismissed."

"By 'the big partners,' who do you mean?"

"Dale Masterson and Mark Hamilton. They founded the firm and they're in control. None of the other partners have any real power. They make a lot of money but they knew when they joined the firm that they might be on the letterhead but Mr. Masterson and Mr. Hamilton are in charge."

"Okay, so you think Christine was killed because she was going to expose the fraud?"

"I don't have any proof, but if they were afraid that Christine had told Tom about the fraud it would explain why they had to frame him for the murder. He'd be so distracted by his arrest that he wouldn't be able to pursue an investigation. And who would believe him anyway if he was a convicted murderer?"

"You've given me a lot to think about," Amanda said.

"I can't prove a word of anything I've told you. So please keep me out of the case."

"I will. And I may have a way of finding out if the firm is in as much trouble as you think it is."

"But it's not. We're Global's lawyers. They hired the firm. Christine was going to talk to the people at Global but she never got the chance. The influx of cash can be used to solve most of the firm's problems and the partners can fix the books. By the time you get a court order, everything will look fine."

"Kate's looking for you," the receptionist said when Amanda returned. Amanda walked down the hall.

"Guess where I was?" she said when she walked into Kate's office.

"I have no idea."

"Brittney Vandervelden and I just had a secret rendezvous at Lloyd Center."

Kate listened carefully while Amanda told her about her meeting with Christine Larson's secretary.

"It looks like the partners at Masterson, Hamilton had millions of reasons for wanting Christine Larson dead," Kate said.

"But proving the senior partners in one of the most powerful law firms in the state had another partner rubbed out—if they did—will not be easy," Amanda answered. "By the way, have you run down Carol White?"

"No. But I found an address for her." She shook her head. "She's living in an apartment house that's one step away from being condemned. Talk about bottom of the barrel. Anyway, when she didn't answer her door I slipped the manager a few bucks for a look at her apartment. It's a pigsty, and I don't think she's been home for a while. The food in the refrigerator is producing penicillin, and I don't even want to talk about the smell. I knocked on doors. None of her neighbors say they've seen her around but that doesn't mean much in a place like that. Most of her neighbors belong to the subclass of society that never tells the truth to anyone, especially cops or investigators. But my guess is she's not staying there anymore."

"Damn. I'm sure White lied to Nowicki."

"I do have something for you on White, but I don't know how much it helps. I looked through the court files in the cases where she was a defendant or an informant. If she testifies, you'll grow old telling a judge or jury about her priors and if she testifies her occupation is drug addict, streetwalker, or shoplifter, she won't be committing perjury."

"Anything violent?"

"Nah, it's all petty shit. The worst thing she's been busted for is distribution, but they were all small amounts. She was probably selling so she'd have the money to buy more heroin."

"What about informing? Has she done it a lot?"

"A fair amount, usually when she needs to work off a beef. And she's been doing it off and on for a long time. The first time was ten years ago when Greg

Nowicki and his partner, Reginald Kiner, used her to bust Diego Chavez, a mid-level drug dealer. Four years later, White got probation after selling to an undercover cop. The amount she sold should have landed her in prison but the charges were dismissed after White helped Nowicki jack up a college kid who was selling at Reed College. There are two more times Nowicki used her as the affiant in a search warrant affidavit before we get to Tom's case."

"Okay. Well keep looking for her; let me know if you have any success. I'm certain Tom was set up, and finding White is the key to proving it."

Chapter 14

The brutal murder of a partner in one of Portland's largest law firms by a paralegal who might have been her lover was a juicy news item, and the spectator benches of the Honorable David Chang's fifth-floor courtroom were jam-packed. As Amanda walked to the front of the courtroom, she noticed Brittney Vandervelden, Dale Masterson, and several other members of the Masterson, Hamilton law firm scattered among a crowd that included well-dressed society women, a heavily bearded hippie, new deputy district attorneys hoping to learn their trade by watching two top attorneys in action, reporters, and ancient court watchers who attended trials instead of watching daytime television.

Larry Frederick and Cathy Prieto-Smith were bent over law books and legal memos at the counsel table closest to the empty jury box. The assistant district attorneys scrupulously avoided looking at Amanda when she took her seat next to Tom Beatty at the other counsel table.

As soon as all the parties were present, the bailiff rapped his gavel and the judge took the bench.

"This is the time set for motions in *State of Oregon v. Thomas Darrel Beatty*," Judge Chang told the parties. "Are you ready to proceed?"

Larry Frederick stood up. Amanda noted that the prosecutor looked much better than he had at the arraignment.

"The state is ready, Your Honor," Frederick said. The forceful way he answered the judge's question let Amanda know that his desire to put her client on death row had not lessened.

"Amanda Jaffe for Mr. Beatty. We're ready to proceed."

"Miss Jaffe," Judge Chang said, "I received a raft of motions from you. The bulk of them are legal challenges to Oregon's death penalty statute. I assume you're filing these motions to make a record on appeal because I've denied similar motions in other cases, one of which your father handled, and I am not inclined to change my mind about the merits of your arguments. Is there anything you want to add about the constitutional challenges?"

"No, Your Honor. Several of these issues have not been decided by the Oregon or United States Supreme Courts and I'll take them up there if necessary."

"Very well. Now, you've filed a motion for bail. What is your position, Mr. Frederick?"

"We oppose bail, Your Honor, and I'm prepared to put on witnesses who will show how strong our case is."

"Very well. Call your first witness."

"I've talked with Miss Jaffe and we've agreed that I can show the court a photograph of the victim and summarize the autopsy report in lieu of calling Dr. Sally Grace, the medical examiner."

"Is that correct, Miss Jaffe?" the judge asked.

"It is."

The prosecutor pressed some keys on his laptop and several spectators gasped when a horrific picture of Christine Larson's face was projected onto a screen next to the jury box. Both of Christine's blackened eyes were swollen shut, her nose was broken, there were lacerations on her face, the skin on her ears and lips were split, and her upper and lower jaws were broken. Larry Frederick gave the judge a summary of the damage Christine had suffered and concluded by telling the judge that the cause of death was blunt-force head trauma.

After the cause of death was established, Frederick called Greg Nowicki. The detective was dressed in a suit and tie and would have looked like a corporate at-torney if the tattooed talon of an eagle hadn't peeked out of his collar at the back of his neck. After he was sworn, Nowicki told the court about the execution of the search warrant and the discoveries of the victim in Tom Beatty's bedroom and of heroin in his home.

"Are you going to present evidence on the bail question?" the judge asked Amanda.

Amanda had debated calling Dr. Fisher to explain her client's war service and his PTSD, plus some of the people who worked with Tom. After much thought, she had concluded that these witnesses were best saved for the sentencing phase if Tom was convicted.

"No, Your Honor," Amanda said.

"I'll wait to rule on the question of bail until I've heard all of Miss Jaffe's motions," Judge Chang said. "Let's hear Miss Jaffe's motion to suppress the evidence found during the search of Mr. Beatty's house. Do you have witnesses you intend to call, Miss Jaffe?"

"Yes. I also have something I want to put on the record. My investigator has tried to find Carol White, the affiant who provided the information which led to the issuance of the warrant. I wanted her present at this motion, but we've had no luck finding her. I told Mr. Frederick about our problem but he has not produced her."

"Mr. Frederick?" the judge asked.

"Miss White is a drug addict, Your Honor. Detective Nowicki went to her apartment but she wasn't in. I've had officers looking for her since I received Miss Jaffe's request but they haven't been any more successful than Miss Jaffe's investigator. If we find her, I'll notify Miss Jaffe immediately."

"It appears that Mr. Frederick is acting in good faith," the judge said. "Can you proceed with your motion without this witness?"

"Yes, but I'd like a chance to reopen the motion at a later date if Miss White is located and I feel it's necessary to complete my record."

"That seems reasonable. Any objection, Mr. Frederick?"

"No, Your Honor."

"Then let's proceed. The search was executed pursuant to a warrant, so you have the burden of proof, Miss Jaffe. Who is your first witness?"

"Mr. Beatty calls Greg Nowicki."

Once he took the oath and was seated, Amanda began. "Detective Nowicki, you've told the court that you executed a search warrant at Mr. Beatty's house, but I'd like to go into a little more detail. How did you learn that Mr. Beatty was supposed to have drugs in his home?"

"Over the years, I have developed a relationship with several individuals who supply information to me about the narcotics trade. Carol White is one of my informants. She gave me the information I placed in the affidavit."

"How long has Miss White acted as an informant?"

"Let me see. I believe I arrested her for the first time nine or ten years ago, and she's supplied me with information off and on since then."

"When does she do this?"

"Usually after she's been busted and needs a favor."

"And she'd been arrested recently?" Amanda asked.

"Yes, for possession, but she was out on bail."

"Did you contact Miss White about Mr. Beatty or did she come to you?"

"She called the station and told me she had read about Mr. Beatty's arrest for assault and knew something about him I might find interesting. We arranged a meet."

"And it was during this meeting that she gave you the information you set out in your affidavit?"

"Correct."

"Miss White is a drug addict. Isn't it true that drug addicts are untrustworthy?"

"Some are and some aren't. In my experience, Miss White has been truthful in her dealings with me."

"So you took her word for what she told you?"

"Yes."

"Did you check her story?"

"As much as I was able."

"Miss White said that another junkie told her that Mr. Beatty was a dealer?"

"Yes."

"Did you talk to this junkie to see if that was true?"

"No."

"Why not?"

"I did ask for a name but Miss White could only remember his first name—Frank—and her description was fairly general. She didn't know how to contact Frank."

"Have you had any other person in law enforcement or any other informer tell you that Mr. Beatty was dealing heroin?"

"No."

"So the only evidence you had that Mr. Beatty was dealing drugs was the word of a drug addict who was desperate to work off a beef?"

"Miss White described Mr. Beatty's house accurately. The fact that she could tell me where he lived was important, because the house is not near the area where she says she bought from him on most occasions and it's not in an area frequented by drug addicts."

"Did you try to see if you could find any witnesses who could back up Miss White's claim that she bought drugs from Mr. Beatty?"

"No."

Amanda paused to consult her notes. "Did Alan Hotchkiss accompany you when you executed the warrant at Mr. Beatty's home?"

"Yes."

"Did he ride in your car with you?"

"Yes."

"Did Detective Hotchkiss read the warrant and the affidavit?"

"Yes."

"When was this?"

"In the car on the way to Mr. Beatty's residence."

"So after the warrant was issued but before the search?"

"Yes."

"Did Detective Hotchkiss make any comment about the affidavit before you entered the house?"

Nowicki started to answer. Then he paused and frowned. "I . . . I don't think so."

"What made you pause?"

"He never said anything when we were driving and I was trying to remember if he said anything after that. If he did, I probably didn't pay attention because we were preparing to enter the house. Detective Hotchkiss told me that Mr. Beatty is an ex-soldier with a lot of combat experience. I was concentrating exclusively on how to enter in the least dangerous manner and I was preoccupied with keeping everyone safe."

"So it's possible Detective Hotchkiss made some comment about the facts in the affidavit after the two of you left your car?"

"Like I said, if he did I don't recall the comment."

"Nothing further," Amanda said.

"Mr. Frederick?" Judge Chang said.

"No questions."

For the next half hour, Amanda questioned the SWAT team members who were at the front of the house when entry was made. She posed general questions about the search, seeding in the questions she really wanted an answer to in a disinterested tone. Amanda struck out with the first four witnesses before striking pay dirt when Harold Fernandez took the stand. After several general questions about Fernandez's training and years on the force, Amanda led the officer into the area in which she was really interested.

"Where were you in relation to Detectives Nowicki and Hotchkiss prior to entering Mr. Beatty's house, Officer Fernandez?"

"We were on the front porch. Detective Nowicki was pressed against the wall next to the left side of the door if you were facing the door. I was in the same position but on the right side of the door and Detective Hotchkiss was next to me."

"So you were between the two detectives?"

"Yes."

"If Detective Hotchkiss wanted to say something to Detective Nowicki he would have to talk past you?"

"Yes."

"Please tell the judge what Detective Hotchkiss said to Detective Nowicki and what Detective Nowicki said to Detective Hotchkiss just before entry was made," Amanda said. Then she held her breath.

"We were getting ready to go in when Detective Hotchkiss said something about there being a problem with the affidavit for the search warrant, something about one of the dates."

"Was he specific about which date?"

"No."

"And what did Detective Nowicki say to Detective Hotchkiss?"

"He said, 'Not now,' because we were ready to go in."

"Was there any more conversation about the affidavit?"

"No. Detective Nowicki knocked and we entered and that was that."

"My next witness will be Detective Alan Hotchkiss, Your Honor."

Moments later, the detective entered the courtroom, took the oath, and sat in the witness box. Amanda threw Hotchkiss a series of softballs before easing into the meat of her examination.

"This is not the first time you've been involved in a case in which Mr. Beatty was a defendant, is it?"

"No."

"Just a short time ago, Mr. Beatty was arrested because of a fight in the Lookout tavern, was he not?"

"Yes."

"Isn't it true that you had more than a casual interest in that case?"

"I investigated it."

"Do you remember a meeting in the office of Mr. Frederick at which he, you, and I were present?"

"Yes."

"I asked for a dismissal of the case because I believed that Mr. Beatty had acted in self-defense, did I not?"

"Yes."

"You vehemently opposed dismissing the case, didn't you?"

"I felt that your client had gone too far and used too much force."

"When I pointed out that Mr. Beatty was a decorated soldier who had defended our country in combat, did you ask Mr. Frederick if he was buying 'this John Wayne crap'?"

"I may have said that."

"So you had strong feelings about dismissing the case?"

"Yes."

"This assault case was fairly recent, wasn't it?"

"Yes."

"Would it be fair to say that the case is fresh in your mind?"

"I guess."

"And you had even fresher recollections about it on the evening of the search because the events were even closer to that date than they are to this day?"

"I guess."

"Detective Nowicki testified that you read the search warrant and the affidavit in support of it on the way to Mr. Beatty's house. Is that correct?"

"Yes."

"Did you notice anything odd in the affidavit?"

"Odd?"

"Was there anything in the affidavit that concerned you?"

"I'm not sure what you mean," Hotchkiss said, but it was obvious that he was stalling and the judge took a hard look at him.

"May I approach the witness, Your Honor?"

"Yes, Miss Jaffe."

Amanda walked to the witness box holding several documents.

"I'm handing the witness defense exhibit 4, a police report concerning the fight at the Lookout tavern. What was the date that the fight occurred, Detective Hotchkiss?"

"June sixth."

"And you knew that because you were heavily involved in investigating the case?"

Hotchkiss didn't answer.

"Well, Detective?"

"I did know the date of the fight."

"Mr. Beatty arrived at the tavern on June sixth around five p.m. and was arrested there and transported to jail, where he spent the night?"

"Yes."

"I'm handing Detective Hotchkiss defense exhibit seven, a copy of the affidavit in support of the search warrant that was issued for Mr. Beatty's house," Amanda said. "Please read it, Detective."

Amanda waited until Hotchkiss was through.

"In the affidavit, what dates and at what times does Carol White claim she bought heroin from Mr. Beatty."

Hotchkiss stared at the affidavit. When he answered, there was a slight tremor in his voice.

"She said that she bought heroin from Mr. Beatty after dark on the evenings of May ninth, May seventeenth, June sixth, and July fifth."

"Is it dark in early June at five p.m.?"

"No."

"You knew that Mr. Beatty arrived at the Lookout tavern around five p.m. on June sixth, did you not?"

"Yes."

"And he was in the tavern or in jail after five p.m. on the evening of June sixth, wasn't he?"

"Yes," Hotchkiss answered grudgingly.

"When you were standing on Mr. Beatty's front porch just before the police entered his home, Officer Harold Fernandez was standing between you and Detective Nowicki, was he not?"

"Yes."

"Officer Fernandez testified under oath that you told the detective that there was something wrong with a date in the affidavit. What did you mean by that?"

Hotchkiss cast a quick look at Larry Frederick.

"The district attorney can't help you, Detective," Amanda said.

Judge Chang leaned forward and gazed at the witness intently.

"When you saw Carol White's claim that she had purchased heroin from Mr. Beatty after dark on the evening of June sixth, you knew that could not be true, didn't you?" Amanda said.

"I . . . I did have some concerns."

"Were you sufficiently concerned to tell Detective Nowicki, as Officer Fernandez testified, that there was a problem with a date in the affidavit?"

"I . . ." Hotchkiss looked grim. "Yes."

"And this information was known to you after the warrant was issued and before entry was made?"

"Yes."

"No further questions."

Judge Chang looked concerned. "Any cross, Mr. Frederick?"

The prosecutor looked upset. "May I have a brief recess, Your Honor. This line of questioning has come as a surprise."

"I'd object to any recess," Amanda said.

"This is very disturbing, Mr. Frederick," Judge Chang said.

"I don't see how it has any bearing on the validity of the search," Frederick said, but it was obvious that he was flailing around.

"To the contrary," Amanda answered. "This is a clear case for a shadow challenge."

Judge Chang's brow furrowed. "I'm not familiar with that term, Miss Jaffe."

"That's probably because an opportunity for this type of challenge to a search rarely presents itself. The term comes from a poem by T. S. Eliot. 'Between the idea and the reality, between the motion and the act, falls the shadow.'

"Let's assume that the police get a search warrant that's completely bulletproof; there's clear probable cause stated in the affidavit. Then between obtaining the warrant and executing it the police learn something that undermines probable cause. An easy example is a search warrant issued in a terrorism case during a Jewish holiday. In the affidavit in support of the warrant the police swear that the home owner is a Muslim. Then the police arrive at the house and see a mezuzah on the door and a menorah in the window. In a situation like that the police are obligated to go back to the judge with this new information so the judge can decide if probable cause still exists."

"Do you have any case law in support of this theory?" the judge asked.

"I do. Close to home is the Washington case of *State v. Reichenbach*. The police obtained a warrant based on information that the defendant was going to buy drugs, but after the warrant was issued the police were told that the defendant had been unable to obtain the drugs. The warrant was executed anyway and the court held that the officer's failure to inform the issuing magistrate of this new information rendered the warrant invalid at the time of its execution.

"In *United States v. Marin-Buitrago*, the Federal Second Circuit stated, 'Certain restrictions are placed on the execution of search warrants to ensure that probable cause, as well as veracity of the information in the affidavit, exists when the warrant is executed.' And the Sixth Circuit held in *United States v. Bowling* that probable cause must exist when the warrant is issued *and* when it is executed. The court said that when new facts come to light, the officers have an obligation to inform the issuing magistrate of the change of circumstances."

"Mr. Frederick," Judge Chang said, "I'm very concerned that Detective Hotchkiss did not insist on telling Detective Nowicki that he had good reason to believe that one of Miss White's statements was not true before the warrant was executed."

"That was only one statement out of many. Miss White may have made a mistake about that one date."

"That's true, but Mr. Beatty was not home so there was no urgency to enter. Detective Nowicki could have phoned the issuing magistrate to see if this new information would change his mind about probable cause."

"No one knew where Mr. Beatty was and when he would return. He could have been lying in wait inside the house."

"Your Honor," Amanda said, "if Mr. Beatty was inside no one would have been in danger if the entry wasn't made, and the entry could still have been made if Mr. Beatty showed up before the warrant was executed if the magistrate told Detective Nowicki to go ahead after he'd been apprised of the lie in the affidavit."

Larry Frederick started to say something, but Judge Chang held up his hand. "Give me a minute to think," he said, and the attorneys sat down.

"What is he going to do?" Tom Beatty asked anxiously.

"I'm not sure," Amanda answered. "I've made a good point but I could also argue the other side of the issue. It's a close one. Judge Chang will have to throw out all of the state's evidence if he rules for us. That's a tough call in a murder case."

"I'm going to suspend this hearing until next week so you and Miss Jaffe can brief this issue," the judge said. "And I want Carol White in this courtroom when we resume."

Amanda stood. "Your Honor, will you rule on my motion for bail in light of this change of circumstances concerning the validity of the search?"

"I'm not going to decide bail now," the judge said. "But I will hear your bail motion when we reconvene to discuss the validity of the search."

"What happened in there?" Larry Frederick asked Alan Hotchkiss and Greg Nowicki as soon as they were in Frederick's office with the door shut tight.

"Greg came to me before he got the warrant," Hotchkiss said. "He asked me if I wanted to be present when we searched Beatty's house. I read the affidavit for the warrant for the first time on the way and I was almost at Beatty's house when I saw the June sixth date. I didn't get it at first. Then, just before we went in, I realized that White couldn't have bought heroin from Beatty after dark on the evening of June sixth because he was in jail. I tried to tell Greg but he told me to wait because he was concentrating on the entry."

"Is this going to screw up the arrest?" Nowicki asked.

"I don't know. I've never had an issue like this so I'll have to hit the law books."

Then he looked at Nowicki. "What I do know is that we have to find Carol White."

Chapter 15

Two days after Amanda and Larry Frederick submitted their briefs, Judge Chang's secretary phoned Amanda and told her that the judge wanted her in his courtroom as soon as possible. This time there were not as many spectators but Amanda noticed Dale Masterson sitting on the last bench.

Tom Beatty was seated at the counsel table. Two guards were standing nearby. Alan Hotchkiss and Greg Nowicki were sitting at the other counsel table with Larry Frederick.

"What's going on?" Beatty asked when Amanda sat beside him.

"I have no idea," she answered just as the judge took the bench.

"Let the record show that we are in court in *State v.*

Beatty. Mr. Beatty and Amanda Jaffe, his attorney, are, as are Deputy District Attorney Larry Frederick and Detectives Greg Nowicki and Alan Hotchkiss.

"Mr. Frederick, please tell Miss Jaffe what you told me roughly one half hour ago."

"A dead woman was discovered under the Burnside Bridge yesterday morning. The woman has been identified. It's Carol White."

Amanda was stunned. "How did she die?"

"A heroin overdose."

"Was she murdered?" Judge Chang asked.

When Frederick answered, he sounded subdued. "There was some bruising on her arms, but the medical examiner says she can't say that Miss White was attacked. The first responders didn't see anything unusual, either. The ME's best guess is that she overdosed by mistake or committed suicide."

"This doesn't change anything, Your Honor," Amanda said. "My motion to suppress doesn't rely on Miss White's testimony."

"I agree," Judge Chang said. "Mr. Frederick, I asked you to bring the detectives with you because I have some questions I want to ask Detective Nowicki."

"Detective," the judge said once Nowicki was sworn, "I am very troubled by this case, and I need your answers to several questions to assist me in reaching a decision. In the affidavit in support of the warrant, you state that Miss White told you that the defendant told her that he was getting his heroin from a drug ring that included men he'd served with in Afghanistan who'd developed ties with warlords when they were stationed there."

"Yes."

"Did you find any information that supported her statement?"

"No."

"I assume you have agents in the Drug Enforcement Administration that you talk to about cases."

"Yes, Your Honor."

"Did you ask any of them about Mr. Beatty and this alleged international drug ring?"

"I did, but they had no information about the defendant or the ring."

"Miss Jaffe submitted a memo in support of her motion for bail in which she alleges that there is strong evidence that Mr. Beatty was set up. Is she correct that there was an absence of blood spatter at the crime scene?"

"That's correct," Nowicki answered reluctantly.

"That would be inconsistent with Miss Larson's having been murdered on Mr. Beatty's property?"

"Yes."

"So Miss Larson was most probably killed elsewhere and brought to Mr. Beatty's home after she was dead."

"Yes."

"And is there surveillance footage showing Mr. Beatty at the Masterson law firm on the evening you conducted the search?" the judge asked.

"Yes."

"This supports Miss Jaffe's contention that the real killer lured Mr. Beatty to his office so the killer could plant the heroin and the body in Mr. Beatty's home."

"He could have gone to the law firm to establish an alibi."

"Miss Jaffe also alleges that her client's fingerprints were not found on the wrappings of the heroin you discovered in his basement. Is that true?"

"Yes."

"Wouldn't that be odd if he was selling to a lot of people? Wouldn't he have to take the heroin out of the wrapping and put it in a baggie or bindle?"

"Yes. But he could have worn gloves."

"Did you find any paraphernalia in Mr. Beatty's house that you would expect to find in the home of a drug dealer?"

"No."

The judge shook his head. Then he looked at Larry Frederick.

"This case stinks to high heaven," he said. "It smells of a setup."

"Your Honor, we haven't discovered any reason why anyone would want to frame the defendant. With all due respect, you're overthinking this. We have witnesses who will testify that the defendant and Miss Larson quarreled a few days before she was killed. I believe that the defendant and Miss Larson were lovers who argued, with fatal results."

"If I may, Your Honor," Amanda said.

"Yes, Miss Jaffe," Judge Chang answered.

"Mr. Beatty and Miss Larson were never lovers, and I challenge Mr. Frederick to produce a single witness who will testify that they were involved romantically. They did quarrel shortly before Miss Larson was murdered, but the reason for the quarrel also explains why someone would have killed Miss Larson and framed Mr. Beatty.

"Miss Larson's firm was trying to land a major client, but it was having financial problems. She suspected that someone in the firm was cooking the books to make its financial situation look better than it was. She told Mr. Beatty about her suspicions and asked him to help her uncover what was going on. He had just been arrested on the assault charge. He told Miss Larson he wouldn't help her because he was afraid of losing his job, and she got upset. That's why they argued. If Miss Larson was going to go public about financial fraud at the firm, there are several people who would have reason to want her out of the way. Several people knew about Mr. Beatty's arrest for assault and Miss Larson and Mr. Beatty's quarrel, so he would be the obvious scapegoat."

Frederick laughed. "Miss Jaffe's argument is preposterous. Masterson, Hamilton is one of the state's most successful law firms. And the idea that they would murder a partner to cover up a problem with their books is ridiculous."

"Can you tell me that you have a witness who supports your theory that Mr. Beatty and Miss Larson were lovers?" Judge Chang asked.

"No, Your Honor. But we do have witnesses to the quarrel."

"Can these witnesses say why Mr. Beatty and Miss Larson quarreled?"

"No. They quarreled in Miss Larson's office, so no one overheard what was said."

The judge leaned back and closed his eyes. When he opened them he looked very disturbed.

"I wish some other judge had this case," he said, "but I'm stuck with it and I have to do what I think is right. I'm granting Miss Jaffe's motion to suppress.

Carol White was a heroin addict with a pending case. She had every reason to lie to Detective Nowicki, and we know that she did lie about buying heroin from Mr. Beatty on at least one of the dates in the affidavit. Now she's dead under suspicious circumstances and can't be questioned under oath.

"Furthermore, we know for a fact that Detective Hotchkiss knew that there was a serious problem with the affidavit before the search was executed. Once he realized that there might be a problem with probable cause, he had a duty to tell Detective Nowicki about the problem.

"Now, I appreciate the fact that there was great pressure on the search team to make certain that all of the officers were safe, so talking about the affidavit right before the entry may have been a problem. But once the officers were safely inside and before the house was searched, Detective Hotchkiss should have told Detective Nowicki about the problem with the dates. Detective Nowicki could have called the issuing magistrate and explained the changed circumstances."

"Your Honor . . . ," Larry Frederick started, but the judge waved him off.

"I'm very troubled by the facts in this case, Mr. Frederick. I find Miss White's death especially troubling. I assume your office will appeal my decision. While the case is on appeal you will have time to investigate further. If you submit new arguments or evidence, I'll consider them and make them part of the record. But, right now, my mind is made up. Believe me, I've given my decision a lot of thought, and I feel that this is the appropriate decision given these circumstances."

"Your Honor," Amanda said, "will you reconsider my motion for bail?"

"Yes, I'm going to grant bail with certain conditions while the case goes up to a higher court."

When Amanda walked out of Judge Chang's courtroom, she noticed that Dale Masterson had already left. Alan Hotchkiss was talking to Greg Nowicki in the hall.

"Thanks for helping Alan and me keep our jobs," Nowicki said, his voice dripping with sarcasm.

Amanda looked puzzled.

"Every time you put a killer back on the street, we get repeat business."

"Tom is innocent. If you could step back from this case you'd see that he was framed."

"Hey, I believe you. In fact, every guy I ever sent down was framed, so the odds are in Beatty's favor."

"You should be looking at someone in Christine's firm," Amanda said. "If they were cooking the books, one of the partners would have an excellent motive to silence Christine. If Tom is innocent, someone else is guilty. It's not my job to solve your case for you, but you'll never get Christine's murderer if you stop looking."

The fourteen-story Stockman Building had been erected in the center of downtown Portland shortly after World War I in an era when architects could afford to add gargoyles and cherubs and ornate scrollwork to a facade. The law firm of Jaffe, Katz, Lehane and Brindisi leased the eighth floor and Frank Jaffe's spacious office took up one of the corners. Frank was a dinosaur. One of his few concessions to the twenty-first century was the computer that sat on a corner of a partner's desk he'd picked up at an auction shortly before he started his law practice. The office was decorated with antiques, Currier & Ives prints, and a nineteenth-century oil of the Columbia Gorge.

Amanda's father was a big man with a ruddy complexion and a full head of curly hair that had once been black but was now mostly gray. His nose had been broken more than once in his youth and he looked more like the gangsters he represented than one of Oregon's top criminal defense attorneys. When Amanda walked into his office, Frank looked up from the police report he was reading and smiled. Then he stopped smiling when he saw how glum his daughter looked.

"Judge Chang denied the motion?" Frank asked.

Amanda dropped into the client chair across from Frank. "No, I won."

"You don't look like a lawyer who's just saved a client from the gallows."

"Remember I told you why I thought I had a shot at winning the motion?"

"The affiant lied about buying dope from your client on one of the dates in the affidavit," Frank answered.

"She's dead—a heroin overdose. The ME can't say whether or not she was murdered, but she was a junkie for a long time and . . ." Amanda shook her head. "It's just suspicious, especially given all the evidence that suggests Tom was set up."

"I can see why you're upset, but the affiant's death is a problem for the police. Your job was saving Tom Beatty's life, and you did that."

"That's what's really troubling me, Dad. If Tom didn't murder Christine Larson, someone else did. And if that person went to all this trouble to frame Tom, they really wanted him out of the way. But he's not now—he's out of jail. And that means he could be in danger."

Chapter 16

Dale Masterson felt uneasy during the drive to Reginald Kiner's cabin. There was nothing unusual about that. He always felt on edge when he met with RENCO Oil's head of security. He also felt weird when he used Kiner's first name. "Reginald" was a name for a butler or Harvard preppy, not for a man who ordered the death or torture of people without a qualm.

Mark Hamilton, Masterson's law partner, didn't appear the least bit nervous, but then Mark wasn't normal. That's probably why he got on so well with Kiner. If you didn't know Mark well you would never guess that he was a sociopath who would lie and deceive without any regrets. Mark was generally regarded as one of Oregon's top corporate attorneys and a great guy. His appearance was not threatening. To the contrary, he was short, balding, a little overweight, and had a great smile. Mark could tell the funniest jokes and was sought after as a golf partner. People trusted him right up to the point where the knife slipped in, and sometimes afterward.

Mark had met Kiner many years ago when Kiner was a young officer working narcotics for the Portland Police Bureau and Mark was paying his law school tuition with money he earned selling drugs. Kiner had busted Mark, then let him slide after accepting a payoff. This mutually agreeable relationship continued until Kiner left the police force and started working in the private sector for RENCO Oil, where he was the current director of the company's security division.

The two men renewed their business relationship while Mark was defending a lawsuit for the then-fledgling firm of Masterson, Hamilton. A win would make the firm's reputation, but one recalcitrant witness was threatening to cost the firm millions. As an executive at RENCO Oil, Kiner was respectable enough to have a membership at The Westmont, Portland's most exclusive country club, where Mark was also a member. Mark had mentioned the problem he was having with his case during a round of golf. Kiner had told Mark that he could solve his problem. RENCO operated in some of the scariest areas of the globe and had to use individuals with certain skill sets to solve problems in those scary places. For a price, Kiner said, he could contact one of these people and make Mark's problem disappear. A month later, the lawsuit was settled for eight figures, and Mark and Kiner were two happy fellas.

Masterson, Hamilton had not used Kiner's services often, but Dale had panicked and contacted Kiner when Christine Larson threatened to tell Global Mining about the discrepancies in the law firm's books. With Larson dead and Tom Beatty in jail for her murder, everything appeared to be rosy. Then Amanda Jaffe had mentioned the books while arguing her motion.

Kiner's log cabin was deep in the forest near Mt. Hood at the end of a long dirt road. The security chief insisted on meeting there anytime he was going to take part in a certain type of discussion because the cabin was always swept for bugs beforehand and was surrounded by motion sensors and other high-tech devices that ensured privacy.

"This is fucked up," Masterson muttered.

"Most definitely. And we wouldn't be in this mess if you hadn't asked Larson to make the report. What were you thinking?"

"I thought Global would buy the report if she presented it. I mean, she looked so honest and she'd always been a good soldier. How did I know she'd grow a conscience?"

"Well, she did."

"What are we going to do?" Masterson asked anxiously.

"We're going to relax," Hamilton said.

"How can I relax? That bitch Jaffe told the judge about our books in open court. It's public record."

"And impossible to substantiate, Dale."

As he got out of the car, Masterson noticed an armed guard move out of the foliage and give him the once-over. Masterson was certain that there were other eyes on him too. The door to the cabin opened as the law partners climbed the steps to the front porch, and Kiner let them inside. The security chief, a large man with a commanding presence, wore his gray-flecked hair short. Stubble sprouted on a chiseled face with high cheekbones, a slightly misshapen nose, and a broad forehead decorated by a jagged scar. He wore a pair of khaki pants and a short-sleeved black silk shirt that hung outside his trousers and fit loosely across his broad shoulders.

The cabin was rustic, the walls decorated with the mounted heads of exotic animals that Kiner had killed on every continent.

"Drinks?" Kiner asked.

"Nothing for me," Hamilton said.

"Scotch, a double," Masterson told their host.

"I've got a twenty-five-year-old single malt I think you'll enjoy," Kiner said.

"We've got a serious situation, Reggie," Masterson told Kiner as their host walked over to the wet bar.

"Not anymore," Kiner answered as he poured a stiff shot of amber liquid into a glass of cut crystal.

"What . . . what do you mean?" Masterson asked.

"Tom Beatty will soon cease to exist."

"Oh, God!" Masterson said as he ran a hand across his forehead. First it was Christine, then that White woman. Now there would be another murder.

"Tell me what you think," Kiner said as he handed the glass to Masterson.

"I think we may still have problems. Getting rid of Beatty doesn't cure the fact that Jaffe told the court we cooked the books to get Global Mining as a client."

"The scotch, Dale," Kiner said. "What do you think about the scotch?"

"You have to get a hold of yourself, Dale," Hamilton said. "No one can prove anything about the books. Larson is dead and anything she told Beatty is hearsay."

"What about Jaffe? She knows. She's the one who told the judge."

"We'll keep an eye on her," Kiner said, "but what she knows is also hearsay, and she won't have any reason to pursue her theory without a client to defend."

Masterson felt ill and had a sudden urge to go to the bathroom. He excused himself and walked down the hall.

"Is he going to get his shit together?" Kiner asked.

Hamilton shrugged. "I don't know. Dale can get emotional, but I think he'll be okay."

"He doesn't act like someone who's going to be okay. He acts like someone who'll spill his guts to the first cop who questions him."

"No, no, Reggie, Dale won't fold," Hamilton said, but he didn't sound convincing.

"If you say so," Kiner answered, but Hamilton could tell that his partner was making Kiner nervous, and that wasn't a good thing to do.

Chapter 17

Amanda asked Kate Ross to drive Tom home, and she was waiting in the jail reception area when he stepped out of the elevator at ten p.m. He looked exhausted, and was quiet during the drive.

"Why don't you stop here," he said when they reached the entrance to his cul-de-sac.

"I can drive you to your door," Kate said.

Tom smiled. "Thanks, but I've been locked up for days and I'd like to get a little fresh air."

Kate pulled over to the curb and Tom got out. "Thanks for the ride," he said. "You and Amanda have been fantastic. I can't thank you enough for what you've done for me."

Kate nodded, embarrassed by Tom's gratitude. "Do you need anything? What about food? Anything in your fridge is going to be pretty ripe."

"Thanks, but I'll be okay. Right now all I want is a hot shower and a good night's sleep in my own bed."

"Okay, then. Amanda will be in touch if there are any developments in your case, and call if you have any questions."

"I will."

The sky was overcast, and the only streetlight on his block didn't provide a lot of illumination. Tom's house was dark and his yard was in shadow. He waited until Kate's car was out of sight. Then he moved into the shadows and ran into the woods that bordered his house. Years of combat in very dangerous environments had made Tom hyperalert. That's how he'd spotted the car that had followed Kate from the Justice Center and pulled up a block from the entrance to the cul-de-sac. The odds of a neighbor just happening to be waiting outside the Justice Center at ten at night, then driving to within a block of his home behind Kate's vehicle, were minuscule. Given what had happened to Christine and Carol White, he wasn't taking any chances.

When he was certain he wouldn't be seen, Tom ran to the side window in his bedroom and peered through it. The bedroom door was open and a shadow moved in the hall. Tom shifted to a window that gave him a look into the front room and saw a muscular man in a windbreaker talking on a cell phone. Now Tom knew there was at least one person inside and one person in the car that had followed him from the jail. The odds were high that they were both armed. Tom had two choices: run or stay and fight. If he ran, he might never find out who killed Christine.

Tom went to the shed behind his house where he kept his mower and his tools, and found a wrench. Then he opened the rear door with his key, moved inside, and relocked the door. He hadn't been in combat for several years, but his training was kicking in. He slowed his breathing and crept down the hall until he heard a low voice coming from the front room.

"I just told you. I've been watching the front door since you told me he got out of the car." Pause. "No, he never came up the path and I checked the back door." Pause. "Yeah, it was locked." Pause. "No, I don't know where he went." Pause. "Okay."

As soon as the man stopped talking, Tom hit him in the head with the wrench. He stumbled forward just as the front door opened. A thickset man holding a gun stepped inside. Tom used the man he'd just stunned as a shield. The gun went off and a red stain spread around an exit wound in the stunned man's chest. Tom leaped from behind the wounded man and smashed the wrench down on the gunman's wrist. The gun fell, and

Tom followed with a glancing blow on the side of the head. The gunman staggered backward off the porch and rolled away from Tom. When he stood up he was holding a knife, but he looked dazed.

Tom moved forward in a crouch. The man lunged with the knife, but his movements were sluggish. Tom sidestepped and swung the wrench. Metal connected with bone. As the man lurched sideways, Tom swung with all his might. The knife dropped to the lawn, the killer's eyes rolled back in his head, and he pitched forward. When Tom hit him again, he crumpled to the ground. Tom knelt beside the body and felt for a pulse. There wasn't one. He swore silently. Then he dragged the corpse inside. The other man was still alive, but his breathing was shallow and he was losing blood. Tom knelt beside him and stared into his eyes. The man was fading fast.

"Who sent you?" Tom demanded.

The man stared at him. Tom slapped his face, but it didn't help.

"Who sent you?" he asked again. The man's lips moved but no sound came out. Then his chin dropped to his chest, and Tom knew he was gone.

Tom shut his eyes and slumped onto the floor. He had not wanted to kill. He'd done enough killing. All he'd wanted was information.

Once Tom was calm, he went through the dead men's pockets. Neither one had any identification. Tom stood up and took stock of his situation. Someone had sent trained assassins to kill him, but why, and who was behind this attempt on his life? With both men dead, he would not be able to get quick answers to his questions—but he was going to get answers; that was a fact. One thing he would bet on was that the person who wanted him dead was the same person who was responsible for beating Christine Larson to death, and Tom vowed to make that person pay.

Chapter 18

If you did a Web search for "Trophy Wife," it wouldn't be surprising if you discovered a photograph of Veronica Masterson, Dale Masterson's third spouse. Veronica was a very well preserved thirty-five-year-old with a gym-trimmed body, silky, dyed-blond hair, and enough intelligence to keep a man interested while she figured out novel ways to spend his money. You would think that with an estate situated on several acres, a very wealthy husband, and ample idle time, Veronica would always be in a good mood, but that was not the case when she arrived home at eight thirty on this balmy Saturday evening.

Veronica's day had started well. She'd gotten up at ten, grateful that she wouldn't be groped by her husband, who had an early tee time. After a leisurely breakfast, Veronica had driven to Mark Hamilton's house, where she had screwed his brains out, and vice versa. Talk about not being able to tell a book by its cover. Mark looked like a toad, but he fucked like a bull. Her husband, on the other hand, looked like a bull and, well . . .

After leaving Mark, Veronica had driven into the city, and that was when her sunny day turned gloomy. By the time she arrived at the Westmont Country Club, she was fuming because she had not been able to find a dress or shoes for the children's hospital gala. She had complained to Mary Ann and Anne Marie over dinner and her former sorority sisters had sympathized. There was famine in Africa, chaos in the Middle East, and a pitiful lack of shopping opportunities in Portland, and the women viewed all three disasters as being equally tragic.

Her shopping debacle had put Veronica in a terrible mood that the beautiful day and the martinis she'd imbibed during dinner had not been able to dispel. She was still brooding about life's injustices when she turned onto the long driveway that led to her eight-thousand-square-foot mansion. Once in sight of the house, she saw someone racing across the lawn. The man saw the car and stopped short. Then he jerked up his arm to cover his face—a useless gesture, because Veronica had no trouble recognizing the heavily bearded visage of Brandon Masterson, Dale's twenty-six-year-old son.

The car closed on Brandon and he veered away from it. Veronica stopped in the turnaround in front of her home, stared behind her, and saw Brandon disappearing around a curve. She wondered what the little shit was doing at the house and whether she'd imagined the red stains on his white T-shirt and ragged jeans.

Six months ago, Dale had disinherited Brandon after he'd crashed a party Dale had thrown for the executives of a coal mining company for whom the firm had just won a multimillion-dollar verdict. Brandon had screamed several uncomplimentary statements about Dale's corporate clients and Veronica. His tirade about corporate polluters and Dale's "latest slut" had not ceased even after the security guards had hustled Brandon out the door and dumped him in his Prius.

Moments after Brandon disappeared, Veronica lost interest in him and refocused on the only positive aspect of her shopping adventure. She had wheedled a Caribbean vacation at a very pricey resort out of Dale by withholding sex for several days. As soon as he'd agreed to Veronica's demands, her headaches had miraculously disappeared. Veronica had purchased three very sexy bikinis and several beach and evening ensembles for the trip. She hauled her purchases out of the trunk. The servants had been given the day off so Veronica had to carry her swag up to her bedroom. This added to her annoyance.

After putting away her purchases, Veronica changed into shorts. Then she went downstairs to make herself a drink. The den was at the front of the house, with a nice view of the front lawn. As she walked by it, an odd odor assailed her sensitive nostrils. The stink reminded her of rotting meat, and she wrinkled her nose. Curiosity about the smell led her to open the door to the den.

Veronica Masterson had found her husband sprawled on his back on the carpet in the middle of his den. His tan slacks and bright green golf shirt were spattered with blood, but most of the blood was on Dale's face, which had sustained a horrific beating. Something about the murder scene looked familiar. As soon as Alan Hotchkiss figured it out, he muttered a curse.

"What?" asked Billie Brewster, Hotchkiss's partner. Brewster was a slender African-American woman with close-cropped black hair who had been teamed with Zeke Forbus until his retirement. Now that Hotchkiss was her partner, she usually played good cop to Hotchkiss's really mean cop, because she was as easygoing as Hotchkiss was intense.

"You were on vacation when Christine Larson was murdered."

"The case that Chang threw out?"

Hotchkiss nodded. "She worked in Masterson's firm and she was beaten to death, just like Masterson. Her face was a bloody pulp."

"And you think . . . ?"

"Our suspect, Tom Beatty, was a paralegal at Masterson's firm, and I'd love to know where he was today."

A policewoman walked over to the detectives. "Dr. Clay says Mrs. Masterson is calm enough to be interviewed."

Veronica Masterson had been standing outside her house on the front lawn, screaming hysterically, when the first officers arrived on the scene in response to her 911 call. They had brought her into the library, which was down the hall from the den. When she wouldn't calm down, they had gotten the name of her doctor and he'd arrived shortly after the detectives and the forensic unit. The doctors Hotchkiss saw at Kaiser Permanente didn't make house calls, and he decided that there were many positive benefits to being filthy rich.

Roger Clay was a rugged-looking man in his mid-sixties with curly gray hair and a ruddy complexion. He met the detectives at the door to the library. Hotchkiss looked past him and saw Veronica slumped in an easy chair next to a stone fireplace.

"Mrs. Masterson can answer questions, but I'd like to give her a sedative and get her to bed so . . ."

"We'll try and keep this short. We can talk to her again after she's gotten a good night's sleep," Brewster assured Clay.

"Thank you," the doctor said.

Hotchkiss pulled a chair in front of Veronica. She looked up. Tears had ruined her makeup and her hair was in disarray.

"My name is Alan Hotchkiss and this is Billie Brewster. We're the detectives who are going to find out who did this to your husband."

Veronica jerked up. She looked furious. "I know who killed him. It was that disgusting piece of shit Brandon."

"Who is Brandon?" Hotchkiss asked.

"Dale's son. I saw the little bastard running from the house and he had blood all over him."

"Okay, let's slow down here," Hotchkiss said. "When did you see Brandon?"

"When I got home."

"Where had you been?"

"I went shopping. Then I had dinner at the club with two of my friends."

"What club is that?"

"The Westmont," Veronica answered in a tone that let the detective know that she was shocked that he needed to ask.

"Did you drive home after dinner?" Hotchkiss asked.

"Yes."

"When?"

"About eight thirty. And that's when I saw him. I was halfway up the drive and he was running away from the house. When he saw me he froze and threw up his arm, like this," she said, imitating Brandon. "Then he ran away, but not before I saw his T-shirt. It was covered in blood and there was blood on his jeans."

"Why would Brandon murder his father?" Hotchkiss asked.

"He hated him, that's why. Dale disinherited the little prick. And he's crazy. Everything is 'global warming' and 'the environment.' He's always picketing or at some protest, and he hated Dale because Dale represents coal and oil companies. He's a complete nutcase."

"I take it that Brandon doesn't live here."

"Are you kidding?"

"Do you know where he's living?"

"I have no idea. You'll have to ask his tree-hugger friends. He's involved with every environmental group in the state."

"Okay," Hotchkiss said. "I'll let you get some rest in a minute. I just have a few more questions. Can you think of anyone else who might have done this to your husband?"

"No. I mean, he's a lawyer. He sues all the time but they're corporations, you know, not real people."

"Have you ever heard of a man named Tom Beatty?"

Veronica's brow furrowed. "No."

"Mr. Masterson never mentioned him?"

"No, who is he?"

"Just someone who used to work for your husband's firm." Hotchkiss stood up. "We'll want to talk to you again, but it's more important that you get some rest now. I can't imagine how you're feeling."

And Veronica knew he couldn't. Her social life would be in shambles for a while, what with the funeral and a period of mourning. On the bright side, she was going to be a very rich woman, and she wouldn't need to look for a dress for the gala.

Chapter 19

Alan Hotchkiss put out an APB for Brandon Masterson. Then he told Billie Brewster that he wanted to drive to Tom Beatty's house because of the similarities in the way Christine Larson and Dale Masterson had died. On the drive, a patrolman who had checked out Brandon Masterson's apartment radioed Hotchkiss to tell him that Brandon was not at home.

There was no car parked in front of Beatty's house and the lights were out. The detectives approached the front door cautiously. Billie knocked loudly. Beatty didn't call out and they didn't hear anyone moving inside.

"Mr. Beatty, this is Detective Hotchkiss. I'd like to talk to you," Hotchkiss shouted after waiting a minute.

"What do you think?" Hotchkiss asked.

"We can't barge in without a warrant," Billie replied.

Hotchkiss thought for a moment, then he pulled out his phone and made a call. One of Judge Chang's conditions for Beatty's bail was that Beatty report daily to someone at Parole and Probation. It was late, so Jane Lowell wasn't in her office, but the person on duty gave Hotchkiss the number of her cell phone.

"Hey, Jane," Hotchkiss said when he was connected to the person to whom Beatty was supposed to report.

"What's up, Alan?"

"I'm at Thomas Beatty's house. We wanted to talk to him in connection with another case—not the one he's out on bail for. He's not home, and I was wondering if he's been reporting to you like he's supposed to."

"Beatty never reported in. I gave him a day or two to give him the benefit of the doubt. Then I called his number a few times. Personally, I think he's in the wind. That's what I told Judge Chang this afternoon."

"Thanks, Jane."

Hotchkiss then called the judge at home. After they'd spoken a few minutes, he hung up.

"Chang gave us the okay. We can go in."

Hotchkiss tried the door. The knob turned and it opened. They looked at each other. There was no car parked in front of the house and the door was open. That was not a good sign.

Billie walked into the room and fanned it with her gun. No one. She flipped on the light and started forward.

"Stop!" Hotchkiss commanded.

Billie held up and looked where her partner was pointing.

"Is that blood?" Hotchkiss asked.

Chapter 20

J oe Damico put out his cigarette and waved his hand to disperse the smoke into the stairwell of the twenty-third floor. Smoking was prohibited everywhere in the office building where he worked as a security guard, but the few associates on duty on Saturday night in the law offices of Masterson, Hamilton were on the floor below and would never smell the smoke.

Damico checked his watch. It was time to make his rounds. He decided to start on the twenty-third floor, then work his way down. He hadn't seen anyone working on this floor when he'd made his rounds earlier in the evening and he did an indifferent walk-through until a flash of light caught his eye.

The security guard frowned. Had he really seen light seeping out from under the door of Mr. Masterson's office? There was nothing there now. If there had been light, it was probably something from outside the building that had shone through Mr. Masterson's window. Only that didn't make sense—they were twenty-three stories above the ground.

Damico was a retired Portland cop who had been an MP in the Army before joining the police bureau, but he hadn't been in a dangerous situation for years. He felt his gut tighten as he crept down the hall with his hand on his gun.

It was probably nothing. Maybe Mr. Masterson had forgotten a brief or some legal document and had come back to get it. If he had seen a light that was probably the explanation. But why was the office dark now?

Damico paused in front of the door and pressed his ear against it. Nothing. His hand closed on the knob. Should he announce his presence before barging in? Masterson had a reputation. What if he was banging a secretary or one of the young associates? Damico decided it was better to be safe than sorry.

"Mr. Masterson, is that you in there?" he called out.

When no one answered, he called out again. Then he took a deep breath and opened the door. The only light in the room came from Mr. Masterson's computer. The security guard squinted but he didn't see anyone in the room. After a moment, he took a step inside, and the next thing he remembered was coming to on Dale Masterson's carpet.

Billie Brewster and Alan Hotchkiss were on their way back to headquarters when they heard about the break-in at Masterson, Hamilton. When they arrived, there were two marked cars and a van from the crime lab parked at the entrance to the building. An officer had been posted in the lobby, and he told the detectives to go to the twenty-third floor. When they got out of the elevator another officer directed them to Dale Masterson's office. Robbery detectives Alice Herrera and Max Rosenbaum were conferring in the hall outside the office, but they stopped when they saw Brewster and Hotchkiss approaching.

"To what do we owe the presence of two such eminent detectives?" Herrera asked.

"This is Dale Masterson's office, right?" Hotchkiss asked.

"Yeah," Rosenbaum answered.

"He was beaten to death tonight," Hotchkiss said.

"No shit?" Rosenbaum said.

"Yeah," Billie answered. "So what happened here?"

"The security guard was making his rounds and he thought he saw a light in Masterson's office," Herrera said. "When he went in to investigate he saw a light coming from Masterson's computer. Then someone coldcocked him."

"Is he okay?" Billie asked.

"He probably has a concussion," Rosenbaum said. "The EMTs took him to the hospital."

"What was taken?" Hotchkiss asked.

Herrera jerked her thumb toward the office. "Mark Hamilton, one of the partners, is inside doing an inventory. The lab guys are inside, too, so we're giving them some space."

"Does Hamilton know about Dale Masterson?" Billie asked.

"No," Herrera answered.

"Let's get him out here," Hotchkiss said.

Rosenbaum went into the office. A moment later, a harried-looking man followed him out. He was wearing jeans and a sweatshirt and it was obvious that he had been summoned to the law office from his home. Rosenbaum pointed the lawyer toward the homicide detectives.

"I'm Alan Hotchkiss, Mr. Hamilton, and I'm afraid I have some very bad news for you. Mr. Masterson has been the victim of a homicide."

Hamilton's mouth gaped open. He struggled to speak and finally said, "What?"

"Mr. Masterson was killed in his home, this evening."

"Jesus! Do you know who did it?"

"We're investigating some leads," Hotchkiss said evasively. "We came here as soon as we heard about this break-in. We thought it could be connected to the homicide. Do you know what was taken?"

"I don't know what was on Dale's desk when he last left work. He had some expensive paintings on the walls but they're still there. The computer was on, and I called our tech guy. He's looking at it now."

"When was the last time you spoke to Mr. Masterson?"

"We had a phone conversation yesterday about a case. It involves some real estate holdings."

"How did he seem?" Hotchkiss asked.

"Normal. Not upset or worried, if that's what you mean. I think he and Veronica—his wife—were going to a party in the evening."

"What about work? Did he seem worried about any particular person, someone with whom he was litigating, anyone in your firm, a disgruntled employee?"

"No. I mean, Dale was handling some pretty big cases, but I can't think of someone who's involved in his cases who would want to kill him. And I can't think of anyone in the firm or any ex-employee who would be mad enough at Dale to murder him."

"What about his son, Brandon?" Billie asked. "We've been told that they didn't get along."

Hamilton barked out a laugh. " 'Didn't get along' is an understatement. Brandon is a head case. But murder . . . ?" Hamilton shook his head. "Brandon is all talk."

Then he paused. "How was Dale killed?"

"He was beaten to death."

"Then it's definitely not Brandon. Have you met him?"

"No, sir," Hotchkiss said.

"As soon as you do, you'll see he couldn't possibly have beaten Dale to death. Dale is . . . was very physically fit. He was a wrestler in college, and he stayed in shape. Brandon wouldn't stand a chance against his father in a fight."

A sudden thought occurred to Hamilton. "Wasn't Christine Larson beaten to death?"

"Yes," Hotchkiss said.

"What about Tom Beatty? Have you questioned him?"

"Why do you ask? Have you heard or seen anything that would lead you to believe Beatty had a grudge against your partner?"

"No. It's just the similarities in the crimes."

"Mr. Beatty is the first person I thought of but we can't find him."

"He's on the loose?" Hamilton asked nervously.

"It looks like he jumped bail. We have an APB out for him."

As soon as the homicide detectives left, Mark Hamilton went back into Dale Masterson's office to complete his inspection, but his mind was elsewhere.

If Beatty was missing it could be because Kiner's men had taken care of him. But what if they hadn't.

As soon as Hamilton finished in Dale's office he was brought home by the officer who'd driven him to the firm. Once he was inside, he called Kiner. Kiner didn't pick up until the third ring. When he answered it was obvious that he'd been sleeping.

"Why are you calling me?" Kiner asked.

"Someone broke into Dale Masterson's office tonight and went through his computer. While I was at the office a homicide detective told me that Dale was beaten to death tonight."

"You still haven't told me why you're calling."

"The detective said he thinks Tom Beatty may be involved. They can't find him."

"It's late," Kiner stated emphatically. "I want to get back to sleep. Let's not discuss this now. Let's meet at the cabin tomorrow."

"But . . ."

"Do you really want to talk about this over the phone?" Kiner asked, the edge in his voice getting sharper.

There was dead air for a moment. Then Hamilton caught on. "Sure, tomorrow is fine. Sorry I woke you."

The call ended, and Hamilton had some idea about why Kiner had been paranoid about talking on the phone. Either Kiner's men had killed Beatty, in which case he wouldn't want to implicate himself in a murder, or something had gone wrong and Beatty was still alive.

Chapter 21

"Thank you for coming in on such short notice," Judge Chang said when Amanda walked into the courtroom. As she headed down the aisle, Amanda saw Billie Brewster and Alan Hotchkiss sitting with Larry Frederick at his counsel table.

"Now that everyone is here, let's put this on the record," Judge Chang continued. "Court has convened at the request of Deputy District Attorney Larry Frederick, who has filed a motion to revoke the bail of Miss Jaffe's client, Thomas Beatty. Let the record show that Mr. Frederick and Miss Jaffe are present but the defendant is not. Also, Portland police detectives Alan Hotchkiss and Billie Brewster are in the courtroom, sitting with Mr. Frederick.

"Mr. Frederick, this is your motion, so you have the floor."

"Your Honor, I am serving Miss Jaffe with a copy of my motion and an affidavit from Jane Lowell of the Parole and Probation Department. If Miss Jaffe wants Mrs. Lowell to testify in person I can have her here in about twenty minutes."

"Miss Jaffe," the judge said, "you're within your rights to put Mrs. Lowell's testimony on the record, but she told me everything that's in the affidavit yesterday when she alerted me to the fact that Mr. Beatty had failed to meet one of his release conditions by never contacting Mrs. Lowell and not answering his phone when she called him."

"It won't be necessary for Mrs. Lowell to come to court," Amanda said when she was finished reading the affidavit.

"I'm also handing Miss Jaffe an affidavit signed by Detective Hotchkiss in which he states that he and Detective Brewster went to the defendant's house last night to talk to him about a case unrelated to the murder of Miss Larson. Detective Hotchkiss swears that the defendant was not home and his car was not in the area. Additionally, the detectives found blood on the floor in the front room of the defendant's home."

"Do you need the detectives to testify?" the judge asked.

"No," Amanda said when she finished reading Hotchkiss's affidavit, "but I would like to know if the blood is Mr. Beatty's."

"Detective?" the judge asked.

Hotchkiss stood. "The blood is at the lab being analyzed and we haven't gotten a result yet."

"Anything else, Miss Jaffe?" Chang asked.

"No."

"I had reservations when I granted bail in a case this serious, but it seemed appropriate at the time. I did tell Mr. Beatty very clearly that he had to call Parole and Probation every day or his bail would be revoked. It's on the record that he said he understood that condition and several others I imposed. Now he's gone and he never called in, so I have no choice but to grant the State's motion. Do you have an argument you think will persuade me to keep Mr. Beatty out on bail, Miss Jaffe?"

"No, Your Honor. But I would ask the court to hold a hearing on the issue if Mr. Beatty is put back in custody. The blood in the entryway bothers me. If Mr. Beatty was wounded or in danger, he may have an explanation that would satisfy the court."

"Of course, Miss Jaffe. If he turns himself in or is rearrested, you can file another motion for bail and I'll hear everything your client and you have to say. But for right now, Mr. Beatty's bail is revoked."

When court adjourned a few minutes later Amanda started to leave, but Billie Brewster caught up with her.

"If your client gets in touch, do the smart thing and advise him to turn himself in," Billie said.

"If he gets in touch I'll do that."

Billie was about to say something else when her phone rang.

"See you around," Billie said as she answered it.

"Are you investigating the murder of someone named Dale Masterson?" the desk sergeant at the Portland Police Bureau asked.

"Yeah, why?"

"His son just showed up and confessed. We have him in an interrogation room. I thought you'd like to know."

Amanda was in a terrible mood when she left the courthouse. She liked Tom Beatty, and the fact that he was missing, coupled with the blood the detectives had found in his front room, had her worried. As soon as she got back to her office she began to look for Kate Ross, but no one knew where she was. Amanda was headed to her father's office when she remembered that he was in court in Washington County.

Lacking someone to vent to, Amanda went to her office and slumped in her chair. That's when she realized that the person she really wished she could talk to was Mike. Mike always knew the right thing to say to make the blues go away, like when he'd talked her out of her funk the day she was upset about the way Larry Frederick was stonewalling her.

Amanda started to reach for the phone, but she hesitated.

"Why are you hesitating?" she asked herself.

"Because you're scared," she answered. "Scared of commitment; scared of losing your independence.

"Would that be so bad if you committed to someone who really loved you and cared for you—someone you loved back?" she wondered.

Amanda took a deep breath and dialed Mike's office.

"Let's try it," she said as soon as he answered. "But can we stay at my condo? I really like my condo."

"No problem. Uh, when do you want me to move in?"

"It's Friday. You could move in tomorrow."

"Tomorrow it is. And thank you," Mike said.

Amanda hesitated. Then she took a really deep breath and said it.

"When you asked me about moving in, you told me you loved me and I didn't say it back. But I'm saying it now. I love you, Mike. That's why I think this will work."

"Me too, and thanks for telling me. I've been having a bad day, but the sun just came out."

Chapter 22

When Billie Brewster entered the interrogation room, Brandon Masterson was slouched in his chair with his scrawny arms folded over his sunken chest and his lips curled into a superior smile. The suspect's long hair was unkempt and unwashed, and the beard that hid most of his face displayed trapped pieces of food. Most off-putting was the fact that Brandon had not bothered to change out of his blood-smeared T-shirt and jeans.

Billie developed an intense dislike for Brandon as soon as she saw him. She knew this was unprofessional, so she tamped down her feelings and kept her composure even though the suspect's smug attitude and disgusting appearance pushed several of her buttons.

"Hi, Brandon," the detective said. "How are you doing? I gather you've been in here for a while. Do you want some food, coffee, a soft drink?"

"Chamomile tea and a scone would be great," Brandon replied, his tone dripping with sarcasm.

Billie smiled, refusing to take the bait. "You're in luck. There's a Starbucks a few blocks from here. I'll send someone over."

Brandon stared across the table at the detective. "Let's get this over with."

"If that's what you want. First, though, I've got to read you your rights."

"Consider them read. I know I can remain silent and that anything I say can be used against me in court and I know I have a right to an attorney and one will be provided free of charge if I can't afford to hire an attorney. I'm waiving all those rights and I'm not being coerced. Is there anything I've missed?"

"No, Mr. Masterson, that covers everything. So, what do you want to tell me?"

"I killed Dale Masterson this afternoon."

"How did you do that?"

"I beat him to death."

"Why did you kill your father?"

"I was acting in defense of other people."

"And who might they be?"

"Every living soul on this planet."

"I'm not following you. Can you explain that to me?"

Brandon's features morphed from disdain into pure hate.

"Do you realize that our planet is dying? The ozone layer is being depleted at a rapid rate, raped by greenhouse gases and carbon emissions from coal, causing global warming that is shrinking the polar ice caps and destroying arable land. Oil spills and chemical pollutants are poisoning the food supply in our rivers and oceans. We will soon have no food to feed anyone but the very rich."

"Just how is global warming connected to your father?" Billie asked.

"My father's law firm represents oil companies and coal mining companies *for profit*! He built his fancy mansion and bought his sports cars and his slut wife's fancy clothes with money he earned from murderers. He was no better than a Mafia don. No, I take that back. The Mafia never tried to murder an entire planet."

Brandon took a deep breath, leaned back in his chair, and stared at Billie, daring the detective to contradict him.

"I get it now, but how does killing your dad stop global warming? The corporations are still polluting whether he's alive or dead, and his firm will keep representing them."

"It sends a message that you will pay for your sins. If more CEOs and unethical lawyers start dying, maybe the CEOs and corporate lawyers who are still alive will think twice about what they're doing."

"So you're hoping that your action will start a jihad against the polluters?"

Brandon flashed Billie a wide smile. "Exactly!"

"That's certainly an interesting approach to saving the planet. So, you want to walk me through your . . . act of civil disobedience. Why were you at your father's house today?"

"Global Mining, his latest client, is one of the worst polluters on the planet, and he was instrumental in bringing these vampires to his firm. I went to try and get him to realize that representing Global was like representing the companies that made the ovens for the Nazi concentration camps."

"Did you tell your father you were coming?"

"No. I knew he wouldn't see me if I told him."

"What happened when you got there?" Billie asked.

"He kicked me out last year when he disinherited me but he never changed the locks. I used my key and came inside."

"Was there anyone else at home?"

"No."

"What did you do once you were inside?"

"I went to the den," Brandon said, but he faltered and his eyes got a faraway look.

"What happened next?" Billie prodded.

Brandon licked his lips and refocused. "He was sitting at his desk, working on something. As soon as he saw me he jumped up and ordered me out of the house. I . . . I told him he had to stop representing Global Mining but he paid no attention to what I was saying. He came around his desk and walked toward me. I was afraid he was going to attack me so . . . so I hit him and we fought and I knocked him down and . . . and I don't remember much after that except running out of the house."

A few questions suggested themselves to Billie, and she was tempted to ask them, but she had her confession so she decided to pass.

"Thank you for being so honest, Brandon. I appreciate that. I'm going to have an officer take your clothes so we can have the lab test the blood. I'll try to get the jail to find a jumpsuit that will fit. I'll also have a statement typed up for you to sign. And I did mean it about the food. You've got to be hungry, unless killing your father also killed your appetite."

The interrogation room was wired for sound, and an inconspicuous camera in a corner near the ceiling transmitted a picture of the interview to Alan

Hotchkiss, who was watching and listening in an adjoining room.

"What do you think?" Billie asked as soon as she entered.

"If the blood on his clothes matches Dale Masterson's blood, I think we've closed another case."

Billie didn't say anything.

"Okay, I'll bite. What's bothering you?" Hotchkiss said.

"Dale Masterson was a big, muscular guy, and Brandon . . . I just don't see him getting the better of his father in a fight."

Hotchkiss shrugged. "That's what Masterson's partner said, and it makes sense on paper, but weird things happen in real life. Masterson may have been bigger and more muscular than his son but he was also a lot older, so he'd have slower reflexes. Maybe junior got in a lucky punch that knocked Masterson down."

Billie shook her head. "Something about his story doesn't ring true. I'm worried there's something else going on here."

"Hey, Billie, we're not talking about some petty misdemeanor where the kid is gonna get work release or a fine. Young Mr. Masterson just confessed to a crime with a possible death penalty. You don't do that for fun."

"Still . . ."

"Be honest. How many cases have you investigated that have been tied up in a neat bow? There are usually some unanswered questions when a perp says he didn't do it. But there tend to be very few loose ends when the guy we arrest confesses. Now, I'm not suggesting we stop looking into this thing; Brandon obviously has a few screws loose. But absent another viable suspect or some forensic evidence that points to a false confession, I'm going with the guy who had a motive, the means, and the opportunity, who was seen running from the scene of the crime and has just confessed."

Chapter 23

Mike had moved in on Saturday. Moving his things from his apartment had been exhausting and they'd gone to bed early. Sunday was supposed to be beautiful and Mike and Amanda had plans to sleep late, then visit a few Willamette Valley vineyards after they got up, but part of their plan went up in smoke when the answering service put through Sarah Hartmann's call at seven thirty in the morning.

Normally, Amanda would have asked Hartmann to come in on Monday morning, but her interest was piqued when Mrs. Hartmann told her that her son was accused of beating Tom Beatty's ex-boss to death, by the same method used to murder Christine Larson. Amanda agreed to meet Hartmann at nine, figuring that she and Mike could still get on the road by noon and make a day of it.

The Stockman Building was locked on Sundays and Hartmann was waiting on the sidewalk. Amanda introduced herself as she unlocked the street door and ushered Hartmann into the lobby.

"I'm sorry to have to ask you to meet on a Sunday," Hartmann said, "but I didn't find out that Brandon had been arrested until I read the paper this morning."

"There's no need to apologize," Amanda said as they stepped into the elevator. "You're a mother, and your son is in a lot of trouble."

"Thank you for being so understanding."

Neither of them spoke on the ride up to the law office, and that gave Amanda a chance to study Hartmann. The woman was nervous and she fidgeted with her purse as they ascended. Her blond hair was expertly styled and she was wearing designer clothes, so Amanda deduced that she had money. Nothing else Amanda observed called that deduction into question. Amanda put Hartmann's age in the late forties or early fifties, but the work she'd had done would have fooled a lot of people into thinking she was ten or more years younger and her figure was trim and athletic. That suggested she worked out at an athletic club regularly, which meant that she had the leisure time and means to take care of herself.

"Have you spoken to Brandon since his arrest?" Amanda asked when they were seated in her office.

"No, and I'm not sure he would speak to me."

"Can you explain that?"

"Brandon and I have been estranged for some time." Hartmann paused. "Our family dynamic is . . . complicated."

"What is your relationship to Mr. Masterson?" Amanda asked.

"I was Dale's first wife. Dale was a bastard. I'm not the least bit sorry he's dead. I worked to pay his tuition for law school and he repaid me by dumping me for some society bitch who could help him get into the best country club and had the contacts to further his career. Then he screwed me when we divorced. Brandon was young, but old enough to see what his father had done to us. We went from living in a nice house to an apartment. Dale missed a lot of child support and alimony payments and I had to beg and threaten to get him to pay. Brandon had to leave private school for a public school. He's never done well socially and it was hell for him.

"Dale was an absentee parent. When he was around, he was cruel and abusive to both of us. He was very macho and Brandon was always weak and introverted as a child. Dale forced him to play sports, then he would belittle him when he failed. He also struck him on occasion, and he physically and verbally abused me as well."

"Why do you think Brandon won't talk to you?" Amanda asked.

"Brandon was twelve when Dale left us. He was socially inept and lived on his computer. When he learned that Dale represented coal and oil companies, he rebelled by becoming a fanatic environmentalist. I don't approve of everything he does but in a way I was glad, because he left the house and got involved with people when he protested instead of staying in his room all day."

Hartmann stopped talking and looked down at her lap.

"What caused the rift between you and your son?" Amanda asked gently.

"I did something for which he has never forgiven me. I married an attorney from Dale's old firm. I knew Richard socially when I was still married to Dale. Dale left us shortly after breaking away from his old firm. Richard was recently divorced and we'd always been friendly. I was also desperate to provide for Brandon. Richard is a good man, but Brandon never forgave me for marrying a lawyer who represented the companies he despised. He moved out as soon as he graduated from high school. We tried to help him with his college tuition but he wouldn't accept any money from us."

"So he went to school?"

Hartmann nodded. "Community college. He worked his way through and transferred to Portland State for his last two years. He has a degree in environmental science."

"Will Brandon let you pay me to represent him?"

"I don't know. He may refuse and insist on getting a public defender."

Hartmann looked down for a moment. Amanda heard her gulp in air. When the woman looked up there were tears in her eyes.

"I just want what's best for him. I love him so."

The guard led Brandon Masterson into the contact visiting room. As the prisoner was taking his seat, Amanda studied him. He was dressed in an orange jumpsuit, and his hair and beard were wild. Amanda frowned. Brandon looked familiar, but she was certain they had never met.

"Who are you?" Brandon asked as soon as the guard left.

"I'm Amanda Jaffe, Brandon, and I'd like to be your lawyer."

"I don't have the money to hire a lawyer, which makes you an ambulance chaser." Brandon's lips curled into a sneer. "How many new clients do you figure you'll get from the publicity my case will generate?"

"I'm here because your mother is very worried about you. She asked me to see you."

"Then we definitely don't have anything to talk about."

"That's where you're wrong. It's time for a reality check. You're charged with aggravated murder. If you're convicted you will receive one of three sentences: life with the possibility of parole after thirty years, which means you'll rot in prison until you are at least fifty-six; life without parole, which means you'll rot in prison until you die; or death by lethal injection. And don't think it will be a picnic if you avoid the death penalty. Your mom told me that high school was hell for you. Well, guess what. Bullies just like the ones who beat you up in high school make up the majority of the prison population, and they live to prey on the weak. If you're lucky you'll only be beaten a few times a week. If you're unlucky, you'll end up as some biker's sex slave. So before you kick me out let's talk, because you are in dire need of the type of help I can give you."

When Brandon didn't answer with a wisecrack, Amanda forged on.

"Check me out and you'll see that I'm in a good firm and I'm doing just fine financially. If I take your case it won't be for the publicity—it will be to help you. I met Dale Masterson when I represented another young man charged with murder who worked as a paralegal in his firm. I thought Mr. Masterson was cold and calculating. And I have the same feelings about the polluters he represents as you do.

"What I'd like to do is just have a talk about you and the fix you're in. You can ask me any questions you want to ask and I'll answer them honestly. After we've talked, you can decide if you want me to help you. If you don't think we can work together there won't be any hard feelings on my part. You have to be happy with the lawyer who represents you, because you're going to spend a lot of time together and you have to have confidence in that lawyer to do his or her best for you. So, do you want to talk?"

"What happened to the paralegal?" Brandon asked.

"I helped him and he's out of jail. I work very hard for my clients, Brandon. I don't always win their cases, but I always give them one hundred percent of my effort and I've gotten more good results than bad.

"Before I came to visit you I read and listened to every report about your case that I could find. The police are saying that Mr. Masterson was beaten to death in the den in his house. Is that true?"

Brandon looked distressed for a moment. Then he nodded.

"They're also saying that Mr. Masterson's wife saw you running from the house and she claims she saw blood on your clothing."

Brandon nodded again.

"In his press conference, the detective in charge of your case said that you came to the police station and confessed to beating your father to death. Did you do that?"

Brandon nodded again.

"Okay," Amanda said. "I'm going to be completely honest with you. Anytime a case involves violence the prosecutors get very serious, and the more evidence of guilt prosecutors have, the less likely they are to want to negotiate a plea. In this case, not only do they have a witness who says she saw you running from the crime scene, they also have your confession. But there are still things I can do for you. The first thing I can do is try to negotiate a plea to a crime less serious than aggravated murder . . ."

Brandon shook his head. "No pleas. I demand a trial."

"That's your right, and I won't be able to advise you whether that's the best way to proceed until I've had full discovery from the DA, but it may not be the best way to go if the evidence is overwhelming."

"I don't care. I'm going to trial if I have to represent myself. I need to make the world understand how my father and the polluters his firm represents are murdering the Earth. That's why I killed him. I know a person is not guilty of murder if they are defending themselves or another person from serious harm. And I was defending all the people of Earth when I killed that bastard, because he was a direct threat to our environment."

"So you want to use your trial to let everyone know about the dangers of pollution?"

"And the vile companies and disgusting lawyers who are killing the planet for profit."

"What if you're found guilty and sentenced to death?" Amanda asked.

"I wouldn't be the first person in history to die for my ideals and the greater good."

"That's true," Amanda said as one avenue of defense occurred to her. It would be worthwhile to have Brandon interviewed by a topflight forensic psychiatrist to see if she had a basis for an insanity defense.

Chapter 24

Kenny Drucker and Larry Getz were supposed to go to summer school because they had flunked several of their eighth-grade classes, but the sun was warm and a light breeze stirred the summer air, making the day too delightful to be spent cooped up in a classroom. Both boys were being raised by single working mothers who always urged them to try hard in school even though they knew in their hearts that their sons would do nothing of the sort. That day, the boys assured their mothers that they would apply themselves diligently to their studies. Then, as soon as their mothers left for work, they filled their backpacks with cigarettes, beer, and marijuana and set out on a day of adventure.

On their way downtown the boys crossed a vacant lot. A car was parked on the other side and the boys would have passed it by if it wasn't for the foul odor that assailed Larry's nostrils.

"What's that smell?" he asked.

"That's some awful shit," Kenny replied as he waved his hand in front of his nose.

"It's coming from the trunk."

Larry leaned down, then pulled back quickly.

"Man, that's gross," he said.

"Let's go," Kenny urged his friend.

"No, bro, something ain't right."

Larry held his breath and squatted next to the trunk. It wasn't locked. Should he or shouldn't he?

"What's in that trunk ain't none of our business," Kenny said.

"Don't be a pussy."

Kenny's reticence decided Larry's course of action, and he raised the trunk to show Kenny that he wasn't afraid. As soon as the trunk lid flipped up, Larry jumped backward so fast that he stumbled and fell on his ass. Then he scrambled away from the car and leaped to his feet.

"What did you see?" Kenny asked.

"There's two guys stuffed in the trunk."

"Are they dead?"

"What do you think is making that smell, fool?"

We got an ID on the dead men in the car trunk," Billie Brewster told Alan Hotchkiss. Hotchkiss was talking on the phone and he raised a finger to indicate he couldn't listen until he was done with his call.

It had taken Billie a while to find the men's identities because neither had a wallet or any other ID on them and the car in which they had been found had been stolen from a shopping mall parking lot.

Hotchkiss made some notes before hanging up. "Okay," he said as he swiveled his chair in Brewster's direction.

"Neil Schaeffer and Richard Schultz," Brewster said. "Schaeffer is thirty-five and Schultz is thirty-three. We were able to identify them because both men are ex-military and their fingerprints were on file. Schultz was an Army Ranger and Schaeffer was Special Forces. Both men saw combat and were honorably discharged."

"What have they done since leaving the military?" Hotchkiss asked.

"They're private eyes, the co-owners of Confidential Investigations."

The tiny storefront office of Confidential Investigations was in a suburban strip mall sandwiched between a shoe repair shop and a Vietnamese restaurant. The detectives had found the door locked and had gotten a key after showing the manager of the mall their search warrant. The door opened into a small waiting area outfitted with a cheap wooden table covered with old copies of sports and outdoor magazines. The table stood between a worn sofa and an uncomfortable wooden chair.

"No secretary's desk," Hotchkiss observed.

"From the décor, I'm guessing they didn't have many customers," Brewster added.

The detectives entered an inner office that held two desks and a metal filing cabinet. The desks were bare of any papers and there was nothing in the in and out boxes. Brewster opened the top drawer of the filing cabinet. There weren't many files in the top two drawers and there were none in the bottom drawer. Brewster opened a few files and frowned as she pawed through them.

"According to the manager, Schaeffer and Schultz have been working out of this office for three years, but it doesn't look like they had enough business to make a decent living," she said.

"Yeah, this place is bare bones, which makes you wonder. Did you see Schaeffer's address?"

"A condo on the waterfront."

"I investigated a case in that building last year. It's very expensive."

"Schaeffer retired from the military. He's single. If he had a decent pension he might have been able to swing it. Or . . ."

Brewster pulled two files out of a drawer. "These boys were working for oil companies in Nigeria and the Middle East."

"What kind of work?"

"The files don't say much but—given their military backgrounds—I wouldn't be surprised if they were security, and that can pay very well."

RENCO Oil owned a ten-story glass and steel building in the center of parkland near the Nike campus in Beaverton, a Portland suburb. Alan Hotchkiss showed his ID at the gated entrance, then waited while the armed guard called ahead to verify the detectives' appointment. The guard directed them to a parking area, and Hotchkiss followed the tree-lined lane to it.

"You've been quiet," Brewster said.

"I know Reggie Kiner."

"How?"

"Before he went private, Kiner was Greg Nowicki's partner."

"When was that?"

"Nine, maybe ten years ago."

"You don't like him?"

"Not one bit. His record with PPB won't show it, but there were a lot of questions that stayed unanswered when he left."

"Such as?" Brewster asked as Hotchkiss maneuvered into a space.

"Missing drugs and disparities between the money confiscated from drug dealers and the money found in the evidence room when their cases came to trial. And then there was the unexplained disappearance of a witness and the shooting death of a drug dealer."

"He sounds like a bad cop."

"He was a bad cop."

"So what's he doing as head of security for an outfit like RENCO?"

"From what I hear about the way they operate overseas, he fits in perfectly."

"Hey, Reg," Hotchkiss said when Kiner's secretary showed the detectives into his corner office. The security chief was wearing a blue hand-tailored pin-striped suit, a blue silk shirt, and a yellow Hermes tie.

"Long time no see," Kiner said as he extended his hand. His grip was as firm as Hotchkiss had expected, and the detective braced for the pressure Kiner would apply. Hotchkiss was as strong and fit as Kiner, and the handshake ended in a draw.

"This is my partner, Billie Brewster," Hotchkiss said.

Kiner nodded to Billie, then motioned the detectives toward a sofa that sat under an elk's taxidermied head. Kiner took a comfortable armchair and crossed one leg over the other.

"What's up?" Kiner asked.

"We're investigating a double homicide. Richard Schultz was beaten and shot, and Neil Schaeffer died from blows to the head. They were found in the trunk of a stolen car."

Kiner's brow furrowed. "And you've come to see me because . . . ?"

"The men are ex-military and they owned a private detective agency. We found records in their office showing that they worked on a Nigerian oil rig for RENCO. The records were vague as to their actual job, but given their military background I'm guessing they provided security."

Kiner frowned. "Those names do sound vaguely familiar. Do you have a photo?"

Brewster held out her smartphone and showed Kiner pictures of the two men after they'd been cleaned up in the morgue. Kiner didn't flinch.

"You know, I think I may have seen them but I can't remember where. When did they work for us?"

"Their files said five years ago."

Kiner stared into space. Then he shook his head.

"I'll get HR to send me their files and I'll get back to you if I think of anything that would help. Anything else I can do?"

Hotchkiss looked at Billie. She shook her head and Hotchkiss stood up. "Thanks, Reg, I appreciate the co-operation."

"No problem."

Kiner watched the detectives leave before returning to his desk. This was an unexpected turn of events, and he did not like surprises. One thing was certain: He'd underestimated Tom Beatty. He'd known he was military but he'd assumed that Schultz and Schaeffer would be able to take care of him since they had been armed and had the element of surprise. He would not make that mistake again.

One question nagged at Kiner. Did Schultz and Schaeffer talk to Beatty before he killed them? If Beatty interrogated them, he probably knew that Kiner had sent them. He'd have to double his bodyguard detail and send some more people to find Beatty. But where would they look? Beatty had elite training and could go to ground where he would never be noticed. He'd start a search, but he would probably have to wait until Beatty came to him.

Kiner thought some more and realized that they had another problem. With Beatty alive, Amanda Jaffe would still have a reason to pursue a theory of defense involving Masterson, Hamilton's books. Killing her would not solve the problem, because Beatty would get another lawyer who would use the books to prove other people had a motive to kill Christine Larson. But Jaffe could be useful. If Beatty contacted her, they could use her to find him. So, the first priority would be to have Jaffe put under surveillance and to tap all of her phones and penetrate her e-mails. Kiner knew just the people for those jobs.

Chapter 25

Amanda had won the 200-meter freestyle at the PAC-10 championships when she swam for Cal-Berkeley and had qualified for the Olympic Trials. After she failed to make the Olympic team, she burned out and stayed away from pools until she returned to Portland to join her father's firm. Though she had lost all interest in swimming competitively, she began to feel that she was turning into a blob, so she'd started swimming for exercise and tried to get in three to four days of vigorous workouts each week before going to the office.

On Monday morning, Amanda thought about Brandon Masterson as she swam her laps. Brandon had agreed to let Amanda represent him as long as she agreed that they would go to trial so he could testify.

Amanda acceded to Brandon's request because the desires of a client were always paramount. An attorney was an adviser who did not suffer any consequences if a case was lost. If Brandon was convicted he faced a lengthy incarceration or death, so he had to make the ultimate choices in his case. To paraphrase an old adage, a lawyer could lead a client to water but could not make him drink. Amanda could advise Brandon on the best way to go in his case, but she could not force him to take her advice. And, from a practical standpoint, there was no sense in trying to change Brandon's mind about going to trial until she knew more about the case.

After her swim, Amanda drove downtown and picked up a café latte at the Nordstrom coffee bar. When she entered her office, she found that Kate Ross had left the discovery in Brandon's case for her. Amanda took a few sips from her latte as she checked her e-mails. Then she read through the police, forensic, and autopsy reports. As she was reading the autopsy report, an odd feeling began to form in Amanda's gut. Masterson's nose had been broken, both eyes had been swollen shut, there was a depressed fracture at the base of his skull, his lower and upper jaws had been broken, there were lacerations on his face, and the skin on his ears and lips had been split.

When she finished reading Masterson's autopsy, Amanda went to the file in Tom Beatty's murder case and reread Christine Larson's autopsy report. The way Dale Masterson was beaten to death was eerily similar to the beating that had killed Christine Larson. It was almost as if the person who killed Masterson had been using Larson's autopsy report as a road map.

Amanda leaned back in her chair and took another sip of her latte. If Tom Beatty was innocent, that meant someone else had murdered Christine Larson. The only motive for Christine's murder that Amanda had been able to come up with involved Christine's idea that someone at her law firm was cooking the books. Christine had told Dale Masterson about her suspicions and she had died soon after. Now Masterson was dead, killed in a manner that mimicked Christine's murder. Were Christine and Masterson murdered by the same person?

Amanda stared into space. There was no reason on earth to believe that Brandon Masterson had murdered Christine. If Amanda could prove that the same person killed Christine and Dale Masterson, it would raise a very reasonable doubt about Brandon's guilt—which meant that this was a theory that needed to be explored.

There were some other items in the discovery that made Amanda pause. All the blood in the den was Masterson's, and no traces of skin or blood from anyone else had been recovered from the crime scene. The obvious conclusion was that Masterson's assailant had worn gloves when he pummeled his victim, and that raised some questions for Amanda that she wanted Brandon to answer.

Amanda also made a note to find out if the blood spatter on Brandon's clothing was consistent with the type of spatter pattern you would find on the clothing of someone who'd beaten a person to death.

Finally, Amanda noted that soil and some kind of berry had been found near the body. She had read an article in a law journal about using pollen to solve cases, but she couldn't remember the details. She resolved to reread it if the soil and berries became important.

Brandon was going to be arraigned in three hours. That gave her enough time to do some work on a memo she was writing in a federal bank robbery case and to grab a quick lunch before heading to the Multnomah County Courthouse. Amanda finished her latte and put the Masterson file to one side.

Amanda had told Sarah Hartmann to wait for her on a bench across from the elevator on the floor below the courtroom where Brandon was going to be arraigned. Hartmann walked over to her son's attorney as soon as Amanda stepped out of the elevator.

"Why did you want me to meet you here?" Brandon's mother asked.

"I wanted to prepare you for the circus we'll find when we get near the courtroom. Reporters, television cameras, and the curious are going to be lining the corridor, and everyone will be firing questions at you as we run the gauntlet."

Hartmann looked nervous. "What should I do?"

"Don't say anything and stay right behind me. We'll be fine once we're inside the courtroom."

"How . . . how does Brandon's case look?"

Amanda touched Hartmann's forearm and looked directly at her. "I'm not going to sugarcoat this, because it won't do anyone any good to avoid reality. Your son is in a lot of trouble. He told the police that he killed your ex-husband, and he was seen leaving the crime scene covered in blood."

Hartmann inhaled.

"There are still things I can do for him, but I don't want to get your hopes up."

"Thank you for being honest."

"Now, let's get going," Amanda said. "Our judge does not appreciate lawyers who are late to court."

The two women climbed the stairs. As soon as they rounded the corner and started down the corridor to the courtroom, a mob surrounded them and started peppering them with questions. Amanda smiled confidently for the cameras as she muscled her way through the crowd, answering the questions with clichés that revealed nothing.

Every seat in the spectator section of the courtroom was occupied, and it seemed to Amanda that every head swiveled toward her as soon as she stepped inside.

"This was probably what it was like in the Roman Coliseum when the Christians were fed to the lions," Amanda said to Hartmann as she threaded her way through the people who were standing in the aisle, waiting for court to begin. Kate Ross had saved a spot for Hartmann on the bench behind the low rail that separated the spectators from the area of the court where business was conducted. Amanda pushed through a gate and walked to her counsel table.

Larry Frederick and Cathy Prieto-Smith were sitting at an identical table.

"We have to stop meeting like this," Amanda said as she set out her laptop and papers.

Larry smiled, and she was glad to see he wasn't upset with her the way he'd been during the Beatty case. Of course, any case with an eyewitness and a signed confession was going to bring a smile to a prosecutor's face.

"Ready to pull another rabbit out of your hat, Amanda?" Frederick asked.

"Not bloody likely in this one, Larry. I'll just be trying to keep Mr. Masterson off death row."

The deputies brought Brandon over to join Amanda. The defendant spotted his mother. She smiled, and he looked uncertain. Then he turned his back on her and sat next to his lawyer. Hartmann's smile vanished, leaving her looking very sad.

The bailiff banged his gavel and Judge Valerie Chastain took the bench. Chastain was a delicate-looking woman in her late fifties who had been a partner in a firm that specialized in employment law. Her gray hair, wire-rimmed glasses, and soft blue eyes made her look like a favorite fun-loving aunt, but Amanda knew from experience that Chastain was a no-nonsense jurist who did not tolerate fools or the unprepared.

"This is the time set for the arraignment in *State v. Brandon Jerome Masterson*," Larry Frederick intoned. "Larry Frederick and Cathy Prieto-Smith for the government, Your Honor. The defendant and his attorney, Amanda Jaffe, are present."

"I'm looking at this indictment, and it charges the defendant with aggravated murder," Judge Chastain said. "Do you intend to seek the death penalty, Mr. Frederick?"

"Yes, Your Honor."

"Okay then, Miss Jaffe. How does your client plead?"

Amanda signaled Brandon to stand. She had told him to answer "Not Guilty" when this moment occurred.

Brandon stood. "Not guilty!" he proclaimed loudly. "I killed my father in self-defense. He was a fascist who was trying to murder the people of Earth by representing polluting coal and oil companies who are destroying our planet for profit."

Amanda laid a hand on Brandon's forearm, but he shook it off.

"Global Mining, RENCO Oil, and his other clients are worse than the Nazis. They—"

Judge Chastain brought her gavel down hard several times.

"Silence your client, Miss Jaffe, or I'll have the guards do it," she yelled to be heard over Brandon's rant.

"Brandon, this is not the time or place to do this," Amanda said.

"I have a right under the Constitution of the United States to free speech. The people have to know that the Earth is being poisoned before the ice caps melt and tsunamis flood this city and—"

Two burly jail deputies pushed Brandon onto his chair.

"Don't hurt him," Amanda said to the guards as Brandon struggled.

"I will not be silenced!" Brandon screamed.

Sarah Hartmann brought a hand to her mouth and struggled to choke back tears.

"Take him out," Judge Chastain ordered, and the guards pulled Brandon to his feet and hustled him out of the courtroom.

"You better have a long talk with Mr. Masterson," the judge told Amanda. "Explain that I will have him gagged and put in chains if he keeps this up. We'll adjourn until Mr. Masterson is under control."

The guards had placed Brandon in a holding cell. When Amanda walked in, Brandon stared at her defiantly.

"Look, Brandon, I know you're on a mission, but you've got to pick your spots. Judge Chastain won't tolerate another outburst. She told me she'll gag you and put you in manacles if you sound off again like that."

"I have a constitutional right to speak about injustice," he repeated stubbornly.

Amanda sighed as she sat down. "Did you listen to what I just said? If I can't promise the judge that you won't start making speeches again she'll order the deputies to gag you. Then you will not only be silenced but you'll also look ridiculous trussed up like a Thanksgiving turkey."

Brandon folded his arms across his skinny chest.

"Look, you'll get your chance to get your point across. When you take the stand at your trial you can explain why you killed your father. That's the time to do it. The reporters will take down what you say and your message will be broadcast to the world. Have some patience. When you act out like you just did, you look deranged and people won't take your message seriously."

Brandon didn't respond. He just tightened his arms across his chest and glared at Amanda, who noticed that there were no cuts or bruises on Brandon's knuckles. That reminded her of something she wanted to go over with him. With luck, he'd be distracted by the discussion.

"While we're here, I wanted to tell you that I read the discovery in your case; I'll get you a copy tomorrow. But I have some questions for you. I've seen the crime scene photographs. They're pretty gruesome. I mean, you really did a tune on your dad's face. Can you tell me how many times you hit your father?"

Brandon looked down. He seemed nervous.

"I don't remember," Brandon said. "I was in a rage."

"Your father was a pretty big guy, and he looked fit. Plus I understand he wrestled in college. But you don't look that marked up."

"Yeah, well, my adrenaline was pumping and I got a lucky punch in early and he went down. After that I don't remember what happened until I was outside."

"If you hit your father enough times to cause the injuries I saw on his face, why don't you have any marks on your knuckles?"

Brandon hesitated. Then he said, "Gloves, I wore gloves."

Amanda didn't remember anything in the discovery about Veronica Masterson telling the police that Brandon was wearing gloves when she saw him running from her house.

"Do you still have the gloves?"

"I got rid of them. They . . . they were covered with blood and I knew they could incriminate me."

Amanda smiled. "You've done a pretty good job of that yourself. I mean, you've confessed that you murdered your father. So why get rid of evidence that would corroborate your confession?"

"I . . . I hadn't made my mind up about confessing until I had some time to think. I made up my mind after I threw the gloves away."

"Where did you throw them?"

"I don't remember. Some garbage can. And don't ask me where it is. I was pretty upset."

"You told the detectives that you acted in self-defense? He was coming at you and you defended yourself?"

"Yes."

"You also told the detectives that you wanted to kill your father as a warning to lawyers who represent polluters and to encourage other people who care about the environment to kill lawyers and CEOs who work for polluters."

"Yes, that's what I hoped killing my father will accomplish."

"So, which is it? Did you go to the house to kill your father or did you go to try and convince him to stop representing Global Mining and he came at you and you acted in self-defense."

"Both. I . . . I was going to kill him if he refused to drop Global as a client."

"Did you bring a gun with you?"

"No, I . . . I don't believe in guns. I'm in favor of banning handguns."

"Did you have a knife or some other weapon with you?"

"No."

"So your plan all along was to beat your father to death?"

Brandon hesitated before answering, "Yes."

"That doesn't make a lot of sense, Brandon. If you went to your father's house to kill someone much bigger and stronger than you, why didn't you bring a weapon?"

"What is this? Why are you interrogating me?"

"I'm not. I'm just trying to get answers to questions raised by the discovery."

"Well, it sounds like I'm being cross-examined."

Before Amanda could answer, the door opened and Judge Chastain's bailiff told Amanda that the judge wanted to know if Brandon was ready to resume the arraignment.

"Can I tell the judge you're going to act in a civilized manner?" Amanda asked.

Brandon didn't look happy but he nodded.

"We're good to go," Amanda said as she stood up.

Moments later, the guards led Brandon into the courtroom and the arraignment continued without incident. Amanda had been through hundreds of these proceedings, so she was on automatic pilot, with only a portion of her brain focused on what was going on in court. The other part of her brain was trying to figure out the answers to several questions the discovery and Brandon's evasive answers had raised.

Chapter 26

Amanda was experienced in death penalty litigation, so the Oregon Criminal Defense Lawyers Association frequently asked her to speak at specialized death penalty seminars. Amanda knew that lawyers who were trying their first death cases would be in the audience. She had tried criminally negligent homicide, manslaughter, and non–death penalty murder cases before she tried her first death case, and she always made the point that the difference between a death case and other types of homicide cases was the same as the difference between an ordinary murder case and a shoplifting case.

Amanda always explained that the approach to a death case had to be different from the approach to any other type of criminal case. Of course, when death was a possible outcome there was no margin for error: If you failed to dot one *i* or cross one *t,* the state ate your client. But there was also a procedural difference in death cases that lawyers new to capital cases had to know about.

In all other criminal cases that went to trial the defense attorney did not think about sentencing unless his client was convicted, because time passed between a conviction and the date that the judge decided the defendant's sentence. A lawyer for a convicted client usually had a month or more to gather evidence she hoped would lead to leniency for her client. What made death penalty cases different was the law that required a jury that convicted a defendant of aggravated murder to also decide if the defendant lived or died. The attorney for a client convicted in a death case did not have the luxury of having a month or more to prepare for the sentencing hearing, because a new trial that focused on the sentence started almost immediately after the jury found the defendant guilty. Regardless of her chances for acquittal, a lawyer handling a death case had to assume her client would be convicted and had to start preparing for the sentencing phase at the same time she prepared for the trial on the murder charge so she would be able to go forward immediately if there was a conviction.

As soon as Amanda returned from the arraignment, she called Kate Ross into her office to discuss the penalty phase investigation.

"You look frazzled," Kate said. "What happened?"

Amanda told Kate about Brandon's antics, and Kate started to laugh.

"It's not funny," Amanda said.

"Yes it is," Kate said. "I can see Judge Chastain's face turning scarlet as she banged her gavel. That woman has no sense of humor."

Kate laughed again. Then she said, "So is our client a nut? Are you going to have him shrunk?"

"The answer to both questions is I don't know. I've thought about having a psychiatrist talk to Brandon but I'm afraid he'd go ballistic if I suggested it. And I'm not sure if he's crazy or just a fanatic environmentalist. A lot of what he says about global warming and the effects of greenhouse gases on the environment makes perfect sense and is supported by scientific evidence. It's the way he makes his points that upsets people. What I'm more concerned about is whether he really murdered his father."

Kate stopped smiling. "You have some doubts?"

Amanda told Kate about the similarity in the way Dale Masterson and Christine Larson were killed.

"And Brandon's story doesn't make any sense. You were with me when we met with Dale Masterson. He was a big guy, muscular, in shape. He was a college wrestler. Brandon looks like a stiff wind would blow him over. Yet he says that he went to his father's house to kill him but didn't bring a weapon. He also says that he wanted to reason with his father but his father attacked him and he beat him to death in self-defense. There's no way Brandon would win a fair fight with his father, but let's say we buy his story about the lucky punch. A guy like Brandon would be terrified if he was in a fight. He'd run like hell after he knocked down his father. I just can't see Brandon sitting astride Dale Masterson and beating him to death."

"What do you think is going on?" Kate asked.

"I think there is a possibility that someone else— maybe the person who killed Christine—beat Dale to death and that Brandon came to Dale's house to confront him about Global Mining and discovered the body."

"And he's taking credit for the murder to get a platform to tell the world about his views on the environment, how evil his father and his father's horrible corporate clients are, even though he might die?" Kate said.

"As nutty as that sounds, I think it's a real possibility."

"What do you want me to do?" Kate asked.

"What you'd do in any death case. The jurors are going to be horrified when they see the crime scene photographs. If Brandon goes crazy when he's on the stand or has outbursts during the trial, they're going to believe that he's a dangerous lunatic. We're going to have to show the jury that Brandon is not a monster. If we don't make the jurors see he's a human being they'll sentence him to death. Let's build a biography of Brandon from the day he was born to the day of the trial. His mother says that Dale abused him physically and mentally. Ask her for the names of people who can testify to the abuse so we can paint Dale as the real monster. And talk to the people in his environmental groups: people who can tell the jury about Brandon's devotion to saving the Earth and can paint him as a caring human being. His mother will be a good starting point. She may know the groups in which he was involved, and friends and teachers who can tell the jury what Brandon was like as a child and teenager."

"Gotcha," Kate said. "Anything else?"

"Yeah, why don't you talk to Billie Brewster and see if she's heard anything about Masterson, Hamilton's financial situation—you know, are the Feds looking at them. And I'd like to know anything you can find out about the break-in at Dale Masterson's office on the evening he was killed."

Chapter 27

O ver the years, Mark had politely listened while Dale complained about his son. Reading an account of the outburst at Brandon Masterson's arraignment made Mark grateful that he didn't have children. Hamilton was almost through the article when his secretary buzzed to tell him that Veronica Masterson was in the waiting room. Mark arranged his face so he looked sympathetic and somber before walking down the hall to the reception area. Veronica was sitting on a sofa, her hands demurely clasped in her lap, the picture of a grieving widow. She stood when she saw him. She was wearing a black designer dress that must have cost a fortune and molded perfectly to every one of her curves. Mark took her hands in his.

"How are you holding up?" he asked with great concern for the benefit of anyone who was listening. He knew she was holding up very well because she'd shown him how much Dale's death had affected her when they had screwed during Mark's condolence call two days before.

"I'm still numb," Veronica answered for public consumption.

"Come on back," Mark told Veronica. Then he told the receptionist to hold his calls.

As soon as the door to his office closed, Veronica pressed her body against Mark and groped him hard between his legs. Veronica's touch was electric, and Mark wondered if this was what it was like to be stunned by a Taser. Then he remembered that they were in a law office peopled by several hundred lawyers and support personnel, and he pulled away.

"Not here," he gasped.

"Oh, Markey, don't be a spoilsport."

"We both know a weakling like Brandon would never be able to beat Dale to death. As soon as the cops figure that out, you're going to be a prime suspect. The last thing we need is a witness who can tell a jury they saw us fucking on my desk."

Veronica pouted. "You used to be fun."

"And I will be again when we can be certain we're not the subject of a police investigation. We have to be very careful."

"I don't know why you're worried. Neither one of us could have killed Dale like that." She shivered. "I have nightmares every time I think about Dale's face."

"No one is going to think we beat Dale to death, but an accessory is just as guilty as the person who commits the crime."

Veronica shrugged. "Well, I have nothing to worry about." Then she smiled coquettishly. "Can you say the same?"

"This is not a subject I want to discuss. So, why are you here?"

"Miles Horvath wrote Dale's will. He asked me to come in to discuss it."

"Ah."

"Do you know what he was worth?" Veronica asked, and Mark couldn't help but notice how callous her inquiry was. When other people were around, Veronica was weepy and needy, but she had not shown the slightest hint of emotion over her loss when they were alone.

"I'd just be guessing, but I'm sure you'll do just fine."

Mark escorted Veronica down the hall to Horvath's office and left them to discuss the will. On the return trip he decided that screwing Veronica was a lot more exciting when Dale was alive. In bed Veronica was fantastic, but he would have to spend time with her out of bed if he continued their affair, and he had no interest in doing that.

Mark laughed. He was certain that Veronica wouldn't be broken up if he ended their relationship. He had no illusions about her feelings for him. He knew she didn't have any.

Chapter 28

B randon's mother had given Kate a list of environmental organizations to which Brandon belonged, and Earth Now was the first place she visited.
Its headquarters were on the second floor of an old,
six-story office building on Front Street across from
the Willamette River. Kate opened the door and
walked into organized chaos. Men and women were
talking animatedly on phones, making notations on
wall charts, stuffing envelopes, and striding purpose-
fully back and forth across a large open space decorated with posters concerning the environment. With
a few exceptions, they were young, dressed in jeans,
and wearing T-shirts decorated with colorful phrases
that either condemned polluters or supported saving
the Earth.

No one appeared to be in charge, so Kate waited until the harried-looking young woman seated at the desk closest to the door hung up her phone.

"Hi," Kate said, "is Bruce Nakamura in?"

"Bruce, yeah," she answered as she threw her thumb over her shoulder toward a door in the corner of the room.

"Could you please tell him that Kate Ross would like to talk to him?"

"Just knock and go in," the woman said before looking down at a list and dialing another number.

Kate crossed the room and knocked on a frame door with a frosted-glass pane in the upper half. Gold lettering on the pane informed her that the occupant of the office was Earth Now's executive director.

"Come," shouted a voice from behind the door. Kate entered and found herself in the presence of a stocky Japanese-American with long black hair who was typing away on a laptop.

"Mr. Nakamura?" Kate asked.

The man looked up.

"I wonder if I can have a few minutes of your time?"

"If you're selling something I'm not interested."

Kate held out her identification. "I'm an investigator working for the attorney who's representing Brandon Masterson on a charge of aggravated murder."

Nakamura stopped typing, leaned back in his chair, and gave Kate his full attention.

"I read Brandon was arrested." He shook his head. Then he pointed to a chair on the other side of his desk. "Sit down, please. How can I help you?"

"This is early days in our investigation so I'm just trying to find out as much as I can about Brandon. I understand he was a member of Earth Now."

"I don't know if I'd say he was a member. His participation with us was erratic. I'm not even sure if he ever paid his dues."

"Did he work in the office?"

"Not really. He did show up for some of our protests, but mostly he'd just drop in when the spirit moved him and rant about something or other."

"Were you surprised when you read that he'd beaten his father to death with his bare hands?" Kate asked.

"That did surprise me. Brandon is irrational about pollution and the environment, really rabid, a screamer and a yeller at a protest, but he's not a violent guy, and beating someone to death . . . No, I can't see him doing that."

"Tell me what Brandon is like."

"He's accurate on his science most of the time, but he's not as smart as he thinks he is. He's also an egomaniac and he's always got to be right. He won't listen to dissenting views. He lectures and he's disruptive if he doesn't get his way. For example, he's bought into some ultra-bullshit environmental theories he's gotten off the Internet, and if you don't buy in too he goes off. And you can't always trust him to tell the truth."

"What do you mean?" Kate asked.

"He makes stuff up. For example, Brandon told me that he graduated summa cum laude. I told that to someone who knew him at Portland State and he said that Brandon was a C student, not some academic whiz. Also, he once claimed he had a master's degree, which he doesn't."

"Did Brandon have a job?"

"I heard he was a clerk at a store that sells TVs and home stereo equipment but I'm not sure. Why don't you ask his mother?"

"She and Brandon are estranged."

"I'm not surprised. He's a tough guy to get along with."

What Kate learned at the other environmental groups on Mrs. Hartmann's list was similar to what Bruce Nakamura had told her. Brandon never put in time stuffing envelopes or making calls, but he did annoy almost everyone he talked to by distracting them from their work with rants about his pet theories on how to save the planet. Kate found the TV store where Brandon had worked, but the owner told her that he'd fired Brandon after a month because of repeated absences, late arrivals, and customer complaints.

Brandon's apartment was on the second floor of a two-story garden apartment complex on the east side of the river in a run-down part of town. There was garbage overflowing from a Dumpster in the parking lot and beer cans littering the asphalt. When Kate got out of her car she heard the sounds of a domestic quarrel coming from one apartment and loud music blasting from another.

Kate opened the door with a key Amanda had given her. The shades were down and the apartment was dark and smelled of sweat and stale food. Kate flipped a switch, and weak light cast a dull glow over half-empty Chinese take-out boxes that stood on a low coffee table. The table sat in front of a sofa that was showing its stuffing and across from an inexpensive TV without a cable box. The type of posters she'd seen at Earth Now were tacked up on the walls. A stained, cheap pea green carpet covered the floor, and it didn't look like Brandon had ever vacuumed it.

The bedroom was no cleaner than the rest of the apartment. Dirty clothes were piled in a corner next to an unmade bed. There were few clothes in the closet and the chest of drawers. But there were books stacked on the floor in the bedroom and living room or lined up on cheap bookshelves. Kate looked at the titles. The subject of most of the books was environmental science, but science fiction and fantasy novels were scattered among them.

It took a moment for Kate to figure out what was missing. When she did, she felt sad. There were no family photographs or photographs of a girlfriend, or any friend for that matter. Kate took one final look around and concluded that Brandon Masterson's apartment was a depressing cave inhabited by a bitter, lonely man.

Chapter 29

Amanda was working on a brief when her intercom buzzed and her receptionist told her that Cathy Prieto-Smith was calling from the DA's office.

"What's up, Cathy?" Amanda said.

"Larry wanted me to call," the assistant DA said. "Brandon Masterson is in the secure ward at the county hospital."

"What happened?" Amanda asked, certain she already knew.

"Mr. Masterson harassed some members of the Aryan Brotherhood during their exercise period and they beat him unconscious."

"How bad is the damage?"

"Mr. Masterson's nose is broken, he's lost a few teeth, and he probably has several broken ribs and a concussion."

"I'm going to go up to the hospital to talk to him," Amanda said. "Can you ask Larry to call and okay the visit?"

"Will do."

"Thanks, and please thank Larry for the heads-up."

Amanda wasn't surprised to learn why Brandon was hospitalized. She could imagine how it happened. Brandon was abrasive and obnoxious and he would have been oblivious to the type of people he was berating. At first, the prisoners would have been amused when this puny weakling began insulting them, as if a Chihuahua had just snapped at their heels. But after a minute or so they would have lost patience with Brandon's continued insults. Brandon was used to arguing with educated, civilized people who used language to respond to arguments. Members of the Aryan Brotherhood would have countered Brandon's arguments with fists and feet, pounding him relentlessly for the sheer pleasure of inflicting pain on a helpless human being.

Amanda got out of the elevator on the third floor of the county hospital and walked over to an orderly dressed in white pants and a short-sleeve white shirt who sat at a wooden table to the right of a thick metal door.

"My name is Amanda Jaffe," she said as she held out her driver's license and Bar Association card for inspection. "I'm Brandon Masterson's attorney, and I'd like to see him. I believe Larry Frederick of the District Attorney's Office called ahead."

"Yeah, you're good to go," the guard said before speaking into a radio. A few seconds later the metal door swung open. Another orderly was waiting on the other side.

"We have Mr. Masterson in a room at the end of the hall," the second orderly said as he escorted Amanda between coffee-colored walls that formed the boundaries of a long hall that smelled faintly of disinfectant. A police officer was lounging in front of another metal door. In the center of the door was a small, square window made of thick glass. The officer stood when he saw Amanda and the orderly approaching. Amanda held out her ID.

"The DA cleared Miss Jaffe's visit," the orderly informed the officer.

"I heard," the officer said.

The orderly unlocked the door to Brandon's austere hospital room, which was outfitted with a hospital bed, two plain metal chairs, and a squat chest of drawers. There were bars on the room's only window and pale light filtered through the grimed glass panes, casting murky striped shadows on the whitewashed wall.

Brandon's bed was cranked up so that he was partially sitting. Bandages covered the top of his head, his nose had been mangled, and his face was covered with bruises.

"Are you okay?" Amanda asked with sincere concern.

Brandon opened his torn lips, revealing gaps where his teeth had been kicked in.

"What do you care?" he managed.

Amanda didn't answer right away. She just stared at her client. He met her eyes for a moment, then looked down.

"Why do you build walls between you and people who want to help you, Brandon? Why do you try so hard to alienate everyone?"

Brandon turned his head toward the wall.

"You asked if I care," Amanda said. "I care because you're a human being who is suffering and I always try to help someone in trouble when I can. You're also my client, and I take my representation of every client very seriously, especially when they're charged with a crime they didn't commit."

Brandon swung his head back toward Amanda.

"You don't have to say a word, Brandon. You've probably been given pain medication, so you're not thinking straight. But try to remember what I'm going to tell you.

"When we met at the jail, I warned you about what prison life would be like. I hope this beating has taught you that you are not equipped to survive behind bars. I told you about the type of people you'd meet in jail. They are bullies and psychopaths. They are not rational. They have no interest in your positions on the environment. They're only interested in using pain to dominate the weak.

"I'm going to leave now. I talked to your doctor and I'm satisfied you'll survive this beating. I don't know if you'll be as lucky the next time. This crusade of yours, this planned martyrdom, is flawed, and I beg you to spend your time in the hospital giving serious thought to how you want to proceed with your case."

Chapter 30

Kate Ross and Billie Brewster had been friends when Kate was a Portland police officer, and they had reestablished their friendship when Billie was involved in the murder case that led to the arrest of Kate's boyfriend, Daniel Ames. Billie would help Kate by giving her inside information when it would not have an adverse impact on a police investigation, and Kate reciprocated when she learned something that would help in a case Billie was working. When they didn't want to be seen together they usually met on the Washington side of the Columbia River at Juniors Cafe, which was not frequented by members of the Portland Police Bureau. Juniors was a throwback where they served strong, black coffee but no lattes, and apple pie à la mode but never tiramisu.

"Since you want something from me, you're buying," Billie said when Kate slid into the booth at the rear of the cafe.

"It's good to know you can be bought," Kate said with a smile.

"For a slice of Juniors apple pie, always," Billie said as she returned the smile.

A waitress appeared at their table and Billie asked for pie and coffee. Kate just ordered coffee.

"I hear Sherman is up for parole," Kate said when the waitress left.

"He is, but I'm not holding my breath."

When Billie was sixteen, her father had deserted the family. Billie's mother had been forced to work two jobs to keep food on the table and a roof over her children's heads, leaving Billie to raise her younger brother. She had tried her best, but Sherman had joined a gang and was now serving serious time at the state penitentiary for armed robbery.

"How's he doing?" Kate asked.

"Just fine," Billie added with a trace of sadness. "Better than he'd do on the outside. He's *somebody* in prison, what with his gangster buddies. Outside the wall he'd be just another fuckup."

Kate felt sorry for her friend. Even though no one else did, Billie blamed herself for not keeping Sherman on the straight and narrow.

"So," Billie said, "why are you bribing me with Juniors pie?"

"It's Brandon Masterson's case. I know Brandon confessed, but Amanda and I have serious reservations about his guilt."

Kate looked at Billie for a reaction, but Billie gave nothing away.

"We think there's a possibility that Masterson was murdered because of something that was going on at his firm."

"Like what?"

"We heard that someone high up cooked the firm's books to make its financial position look better than it was when it was courting Global Mining."

"Alan told me that Amanda made that allegation in court when she was representing the paralegal in the Christine Larson case."

"Have you heard any scuttlebutt that supports Amanda's theory?"

"No. What else makes you think your client is innocent?" Billie asked.

"There's the break-in at Dale Masterson's office on the evening he was killed. That seems like too much of a coincidence."

"True, but your boy could have done it."

"That is a possibility," Kate conceded. "Have you figured out if anything was taken?"

"Masterson's hard drive was copied, but nothing else appears to be missing."

"I assume Masterson's computer was password-protected. How did the thief get in?"

"With Masterson's password."

"So he tortured him for it before he killed him?"

"That's one hypothesis. But he could have known it already. Your client once lived with the victim and would have had many opportunities to learn Mr. Masterson's password."

"You heard Brandon at the arraignment. He hated his father. If he found anything incriminating on Dale Masterson's computer, he would have spread it all over the Internet."

"Maybe there wasn't anything incriminating on the computer," Billie said.

"Have you examined the hard drive?"

"Mark Hamilton, the firm's senior partner, won't let us. He says he's worried about us seeing confidential client information."

"Or evidence that there was something wrong with the firm's books."

"Hamilton says he's going to give us an edited print-out after he's gone through the files."

"Convenient," Kate said. "He'll be able to scrub any incriminating evidence."

"True. But our lawyers say there's nothing we can do about it."

Billie paused to eat a piece of pie. Kate took the opportunity to sip her coffee. When she was finished chewing, Billie looked across the table at Kate.

"You still haven't told me why you think Brandon Masterson didn't kill his father?"

"I'm not sure Amanda would want me to tell you."

Billie nodded. "I can accept that. I'm just wondering if it's not the same things that have me wondering."

"Oh? What might those be?"

"I can't do all your work for you. You can draw your own conclusions after you read the report from the crime lab about the blood spatter. But there's another reason beside the blood spatter that makes me think your boy may be innocent, and you're not going to like it."

"Oh?"

"The MO in Masterson's murder and the MO in Christine Larson's murder were so similar that Alan and I took a ride to Tom Beatty's house to talk to him. When we got there we found blood in Beatty's front room and had the crime lab analyze it. Just before you called to ask me to meet you here, I got a call from the crime lab. They made a match."

"Don't keep me in suspense."

"A few days after Beatty was released on bail, Richard Schultz and Neil Schaeffer were found in the trunk of a Chevy. Schultz had been shot to death and Schaeffer had been beaten to death. The lab matched Richard Schultz's blood to the blood on Beatty's floor."

"Who is Richard Schultz?"

"He and Schaeffer were private investigators."

"What connection does my client have to these guys?"

Billie raised an eyebrow. "You mean besides Schultz's blood being found in Beatty's house?"

"Don't be a wiseass. I should have asked if you've found any other connection between Beatty and Schultz."

"There is one, but it's tenuous. Both dead men are ex-military who worked security for RENCO Oil in Nigeria."

"Why is that a connection?" Kate asked.

"RENCO is a client of Masterson, Hamilton and Beatty worked at the firm. What's bothering me is that it's starting to look like Mr. Beatty likes to kill people. We've got Christine Larson in his bedroom beaten to death, Dale Masterson beaten to death in a way that mirrors Larson's murder, and two men murdered and stuffed in the trunk of a car, one of whom was beaten to death. Oh, and there is that poor bastard he beat up at the Lookout."

"You've definitely given me something to think about."

"Think hard. You and Amanda need to know who you're dealing with."

"Thanks, Billie."

"Yeah, well, despite the fact that you and your boss are representing the bad guys, I don't want to see you dead . . . although that *would* help my conviction rate."

Chapter 31

When the Jaffes needed an independent forensic expert, they used Paul Baylor, a slender, bookish African-American with degrees from Michigan State in forensic science and criminal justice. Paul had worked at the Oregon State Crime Lab for ten years before leaving to set up his own shop.

The offices of Oregon Forensic Investigations were located in an industrial park a few blocks from the Columbia River. Amanda walked up a ramp that led to a concrete walkway that ran in front of an export-import business and a construction firm. The last door on the walkway opened into a small anteroom furnished with two chairs that stood on either side of a low table covered with scientific journals. When Amanda walked in, Baylor's secretary looked up from a report she was typing and smiled.

"Paul's expecting you," she said as she pressed the button on the intercom. Seconds later, the forensic expert walked out of a back room.

"Long time no see," he said.

"Dad and I haven't had any cases with tricky forensic evidence lately."

"Well, this time you gave me a real mystery to solve," Paul said as he ushered Amanda into the spacious back room that held his lab.

"Oh?"

"Have a seat," Paul said, gesturing toward a chair on the other side of an old desk. While Amanda settled into her chair, Baylor opened a file.

"Let me get the easy stuff out of the way. I went to the state crime lab and looked at the evidence. The blood spatter pattern on your client's clothing is inconsistent with the blood spatter pattern you'd expect if he was in a fight that caused so many open wounds. The blood on his shirt and pants is from the victim, but the patterns are consistent with someone who wiped blood on their clothes or knelt in blood."

"Great!" Amanda said. "Now, what's the mystery?"

"There was a type of blackberry found in the den near Dale Masterson's body. The berries were mashed up and mixed in with some soil. The crime lab didn't analyze them because your client confessed and the detectives told them it wasn't a priority, but I got curious.

"It turns out that the berries are from pokeweed, or *Phytolacca americana*. It's a nonwoody perennial that can grow from three to ten feet tall."

"Why is that important?"

"Pokeweed doesn't grow in Oregon. It's most commonly found in the eastern United States or southeastern Canada. It does grow as far west as Texas, but it is not found in the Pacific Northwest."

"Then what were its berries doing in Dale Masterson's den?"

"Exactly the question I asked myself. So I called some botanists I've worked with. They'd never heard of pokeweed being found anywhere in Oregon.

"I asked them how the berries could have been transported to Masterson's den. One theory they came up with was that someone was near a pokeweed and stepped on some of the berries that were in mud. Each berry contains seeds, which are, by the way, poisonous to humans. If the seeds were lodged in the mud and the mud dried, trapping the seeds, they could be carried to Oregon. If the person who stepped on the seeds took off his boots right away and didn't wear them again until they were back here, the seeds might fall out and grow here.

"Another way the berries could have gotten here is if they were brought to a nursery in the state, but I've checked and none of the nurseries I called had pokeweed or could think of why anyone would want it."

"So we don't know where the berries came from?"

"Actually, I do. One of the last people I spoke to was Nellie Norwood. She's with the Forest Park Conservancy and she got very excited when I told her why I was calling. Three years ago, two hikers with an interest in plants were in a remote part of Forest Park and found a plant they couldn't identify, so they brought it to Nellie. She looked up the plant, discovered that it was pokeweed. and was surprised to find it growing in the park."

A queasy feeling started to grow in the pit of Amanda's stomach.

"Can you show me where the pokeweed grows?" she asked.

"I can," Baylor said as he unfolded a map of Forest Park. "I guessed you might ask so I had Nellie show me where she found the plant." He put his finger down on a red X he'd drawn on a section of the map. "The only place in Oregon you can find pokeweed is right here."

Chapter 32

The next morning, Amanda dressed in jeans, a windbreaker, and hiking boots, filled a backpack with water and trail mix, and drove toward one of the trailheads in Portland's Forest Park, a five-thousand-acre recreational area with eighty miles of hiking trails and fire lanes that is the largest forested natural area within city limits in the United States.

A warm rain was pounding down when Amanda parked in the lot near the trailhead closest to the remote area of the park where the pokeweed had been found. Before she got out of the car, Amanda checked the snub-nosed .38 that was tucked into a holster secured to her belt. She had survived several close calls while involved in some of her more challenging cases, and she wasn't going to confront Tom Beatty unarmed.

After pulling her hood over her head and hunching her shoulders against the downpour, Amanda started along a narrow dirt track that the heavy rain had churned into a muddy bog. The trail wound through a forest of towering Douglas firs and western hemlocks, and Amanda was soon stepping around or climbing over fallen trees covered with iridescent emerald-hued moss that dripped with moisture. It was humid, and the thick canopy trapped the heat. Amanda's skin became sticky under the windbreaker and she was constantly ducking away from the jutting limbs that would attack the trail.

Amanda had programmed her GPS with the coordinates for the area of the forest where the pokeweed had been found. Five miles in, she was forced to leave the trail and follow a stream through the thick forest. At one point, Amanda stumbled on a slippery rock and slid into the stream, just catching herself before she soaked her jeans. When she paused to catch her breath, she thought she heard a branch crack. She stood and listened but the pounding rain made it hard to detect the presence of other hikers. When she was convinced that her imagination was making her paranoid, Amanda forged on.

After a mile, the rain let up just as Amanda left the stream. The dense underbrush made walking difficult.

Amanda scrambled up the slippery side of a muddy embankment and stopped short when she saw several tall plants whose green, spear-tipped leaves held clusters of shiny purple berries.

"Pokeweed!" Amanda whispered excitedly. Her exhaustion faded and she forged forward through the underbrush with renewed energy until she suddenly found herself in a narrow clearing surrounded by dense foliage. A tarp, supported by limbs sawed off nearby trees, covered a sleeping bag and a fire pit. Amanda turned slowly, surveying the area for any sign of the person who lived in the camp.

Amanda had noticed a large backpack and a duffel bag under the tarp. She called Tom's name. When no one answered, she ducked under the tarp and squatted next to the duffel. She felt guilty and uncomfortable going through the contents, but she needed to know if this was Tom's camp or if it belonged to a homeless person. The duffel was stuffed with books and changes of clothing. Buried at the bottom was a passport in Tom Beatty's name.

"Where's your boyfriend?" a voice said.

Amanda whirled around. Two men were standing in the clearing. They were rugged and muscular and dressed in camouflage fatigues. They had moved so stealthily that Amanda hadn't heard them until they were right behind her. One of the men was carrying a large knife, and the other held a .45-caliber automatic at his side.

Amanda stepped out from under the tarp and straightened up.

"Who are you?" she asked, trying hard to keep a tremor out of her voice and failing miserably.

"That's not your concern, little lady. What should concern you is what will happen if you don't tell us where Tom Beatty is hiding."

"I have no idea. I thought he would be here, but he's not," Amanda said, stalling for time so she could work a hand behind her back to her gun.

"We'll soon find out if you're telling the truth," the man with the knife said. "I don't think you'll hold out for long under torture."

"Please don't hurt me," Amanda begged as she shifted her left shoulder toward the men to hide her right hand, which was snaking toward her weapon.

The men grinned at each other, enjoying Amanda's plea for mercy. Then the man with the gun stopped smiling and Amanda gaped at the tip of a wooden spear that had been rammed through his body.

The other man had just started to turn when a rock smashed into his skull. He staggered but didn't go down. The rock descended again. The skull split, the knife tumbled to the ground, and the man crumpled next to it.

Meanwhile, the speared man looked down uncomprehendingly at the blood spurting from his chest wound. He dropped the gun and grasped the spear with both hands, staggering in circles as he tried to wrench it out of his body.

Tom Beatty picked up the fallen knife and held it at the man's throat.

"Who sent you?" Beatty demanded, but the man was past answering. He sagged against Beatty, his eyes closed, and his last breath escaped.

Beatty dropped the body and stared at it in frustration. The prehistoric horror Amanda had just witnessed paralyzed her and she could only stare at Beatty, his face smeared with mud and his body cloaked with dripping leaves. Then she remembered her gun, and yanked it out of her holster.

Beatty paid no attention to the weapon. "What are you doing here?" he demanded.

Amanda's mouth was dry and her voice cracked when she finally managed to speak.

"I was looking for you."

"How did you know where to find me?"

"Pokeweed. It's an eastern plant and the only place it grows in the Pacific Northwest is in this part of

Forest Park. You tracked some of its berries into Dale Masterson's den."

Amanda tightened her grip on her gun, unsure how Beatty would react when she asked the next question.

"Did . . . did you kill Dale Masterson?"

Beatty didn't answer. He just stared at her, looking terrifying.

"Tom, you're in big trouble. The judge revoked your bail and you're a fugitive. And they found blood in the front room of your house that's been matched to one of two murdered men who were found in the trunk of a car."

"Who were they?"

"They were private detectives, but they were also ex-military and they worked security for RENCO Oil."

Beatty scowled but didn't say anything.

"I want to help you, Tom, but you've got to turn yourself in."

Beatty looked at Amanda. "Leave," he ordered.

"Tom . . ."

"Leave now."

"But what about these men?" she asked, realizing how inane her question was. The men were beyond help.

"Leave now," Beatty repeated.

Amanda wanted to say something, but fleeing from this massacre before she became part of it was the sane thing to do. She circled in the direction she'd come from, her gun pointed at Beatty. He didn't pay any attention to the gun, but he did keep his eyes locked on hers. Amanda backed into the undergrowth. Then she turned and ran.

Amanda staggered into the parking lot, numb from fatigue, soaking wet, her face scratched and bleeding. She wrenched open the car door, then locked herself in. Her hands shook as she started the engine, and her mind was reeling from the horror she'd witnessed.

Exhaustion and fear kept her from thinking straight, and she had to try extra hard to focus on the road. As soon as she was in a populated area, Amanda pulled into the crowded parking lot of a supermarket and leaned her head against the steering wheel. When she closed her eyes, she saw Tom Beatty drive a spear through the body of a human being, then club another man to death with a rock. Her breathing grew shallow, and she had to fight to keep from throwing up.

Once Amanda was back in control of her emotions, she started to relax, but a sudden thought caused her heart rate to accelerate again. Amanda looked around the parking lot. It dawned on her that the dead men had followed her to Tom's camp. How did they know where she was going? Was she under surveillance? Was there a tracker on her car? Were there other men who knew that she was sitting in this parking lot? Even though crowds of people surrounded her, she did not feel safe.

Amanda's brain was full of cobwebs and every thought was an effort. She knew that she had to get some sleep, but she also knew that she would have to meet with Kate Ross before she could think about sleeping.

Chapter 33

A manda ditched her car in case there was a tracking device in it. She thought about going to her
condo but rejected the idea. Mike was home. If she was
being followed she didn't want to lead anyone to him.
Amanda took a cab to the apartment Kate shared with
Daniel Ames. Daniel was at the coast, taking deposi-
tions so Kate was alone.

"What happened to you?" Kate asked as soon as she
opened her door.

"I'll tell you in a minute, but I want to wash up first.
Can I use your shower?"

"Sure. I'll get you a towel and a stiff drink. You look
like you can use one."

Twenty minutes later, Amanda was warm and comfortable in fresh socks and one of Daniel's warm-up

suits while her clothes tumbled around in Kate's washing machine. She called Mike to let him know she might be late. Then she nursed the glass of scotch Kate handed her while she told Kate everything that had happened in Forest Park.

"When I was calm enough to think, I realized that I needed your help," Amanda said.

"Oh?"

"Those men followed me to Tom's camp. That means they had me under surveillance. I've never felt I was being tailed. I think it's more likely that my condo, office, or phones are bugged."

"And you want me to perform a sweep?" Kate asked.

Amanda nodded. "Can you come to my condo now?"

"I keep my equipment at the office so we have to stop there. I can sweep your office first if you're not too exhausted."

"I'll be fine," Amanda said, even though she would have given all her worldly possessions for the chance to dive into a nice warm bed.

"We can go as soon as your clothes are dry."

"Bring your gun. You'll have to be very alert. Christine Larson and Dale Masterson were brutally beaten, and I'm betting that Carol White was also murdered. The people behind this are not fooling around."

"Are you convinced that Tom isn't responsible for those killings?"

"I'm pretty certain he didn't kill Christine or Carol White. That was probably the work of the people who framed Tom for Christine's murder."

"What about Dale Masterson?" Kate asked. "The pokeweed berries put him at the crime scene."

Dale Masterson's beating had been a carbon copy of the way Christine had been murdered, and Amanda remembered Tom's swearing to avenge Christine's death. She also remembered that he had not answered her in Forest Park when she asked him if he'd killed Masterson.

"You know you've got a big conflict-of-interest problem, right?" Kate continued.

"That occurred to me."

"Brandon is innocent if Tom killed Dale Masterson, but both Tom and Brandon are your clients. You can win Brandon's case by sending Tom Beatty to death row, but you can't do anything to help one client if it will work against another client."

"I took an ethics course in law school," Amanda answered defensively.

"Then you know you're between a rock and a hard place."

"I'm too tired to think about this now."

"You should talk it over with your dad," Kate advised.

"I can't. I know what he'll say. He'll tell me to get off both cases and lead the police to the campsite, but I won't do that." Amanda shuddered. "You weren't there. You didn't hear those men. I don't even want to think about what they would have done to me if Tom hadn't saved me." She shook her head. "I can't betray a man who just saved my life."

The law office was bugged, and Kate found a tracking device on Amanda's car. Once she removed it, Amanda drove to her condo, with Kate following. As soon as Amanda told Mike what Kate was doing, he wanted to know *why* she was sweeping the condo for bugs. Amanda wanted to answer his question but couldn't, so she stonewalled by playing the client confidentiality card.

An hour later, Kate showed Amanda what she'd found in the condo. Amanda herded her investigator into her home office and shut the door on an angry boyfriend.

"This stuff is state-of–the-art," Kate said. "That means that you're dealing with people who have money and connections."

"Didn't Billie tell you that the two men who were found in the trunk of the car were ex-military men who had worked security in Nigeria for RENCO Oil?"

"Yes."

"The men who followed me looked like they had military training, and RENCO would have the means and money to secure state-of-the-art surveillance equipment."

"That's something we need to consider. Meanwhile, I'm going to call in a friend who used to work for military intelligence and NSA. He'll go over the condo, your car, and the office to make sure I haven't missed anything. I'll ask him if he has an idea about who might have access to this type of equipment."

"Thanks, Kate."

"Now, you are going to get to bed before you drop dead."

"I won't argue with you. I'm out on my feet. I'll see you at the office."

Mike had been quietly angry at being shut out by Kate and Amanda, but he hadn't asked her any questions when she'd collapsed into bed shortly after Kate left. Amanda staggered out of her bedroom at nine-thirty the next morning and found a note from Mike saying he had gone to the office.

Amanda was upset when she thought about Mike's reaction, but she couldn't blame him. Then she thought about how the evening would have played out if Mike were still living at his apartment. Mike wouldn't have been there, so he wouldn't have been in danger from assassins and wouldn't have asked her to talk about things she didn't want to talk about. Amanda sighed. Living together in a serious relationship was complicated.

But she didn't have time to think about any of that now. Her first priority was visiting an old . . . well, "friend" didn't exactly cover the relationship.

Chapter 34

The Jungle Club was housed in a square pink and green concrete box that sat in the middle of a parking lot on a busy intersection on Columbia Avenue. The gaudy neon sign was turned off during the daylight hours. Once the sun went down, a naked woman was clearly outlined in flashing lights that also spelled out GIRLS, GIRLS, GIRLS, leaving no doubt about what the curious would find inside.

Amanda parked in the lot at noon, when the patrons would be hard-core perverts who would be too busy ogling the strippers to pay much attention to her. Once she was inside, Amanda realized that any fears she had that she would be recognized were groundless. The club was kept dark so the voyeurs wouldn't notice the age of some of the dancers, and any customer who pulled his eyes away from the gyrating ecdysiasts to peer in her direction would not have enough light to make her out.

The bouncer at the door was an old client. He greeted Amanda warmly before pointing her toward Martin Breach's office, which was at the back of the club at the end of a short hall. Martin kept the music cranked up loud enough to be disorienting, on the theory that the cacophony would make life very difficult for eavesdropping FBI, DEA, or PPB agents, so Amanda had to pound on the office door to get his attention. After four thumps it opened, and Art Prochaska glared at her.

Prochaska, Breach's right-hand man and only friend, was a giant with thick lips, a broad nose, and pencil-thin eyebrows. In his days as a collector for the mob he had used his huge bullet-shaped head to stun recalcitrant debtors. As soon as Prochaska recognized Amanda, he broke into a grin. Amanda had beaten a murder charge for Prochaska, who had, in this rare instance, been completely innocent.

The walls of Breach's office were decorated with pictures of strippers who had performed in the club and an out-of-date calendar from a motor oil company that he never replaced. The rickety furniture was mostly secondhand and the décor was designed to deflect attempts by the Feds to run a net worth on him.

"Look who's here," Art called over his shoulder.

Martin Breach had started out in the trenches with Art, breaking legs for Benny Dee, before staging a coup d'état during which Benny mysteriously disappeared, never to be seen again. Now Breach ran the most efficient and ruthless crime organization in the Pacific Northwest.

Breach's sandy hair was thinning, his drab brown eyes were watery, and he had a pale, vampirish complexion because his skin rarely came in contact with sunlight. He had hideous taste in clothes, and his loud, mismatched outfits made him look like a clown. Over the years, several enemies had treated him with disdain right up to the point where they'd found themselves strapped to a table, listening to Breach tell really stupid jokes while going to work on them with a power drill.

Amanda had mixed feelings about Breach, and no illusions. She knew he was a ruthless criminal, but she also knew that he cared for her in a weird way and had helped her out on a few nerve-racking occasions.

Amanda got another big grin from the crime boss. "You look great," he said. "Take a seat."

Amanda lowered herself cautiously onto a straight-back wooden chair that looked like it might give way at any moment.

"So what brings you to my den of iniquity?" Breach asked with a smile.

"I have a serious problem, Martin. Two men tried to kill me yesterday."

Breach stopped smiling. "What happened?"

"I have a client who's on the run. The police want to find him, but so do the men who attacked me. They bugged my home and office and followed me when I hiked deep into Forest Park. I've been told that the bugging equipment is state-of-the-art and I'm guessing that the men were ex-military. I never knew they were tailing me."

"What did they do to you?" Breach asked.

"They . . . they threatened to torture me if I didn't tell them where to find my client."

Breach's features hardened, and Amanda got a glimpse of the way Martin's victims saw him when he wasn't playing the jolly fool.

"How did you get away?" he asked.

"My client took care of them."

"Oh?" Breach said as he cocked his head to one side.

"They're dead."

"If they're dead why do you need my help?"

"You know Mike Greene?"

"The DA who prosecuted Art."

"Yeah, well, he's my boyfriend. We're living together."

"I thought he was an okay guy even though he wanted to send me to death row," Prochaska said.

"Thanks, Art," Amanda said. She turned back to Breach.

"I'm certain the men who tried to kill me were hired help, so whoever sent them could send someone else. If they want to get to me they might try to threaten me by going after Mike, but I can't tell him what happened in the park because he's a prosecutor and he'd have a duty to tell the police. Mike won't know he's in danger, so I need someone to watch his back until I can figure out who they worked for and whether we're still in danger."

"And you've come to me because . . . ?"

"Can you still get in touch with Anthony?" Amanda said, naming a highly trained assassin and bodyguard who had saved her life when she threatened to expose a criminal conspiracy composed of powerful and ruthless men.

Martin squinted at Amanda. "It's that serious?"

Amanda nodded.

Martin frowned. "I haven't had any contact with Anthony since he babysat you when you had that problem with the Vaughn Street Glee Club, so I have no idea where he is or what he's up to."

"But you can get in touch with him?"

"I can try. Meanwhile, I'll have one of my people watch Mr. Greene's back."

"Whoever sent those men after me is ruthless and probably responsible for several brutal murders. I don't want to endanger any of your men."

"The person I have in mind for the job is used to dangerous situations. And I would feel awful if anything happened to my favorite mouthpiece's boyfriend when I could have prevented it."

"I don't know how to thank you, Martin."

Breach grinned. "An invite to the wedding would be nice, and so would a discount on your legal fees if I ever need your assistance."

Amanda smiled back. "No one's getting married just yet, but the next time you or one of your henchmen are busted, you'll get the repeat-offender discount."

Chapter 35

Alan Hotchkiss was working on a police report when his phone rang.

"Alan, it's Holly Reed from the crime lab."

"Hey, Holly, how you doing?"

"Great. I just solved a problem generated by evidence in the Masterson case that's been driving me crazy."

Hotchkiss swiveled his chair and propped his heels up on his desk.

"What did you find?"

"Do you remember those berries we found in Dale Masterson's den?"

"Not really."

"They were mashed up in some soil on the rug near his desk. I didn't pay much attention to them at first, and then when I finally got around to studying them, I couldn't figure out what plant they were from."

"And?" asked Hotchkiss, who was anxious to get back to his report and not the least bit interested in berries.

"They're from a pokeweed."

"And I should care because . . . ?"

"They're rare, Alan. In fact, you can only find them in one place in Portland."

Hotchkiss lifted his heels off his desk and sat up.

"You've got my full attention, Holly."

"You're the detective and I'm just a techie drudge, but if I was a detective I would conclude that there is a good possibility that the person who murdered Dale Masterson was in a remote part of Forest Park shortly before Dale Masterson was murdered."

"Tom Beatty!" Hotchkiss said.

"Figuring out whodunit is your job, Sherlock."

"I owe you one," Hotchkiss said.

"No, you owe me two. I got my info from Nellie Norwood at the Forest Park Conservancy and she told me that I was the second person she'd told about the pokeweed and where it grows. The first person was Paul Baylor."

"Son of a bitch!" Hotchkiss swore. He knew Paul from Paul's time in the Oregon State Crime Lab, and he also knew that Baylor was the person Amanda Jaffe used when she needed a forensic expert.

"Detectives Brewster and Hotchkiss are in the waiting room," Amanda's receptionist said, "and they'd like to talk to you."

The two detectives pushed their way into Amanda's office seconds later. They were dressed in windbreakers, jeans, and muddy hiking boots.

"Where is Tom Beatty?" Hotchkiss demanded the minute he set foot in Amanda's office.

Amanda expected Hotchkiss to be rude, but Billie Brewster looked as angry as her partner. Normally she would have thrown out anyone who stormed into her office like this, but something was definitely up, so Amanda reined in her anger.

"What's going on?" Amanda asked.

"What do you know about pokeweed?" Hotchkiss asked.

"Why do you want to know?" Amanda asked, fighting hard to keep a placid expression on her face.

"You know damn well why we want to know," Hotchkiss said. "We've just come back from a remote area of Forest Park that happens to be the only place in Oregon where you can find pokeweed. Want to guess what else we found? I'll save you the trouble. We found two dead men in a shallow grave and the remnants of a campsite."

"This has gone far enough, Amanda," Brewster said. "We know Nellie Norwood at the Forest Park Conservancy told Paul Baylor about the pokeweed and where it grows. That's Beatty's camp, isn't it?"

Amanda felt sick. Suddenly her potential conflicts problem was full-blown reality.

"You have to leave," she said without conviction.

"Amanda, Beatty is no longer someone who may have been framed for Christine Larson's death," Billie said. "He's become a mass murderer. How many more people have to die because you refuse to help us catch him?"

"I have to think," Amanda said.

"Well, don't think too long," Hotchkiss said, "or the next victim is on you."

Chapter 36

As soon as the detectives left, Amanda's receptionist told her that Brandon Masterson had just called and left a message on Amanda's voice mail. Amanda accessed the message. Brandon sounded subdued and frightened.

"Hey, um, can you come see me, please? If you can come up right away, I'd . . . Please."

Amanda replayed the short message. Brandon sounded desperate, and a trip to the hospital would distract her from her dilemma. Amanda told the receptionist that she was going to the hospital to visit her client.

Amanda walked into Brandon's hospital room and took a good look at his face. Brandon's bruises had faded to dull purple and jaundice yellow, but he still looked like someone who had been badly beaten.

"Thank you for coming," her client said. He sounded subdued, and Amanda noticed that the arrogance that had characterized his demeanor had drained away, leaving him pale and scared.

"I listened to your voice message," Amanda said. "You sounded very upset."

"I . . . I have something I have to tell you."

"Go ahead," Amanda said as she carried a metal chair to the side of her client's bed.

"I didn't do it. I didn't kill my father."

"I never thought you did," Amanda said. "Tell me why you confessed to such a horrible crime."

Amanda was certain she knew the answer to her question, but she wanted to hear it from her client. Brandon's chin sunk to his chest and he stared down at his blanket. When he spoke, his voice was barely above a whisper.

"I hate . . . hated my father, and I wanted to use my trial to tell the world what a bastard he was and how much harm he was doing to the Earth."

"What made you change your mind about claiming you killed him?"

Brandon choked up and started to weep. "I can't go back there. I had no idea . . ."

Brandon looked up. Tears stained his cheeks and he looked completely lost.

"They beat me. I've never been beaten like that. The pain was awful. I was so helpless, so humiliated."

Amanda reached out and placed her hand over his. "It's okay, Brandon. I know people at the jail. I'll try to keep you here as long as I can, and I'll make sure you're safe if you have to go back."

"Thank you."

"Now, let me ask you something. Veronica Masterson saw you running away from your father's house, and you had blood on you. How did the blood get on your clothes?"

"I got in the way I said, with my key; they hadn't changed the locks. I called out when I was inside because I didn't know where he was. No one answered, so I went into the living room. Then I went into the den. That's where I found him, on the floor."

"And the blood?"

"There was blood all around him. He . . . he looked dead, but I couldn't be sure so I dropped to my knees next to him. That's when I got some of the blood on my jeans." Brandon shook his head as if he was trying to clear away the image of his father's battered face. "I'm not too clear on what I did after that. I was in shock, I wasn't thinking. I did touch him. I was looking for a pulse. I think I shook him. Then I jumped up and saw the blood on my hands. I wiped it on my shirt and pants as I was backing out of the den. Then I panicked and ran. I was running back to my car when Veronica drove up."

"Did you see the person who killed your father?"

"No, I didn't see anyone. He must have left before I got there."

Amanda paused as she debated bringing up a subject that had to be discussed. Then she took a deep breath and plunged in.

"I have a problem. It might not be possible for me to continue to represent you."

"What? Why?" Brandon asked. He sounded panicky.

"I represent a client who may have killed your father."

"Who?"

"I can't tell you or anyone else his name, because he's my client and some of the evidence I have is statements he made to me that are privileged.

"Normally in a case like yours I would argue to the jury that someone other than you killed Dale Masterson, only I can't do that because it would be unethical to show the jury evidence that proved my other client is a killer. You see my problem? In this type of situation it is the best practice for the attorney to resign from both cases and have the clients hire new attorneys."

"No, I don't want another attorney. I want you to represent me."

"I may not have a choice, Brandon."

"Don't desert me, please. I trust you. You've been so straight with me."

"This is a death penalty case, Brandon. Your life is quite literally at stake. You don't want a lawyer representing you who has one hand tied behind her back."

"Can't I sign a waiver? Can't I tell the judge I want you even though you have a conflict?"

"You could sign a waiver, but I don't think that would end it. I'm not going to stay on your case if I think it will lead to you being executed. I couldn't live with myself if you died because evidence that could have cleared you was denied to the jury because of my conflict.

"Look, we're both stressed out. I'm going to go now, and I'm going to try and figure a way out of this mess. If I can't, I'll have to resign. While I'm working on this problem I want you to think about what I said. You don't have to make a decision today, but you're probably going to have to make one soon. And remember: Your life could depend on the choice you make."

Chapter 37

Mark Hamilton's second wife had left him for a gynecologist who lived in Malibu, so he was living alone in a two-story Tudor mansion in the West Hills. At eight in the evening a black Cadillac Escalade carrying Hamilton and his security detail wound up the tree-lined driveway to the front of the house. Reggie Kiner had arranged for the bodyguards after Dale Masterson's murder.

At first Hamilton had felt relief at being surrounded by the bodyguards, but then something had occurred to him. He couldn't believe that Brandon had murdered his father. Tom Beatty was the obvious killer. But what if Tom Beatty didn't kill Dale? What if Reggie murdered Dale because Dale made him nervous? Reggie would not want to take the chance that Dale would spill his guts to the police if he were questioned and would have no compunctions about getting rid of Dale the same way he'd gotten rid of Christine Larson and Carol White. Now Hamilton wondered if Reggie had surrounded him with bodyguards to protect him or to make it easy to get rid of him if Reggie decided that he posed a threat.

Hamilton waited in the backseat while the two guards in the front seat got out. Both men were over six feet tall and heavily muscled. They had handguns in their holsters, knives in sheaths, and carried automatic weapons.

One bodyguard stayed with Hamilton while the other used the entry code to get inside Hamilton's house and check for intruders. Twenty minutes later, the guard walked out.

"All clear, Mr. Hamilton. You can go in now. We're going to watch the house in shifts. Bill will take over for me at two-thirty a.m. and we'll all drive you to work in the morning."

"Thanks, Ray. I appreciate your help."

"Hey, Mr. Hamilton, we earn our living keeping important men safe and sound, and we haven't lost anyone yet."

The men surrounded Hamilton and escorted him into his house. As they walked, the bodyguards scanned the area for hostiles. As soon as Mark was inside, Ray left to begin his patrol. Hamilton activated the alarm and went to his den. The curtains were drawn across the only window, and Hamilton adjusted the rheostat so that only a pale glow illuminated the room. There was a wet bar in a corner. Hamilton took a bottle from the liquor cabinet and poured a stiff shot of aged bourbon over a few cubes of ice. He carried his glass to a deep, comfortable armchair and collapsed.

The liquor helped him relax, and so did the fact that he had guards patrolling his grounds. But how long could he go on like this? He felt like a prisoner. Why couldn't Kiner and the police, with all their resources, find one man?

Hamilton closed his eyes and pressed the glass to his forehead. The cold felt good, and he'd started to calm down when a strip of duct tape was slapped across his mouth. Hamilton's eyes went wide and he dropped the glass just before he was thrown to the floor. Tom Beatty wrenched the lawyer's arms behind his back and secured his hands and ankles with more duct tape. Then a sharp blade pressed against Hamilton's Adam's apple.

"I'm going to remove the tape from your mouth and ask you a question," Beatty said. "Lie to me and I will hurt you and ask my question again. Nod if you understand what I just said."

Hamilton's head bobbed up and down.

"I know you're thinking about ways to let your bodyguards know you're in danger, Mark, but get any of those ideas out of your head. I will sever your windpipe the moment you try anything. Do you understand me?"

Hamilton's head bobbed again.

"Okay. Here is my first question. Who was responsible for Christine Larson's murder?"

Tom Beatty pulled the tape away.

"I can't . . . ," Hamilton started. The tape was slapped back across his mouth and Beatty severed the tip of the lawyer's right ear. Hamilton's eyes went wide from the pain and he writhed on the floor.

"That was just a sample of what I can do to you if you don't give me straight answers. Think about how you'll practice law if I put out your eyes and sever your tongue."

Hamilton fought to keep from throwing up. Beatty gave him a moment to compose himself. During that moment, an answer to all his problems flashed into the lawyer's brain.

"I repeat, who gave the order to kill Christine?"

"Dale, Dale did it," Hamilton gasped when the tape was removed.

"Why did you kill Christine?"

"I didn't. I swear. It was Dale. Christine was going to tell Global Mining that he'd falsified our accounts to get their business. We were going to close the deal in two days, and Dale was afraid that Global would back out if Christine told them about the doctored books. It would have cost the firm millions."

"Good. We're making progress. Were you involved in the decision to have Christine murdered?"

"No. I liked Christine, and cooking the books was Dale's idea. I was out of town on a case. He made the decision himself."

"But you knew what he'd done?"

"After it was too late to stop it."

"And the books—you knew they'd been doctored, right?"

Hamilton hesitated, because he wanted Beatty to drag the answers out of him so he would believe what he said. Beatty pricked the skin at his neck enough to draw blood. The new wound hurt, but the pain would be worth it if he got out of this situation alive.

"Okay, yeah, we discussed it."

"Let's move on. Two men tried to kill me at my house after I was released from jail. Two more went after me in Forest Park. I'm certain that they were mercenaries. Who supplied them and who gave the order to kill me?"

"Please," Hamilton begged.

Beatty slapped the tape back on and carved a strip of skin from Hamilton's cheek. The lawyer screamed, but the tape muffled the sound. He rolled on the ground as tears coursed down his cheeks. Beatty pulled off the tape.

"Who supplied the mercenaries?"

"Kiner, Reggie Kiner," Hamilton babbled. "Please don't hurt me anymore. I'll tell you anything you want to know."

"Who is Kiner?"

"He's the head of security for RENCO Oil."

"What does RENCO have to do with Global Mining?"

"Nothing," Hamilton babbled. "I've known Kiner for years, since he worked narcotics for the Portland police and I was in law school. He . . . he helps the firm when we have . . . problems."

Beatty slapped back the tape and broke Hamilton's nose.

"Is that what Christine was to you, you piece of shit, a 'problem'?"

Hamilton's eyes squeezed shut from the pain. He heard Beatty take some deep breaths so he could calm down. Hamilton could tell that Beatty got his emotions somewhat under control, but he could also tell that he was still very, very angry.

"How much did you pay Kiner to kill Christine?" Beatty asked.

"I told you, I didn't pay Kiner—Dale did. Kiner was in Iraq at some oil field, checking on security. Dale called him and said we had a . . . He told him to get rid of Christine and frame you for her murder. I had nothing to do with it. I didn't even know he called Kiner until later, after Christine was dead."

"What was Christine's life worth?"

"I don't know what Dale paid because I wasn't involved. When . . . when we used him in the past, Kiner always charged six figures."

"Where can I find Kiner?"

"At RENCO or at his house, but you'll never get to him at either place. There's too much security. If you promise to let me live, I can help you."

"How?"

"He has a cabin in the mountains. It has heavy security too but it's isolated and surrounded by woods. I can show you where it is."

"How will you do that?"

"When my security detail finds me I'll demand that Kiner meet me at the cabin. You can follow me and find out where it is."

Beatty was quiet for a minute. Then he turned to the lawyer.

"You see how easy it is for me to get to you. Gaining entry to your house was no problem at all. But I don't have to hide in your house to get to you. I was a sniper in the military, and there is no place you can go where I can't kill you unless you decide to spend the rest of your life sealed in a panic room. If this is a setup you will be dead. Do you get that?"

Hamilton moved his head up and down—slowly, because his broken nose ached when he moved. Beatty smoothed the tape across Hamilton's mouth again. The lawyer waited for more questions or instructions. When none came, he rolled onto his side and looked around the den. There was no one else in the room.

Chapter 38

Ray knocked on the front door at 7:30 a.m., the time Mark Hamilton had told the security guard he wanted to leave for his office. When Hamilton didn't answer, the bodyguard tried the knob. The door was locked. Ray pulled out his cell phone and dialed Hamilton's cell. When Hamilton didn't pick up, Ray signaled to the other guard, then entered using the key the lawyer had given him.

The house alarm shrieked when the door opened, and Ray disarmed it. Then he called Hamilton's name. There was no answer. Moments later, Ray walked into the den and found Hamilton lying on the floor. His hands were bound behind him, his ankles were lashed together, and a strip of duct tape sealed his mouth. Blood had crusted on the tip of his ear, a wound in his cheek was leaking blood, and his nose was mashed flat. Ray pulled a knife from the sheath on his belt and slashed the tape that bound the lawyer's ankles and wrists. He removed the gag last because he wanted to delay the tirade he knew would start as soon as Hamilton could speak.

"He was in my house!" Hamilton screamed. "That fucker cut off my ear!"

"I don't know how this could happen, Mr. Hamilton. We checked the house before we let you go in."

Ray helped Hamilton to his feet. The lawyer wobbled and the bodyguard lowered him onto an armchair.

"I want Kiner. Call Kiner," Hamilton ordered.

"Yes, sir," Ray said as he dialed Kiner's cell, only too glad to let Hamilton scream at someone else.

"Beatty attacked me in my house," Hamilton shrieked as soon as Kiner answered. "He cut off a piece of my ear! I've been lying on the floor in my own filth all night!"

"Stop, Mark," Kiner commanded. "You're on a cell phone."

"A phone your men assured me was secure. Of course, they also assured me that I was safe from that maniac."

"You have to calm down. Do you need medical treatment? Ray was trained as a medic."

"I'm not letting any of these incompetent assholes touch me."

"Okay, look, we have to discuss this in person. Not over the phone."

"I'm coming to the cabin. Be there," Hamilton commanded.

"Good idea—the cabin. You shower and change. And please let Ray patch you up. You don't want your cuts to get infected."

An hour and a half later the Escalade stopped in front of Kiner's cabin and Hamilton stormed out. He hadn't said a word during the trip and had sat with his arms folded tightly across his chest, staring out the tinted windows.

Kiner was waiting on the front porch. He ran down the steps and met the lawyer halfway. Ray had stitched up the cut in Hamilton's cheek, sanitized and bandaged the tip of the ear, and reset his broken nose. Those injuries, coupled with a black eye and several bruises, made the lawyer look like the badly defeated loser in a barroom brawl.

"God, you look terrible, Mark. Come inside. I'll pour you a drink."

Hamilton glared at Kiner and followed him into the house without saying a word.

"Tell me what happened," Kiner said as he filled a glass with scotch.

"I'll tell you what happened. Your flunkies fucked up royally. Ray searched the house before letting me go in, and he did a piss-poor job of it. He told me everything was hunky-dory, so I went into the den. The next thing I know I'm on the floor, tied up and gagged, and that lunatic is slicing off part of my ear and breaking my nose."

"What did he say to you? What did he want?"

"He wanted to know who sent the mercenaries to kill him and who killed Larson."

Kiner handed Hamilton the glass, and the attorney gulped down half of his drink.

"What did you tell him?" Kiner asked.

"Not a damn thing. That's why he tortured me."

"You didn't give him my name?"

"No," Hamilton lied. "I convinced him that I didn't know anyone had tried to kill him and I said that Dale gave the order to murder Larson."

"Did he ask you how Dale was able to get in touch with hired killers?" Kiner asked.

"I told him I had no idea how he could do that. I put on a great act, and I'm pretty certain he bought my story."

"So he just let you go?" Kiner asked.

"No, he didn't just let me go. Look at my face. The motherfucker tortured me until I couldn't hold out any longer. Then I gave him Dale and he seemed satisfied."

"He just bought your story and left."

Hamilton could tell Kiner was skeptical.

"You weren't there, Reggie. It was awful. No one has ever hurt me like that. But I held out as long as I could. Then it took some doing to get him to believe I didn't know anything more than Dale. He bought my story, at least for now. But he could come back."

Hamilton dropped his chin and he teared up, something he didn't have to fake, because he was terrified of Beatty.

"I couldn't take it again, Reggie. You have to get him."

"Yes, yes, you're right. I'm sorry this happened. I was certain my men could keep you safe."

"Well, they didn't. I can't live like this. I'm a wreck. I jump at every sound."

"I think you're safe for now. If Beatty was going to murder you he would have killed you last night. Our priority is taking him down. If he's dead, he can't hurt anyone."

Kiner escorted the lawyer to the car and told Ray to drive him back to town. As soon as the car was out of sight Kiner called in one of his guards and told him to check the surveillance cameras and motion sensors for any sign of activity and to organize a search of the perimeter. If Beatty was smart enough to get into Hamilton's house with Ray guarding the grounds, he would be smart enough to have followed Hamilton here.

After he talked to the guard, Kiner thought about Mark Hamilton. He wasn't sure how much the lawyer had told Beatty, but it was clear that Hamilton was terrified. If he cracked and went to the authorities for protection, he would use his only bargaining chip: his knowledge of Kiner's involvement in Christine Larson's murder.

Kiner had been tempted to kill Hamilton at the cabin just now. He didn't know how many witnesses could tell the police about the bodyguards, or if Hamilton had told anyone the identity of the man who had supplied them. He figured that the security camera at the law firm had probably taken pictures of some of his men.

Kiner finally decided that Hamilton had to go, and he wondered if there was some way that he could make the murder seem like Tom Beatty's work.

Mark Hamilton told Ray to take him home. There was no way he was going into the office looking like he did. Hamilton didn't say a word on the return trip. He was too busy thinking about how to get out of the mess Christine Larson had created by sticking her nose where it didn't belong. God, how he wished that bitch had never been born, but she had been, and now there was a real possibility that he would be killed by Tom Beatty or Reggie Kiner.

Hamilton did not delude himself. He had taken a chance by going to Kiner's isolated cabin, and he was certain that he had been inches away from death while he was there, but the only way he could think of to appease Beatty was to lead him to Reggie.

Hamilton had no idea why Kiner had not killed him and buried him in the woods, but he was still alive and he meant to stay alive. Accomplishing that task was not going to be easy. But one thing he had decided was that Kiner had to go. If Kiner stayed alive he would eventually come to the conclusion that he would not be safe until Hamilton was dead. If Kiner was arrested, he would feed him to the sharks to make a deal. How to kill him was the question.

Chapter 39

Tom Beatty had followed Hamilton into the mountains. When the Escalade turned off toward Kiner's cabin, Tom kept going. A mile later, he parked on a logging road and approached the cabin through the woods. While surveying the area around the cabin, he spotted several hidden security cameras, motion detectors, and guards. He didn't want to risk detection, so he scaled a tree and watched through high-powered binoculars.

Hamilton had stayed inside the cabin for an hour before he got in the Escalade with his bodyguards and drove away. Beatty assumed that Hamilton was headed home to recuperate. If he went to his office he would have to explain his injuries to his coworkers, probably by claiming he'd been in an auto accident. After a few seconds, Beatty forgot about the attorney. He didn't care what Hamilton did. The man he was interested in was the man in the cabin.

Beatty was certain that Kiner's men would stop hunting him if he killed Kiner, which he could do with ease from his perch once he got the right rifle. But killing Kiner would not solve all of his problems. Tom did not want to be on the run for the rest of his life. He'd had a stress-free job at Masterson, Hamilton until Christine was murdered. He wanted peace and quiet desperately, but he would never find peace as a fugitive.

Amanda Jaffe had been able to trace him to his camp in Forest Park as a result of the pokeweed berries he had inadvertently left next to Dale Masterson's body. Beatty assumed that the police would eventually make the same connection between the berries and his isolated camp. He had cleaned up the area and buried the bodies of the two mercenaries, but the graves would be easy to find. The MOs of Christine's and Masterson's killings were identical, and once the police found two more dead men, he would jump to the top of the list in Masterson's murder case. If he wanted to return to the peace and quiet he'd experienced before Christine was murdered, he'd have to figure out a way to convince the police that Reginald Kiner had killed Dale Masterson and Christine Larson, and he had no idea how he could do that. Beatty decided that it was time to ask for help. He worked his way back to the ground and headed for his car to make contact with the one person he thought he could trust.

Amanda usually walked to work on sunny days, but she had not slept well and she decided to drive to work with Mike. The couple had not made love last night, both protesting that they were exhausted, and Mike had been quiet during breakfast, burying himself in the newspaper so that, Amanda suspected, he would have an excuse to avoid talking to her.

When Amanda arrived at her office, she dived into work that she'd put on hold because of the Beatty and Masterson cases. Issues in those cases and her problems with Mike tried to worm their way into her thoughts, but she was able to sidestep the attempts by burying herself in an obscure area of immigration law that had become important in a case involving a Guatemalan drug dealer she was representing. When five o'clock rolled around she congratulated herself on a productive day and called Mike to ask if he was ready to drive home. Mike told her he was tied up with detectives who were interviewing two prostitutes who were witnesses in a liquor store robbery and he would get the detectives to drive him home. Mike sounded friendly on the phone, and Amanda took that as a sign that he was not mad at her any longer.

Amanda parked in a garage near her office. She entered the garage and pushed the button for the elevator. The elevator door opened and Amanda got in. Just before the door closed, a heavyset woman wearing jeans and a black polyester Portland Trailblazer jacket squeezed in.

"Sorry," she apologized with a smile.

Amanda smiled back.

"Looks like you did my work for me," the woman said when she saw the fourth-floor button lit up.

"Glad I could help," Amanda replied.

The elevator stopped at 4. The blond woman waited for her to get out, then followed after her as Amanda circled around to the back wall. The woman walked past her as Amanda got to her car. Amanda had just stopped to fish in her purse for her key when Tom Beatty stepped out of the shadows.

"I'm not going to hurt you," he said.

Amanda saw the blond woman standing next to a pickup truck, watching them. Tom followed Amanda's eyes.

"I'm here because I need your help and I couldn't risk going to your office. Please. I just want to talk, then I'll leave. You don't have anything to worry about."

Amanda hesitated. Then she opened the car and got in.

"What do you want to talk about?" she asked when Beatty was seated next to her in the passenger seat.

"I know who's responsible for killing Christine and the attempt to kill me in Forest Park and at my house."

"Someone tried to kill you at your house?"

"Miss Ross and I were followed from the jail when she drove me home. There were two men. Before I disarmed one of them, his gun discharged and killed the other man. Then I . . . I hit the man with the gun too hard. He died as well."

"These were the men who were found in the trunk of a car?"

"Yes."

"Did you kill Dale Masterson to avenge Christine's death?"

"No, Amanda. I went to Masterson's house to find out who was responsible for killing her. He was dead when I found him in his den. Moments later, I heard the front door open and I heard someone go upstairs. That's when I left."

"Did you break into Dale Masterson's law office?"

"Yes. Christine knew his password and she knew I was good with computers. During our argument, she told the password to me. She wanted me to get into Masterson's computer to see if I could find evidence about the books. When I broke in, I copied his hard drive, but there was nothing on it that helped."

"Who killed Christine and sent the men who tried to kill you?"

Beatty told Amanda everything he'd dragged out of Mark Hamilton, and she listened without comment until he was through.

"So Hamilton told you this highly paid executive sent teams of killers after you and Christine?"

"That's what he told me."

"Out of the goodness of his heart?" Amanda asked.

Beatty looked down. "I . . . I had to rough him up to get Kiner's name."

"He told you about Kiner under torture?!?"

"Yes."

"Jesus, Tom. Even if you had him on tape, nothing he said would be admissible or even believable. People will say anything to escape pain."

"I know that. I just couldn't think of any other way to get what I needed."

"What do you expect me to do with this?" Amanda asked.

"I need you to prove Kiner is behind the killings."

"How am I supposed to do that?"

"I don't know." He sounded desperate. "Maybe you can tell the cops or have your investigator look into it."

"What are you planning on doing? Are you going to stay on the run?"

"I can't turn myself in. I'd be killed in jail."

"I can make sure you're safe."

"You don't know who you're dealing with. These people don't follow any rules. I'm safer staying hidden. And *you* watch *your* back, too."

"I need a way to get in touch with you if something comes up."

Tom handed her a cell phone and a slip of paper.

"If you need me call this number."

Before she could say anything else, Beatty got out and headed toward the stairs. Amanda watched him leave and saw the blond woman walk around the corner and head back in the direction of the elevators.

Amanda pushed the cell Tom had given her into her purse. Then she grabbed her own phone and called Kate Ross. As soon as Kate answered, Amanda told her what Tom Beatty had said.

"What do you want to do with his intel?" Kate asked when Amanda was through.

"My first thought was that we go to Hamilton and grill him. Tom tortured him, so he's probably scared to death. He might crack."

"Not if he's going to end up in prison."

"What do you think we should do?" Amanda asked.

"I'm not sure. Kiner isn't going to admit to anything. The head of security for an outfit like RENCO isn't going to be intimidated."

"I'm too wound up to think straight right now. Let's sleep on this, then talk in the morning."

Amanda wasn't in their condo when Mike got home. He'd picked up some Chinese at a restaurant in the Pearl after the detectives dropped him off and he was starting in on the kung pao chicken when Amanda walked in.

"Want some?" he asked, pointing at the take-out boxes.

"You bet. I haven't eaten and I'm famished."

"I tried to get you on your cell. When I couldn't get through, I bought enough for two just in case you hadn't eaten."

"Thanks. I was working out and I didn't get your voice message until I left the pool."

Mike's eyebrows went up. "Working out at night? That's not your usual routine."

"Yeah, well, I haven't had a normal day and I needed to clear my head."

"Oh?"

Amanda grabbed a plate and chopsticks and sat down opposite Mike at the kitchen table.

"If I say the words 'attorney-client privilege,' will you go ballistic?" Amanda asked.

Mike smiled and shook his head. "No, I will not go ballistic, but I will apologize for the other day. If I was stupid enough to shack up with a defense attorney, I deserve everything I get."

Amanda grinned. "Is living with me that bad?"

"It is trying at times, but worth it. I should have known better than to keep dating you, but I'm stuck with you now so I've decided to make the best of it."

Amanda walked around the table and sat on Mike's lap. Then she gave him a big kiss.

"I don't deserve you," she said.

"Too true," he replied. "Now eat your food before it gets cold."

Chapter 40

Two days after discovering Tom Beatty's campsite and the two dead men, Billie Brewster had driven to Salem for her brother's parole hearing. She was still furious with Amanda Jaffe for protecting Beatty. Alan had told Billie that he was going to talk to the DA about dragging Jaffe into a grand jury, and she was anxious to learn what had happened at the meeting.

Billie was sad during the drive back to Portland. The parole board had denied Sherman's bid for parole as expected, and he had accepted the decision, having known what it would be before he went in. Sherman had shrugged off the loss of freedom as "no big thing," and Billie wondered if he had become one of the institutionalized who welcomed their arrests because it meant a return to an environment where they had no responsibilities except following the rules, and where food and shelter were supplied free of charge. It was this fear that made Billie so sad.

When Billie returned to police headquarters, she looked for Hotchkiss, but he wasn't around. Billie needed a distraction that would help her forget about the depressing events in Salem, so she decided to grab the file in the Christine Larson murder in order to bring herself up to speed on that case. She was reading the transcript of the hearing on Amanda's motion to suppress in the Larson case when she came across Greg Nowicki's testimony. After reading it she walked over to Drugs and Vice and found Nowicki in his cubicle, typing away on his computer.

"Hey, Greg," she said.

Nowicki swiveled his chair toward her and smiled. "What's up, Billie?"

"Al and I ran across an old friend of yours in one of our investigations—Reginald Kiner."

Nowicki stopped smiling. "Kiner was never a friend."

"Oh?"

"Al told you he was shady, right?"

Billie nodded. "He said he left PPB under a cloud."

"A big, dark storm cloud. We could never prove anything, but everyone was relieved when Kiner left the force and went private. So, why are you interested in him?"

"I was reading your testimony in the Beatty motion to suppress, and you said Carol White started informing for you about ten years ago."

"That's right."

"Was Kiner your partner then?"

"Yeah, why?"

"Did he know White?"

Nowicki's brow furrowed. "He might have. Yeah, he did, because she gave us some information we used to bust a dealer we'd been after for a while. Why do you want to know?"

"Just curiosity. The coincidence of Kiner being your partner." She shook her head. "I can't really tell you why, but I wanted to know."

"How is Kiner involved in your investigation?"

"We found two dead men in a car trunk. They were ex-military and RENCO Oil employed them as security. Kiner's the head of security for RENCO."

"I heard that, and I'm not surprised. Reggie would be right at home running mercs in third world countries."

Billie couldn't think of anything else to ask Nowicki, so she left. Amanda Jaffe had argued that Tom Beatty had been framed for Christine Larson's murder, and there was evidence to support that theory. If Beatty had been set up, the first step in the setup occurred when Carol White contacted Nowicki. Kiner knew White was an informant Nowicki trusted. He could have paid her to tell Nowicki that Beatty had drugs in his house.

Billie frowned. She was reaching. Other than some very tenuous connections to the Larson case, there was nothing to suggest that Kiner was involved in it.

Billie was getting ready to settle down with the rest of the Larson file when Holly Reed called from the crime lab.

"Want to hear a weird coincidence?" the lab tech asked.

"Sure."

"You know the two dead guys from Forest Park?"

"Yeah. What about them?"

"The prints came back to a Norman McDonald and a Jeffrey Cook, both ex-military, just like the dead men in the car trunk. On a hunch, I did some checking with the State Department. Both men have traveled back and forth to Nigeria and the Middle East for RENCO Oil."

When Alan Hotchkiss returned thirty-five minutes later, he didn't look happy.

"What happened with the DA?" Billie asked.

"He's not going to put Jaffe in front of a grand jury. He said, and I quote, 'She and her father are too well connected to harass without a hell of a good reason.'"

"Don't look so down in the dumps. I've got something that should cheer you up. I can't prove anything, but I'm beginning to think that Reggie Kiner is more involved in Christine Larson's murder than we thought."

"What have you found?"

"I read the file in Christine Larson's murder case, and I keep on bouncing back and forth between thinking that Tom Beatty is guilty because he killed the men in the car trunk and Forest Park and thinking that he may have been framed for Larson's murder even if he killed the men in the trunk and the park. If he was set up, Carol White is the key. Without her affidavit there's no warrant, and without the search warrant you wouldn't have found the body in Beatty's bedroom.

"If White lied in her affidavit, the person who told her to lie would have a powerful motive to murder her. Greg Nowicki told me that Reggie Kiner knew White and knew Greg had used her as an informant."

"Why would Kiner set up Beatty?" Hotchkiss asked.

"To make it look like Beatty killed Larson."

"Yeah, but why would Kiner kill Larson? There's no proof he even knew her."

"But he did know Dale Masterson and Mark Hamilton. And I just learned that the dead men in the park also had a connection to RENCO. So we know that men who worked for Kiner at one time were in Beatty's house and at Beatty's campsite. What if Kiner sent them there to kill Beatty?"

"Why would Kiner do that? I still don't see the connection."

"It's the books. If Masterson and Hamilton cooked them to get Global Mining as a client and Larson threatened to tell Global, the lawyers would have a powerful motive to kill her and anyone she told about the fraud. Now, I'm making a big leap of logic here, but Kiner was a bad cop who was suspected of killing witnesses. What if Masterson and/or Hamilton knew Kiner could have Larson killed for a price and paid him to take care of their problem?"

"That's not a leap of logic, Billie—that's a fucking rocket trip to another planet."

"Yeah, Alan, but what if . . . Think about it. There are direct connections to Kiner and four dead mercs. Why were mercs in Beatty's house and camp? They weren't there to sell Girl Scout cookies."

Billie waited patiently while her partner mulled over what he'd just heard. After a while, Hotchkiss looked at her.

"Let's say you're right. How do we prove it? If we question Kiner, he'll just laugh at us."

"I agree with you. But Mark Hamilton might crack if we apply enough pressure."

Chapter 41

"What happened to your face?" Billie asked as soon as she and Hotchkiss were seated in Mark Hamilton's law office.

"I was in a car accident," Hamilton said.

"Are you okay?" she asked.

"It looks worse than it is."

"Weird accident, huh?" Hotchkiss said.

"What do you mean?" the lawyer asked nervously.

Hotchkiss shrugged. "The injuries are odd, is all. I mean I can see breaking your nose and cutting your cheek, but how did the tip of your ear get cut off?"

"I . . . I blacked out. I don't have any memory about how it happened so I don't know how I lost part of my ear."

"You reported the accident, right?" Hotchkiss asked. "You have to do that for the insurance."

"Not yet but I'm going to. So, why are you here? I'm pretty busy and I'd appreciate it if you got to the point."

"Yeah, the point," Hotchkiss said. "I don't think you got those injuries in a car accident. I think someone beat you up to make sure you didn't talk to us about (A) your plan to get Global Mining as a client by cooking your law firm's books, (B) the plot to murder Christine Larson when she threatened to go to Global, and (C) the plot to frame Tom Beatty for the killing."

Billie was thrilled to see the color drain from Mark Hamilton's face.

"This meeting is over," the lawyer said.

"There are two ways you can play this, Mark," Hotchkiss said. "You can stonewall us. Do that and we'll get subpoenas for your books and you'll have forensic accountants crawling up your ass for months. When they figure out the scam, there will be grand jury appearances, indictments, and years of attorneys' fees.

"In scenario number two, you cooperate with our investigation. We're pretty certain we know the identity of the man who helped you kill Christine Larson. You can save yourself by helping us nail him."

"I'm not saying another word. Now get out."

Billie stood up to go. "I think you should talk to a really good criminal lawyer before you decide how to play this, because you are in way over your head and we're the only people who can throw you a life preserver."

The detectives didn't say another word until they were alone in the elevator.

"How do you think that went?" Billie asked.

"He's scared to death."

"I agree, and I think this case will turn on whether he's more scared of us or the person who carved him up."

Chapter 42

Kate Ross had majored in computer science at Cal Tech and had been recruited into the Computer Crimes Unit of the Portland Police Bureau right out of college because she was a gifted hacker. She had transferred to Drugs and Vice when she got bored with sitting in an office all day and began to crave more action. The last assignment Kate Ross was given before she left the Portland Police Bureau was to pick up an enforcer for a major drug dealer who was going to testify against his boss in exchange for witness protection. The enforcer insisted on turning himself in at a shopping mall. Kate had warned the DA that it was too dangerous to take custody in the mall, but the DA refused to listen. The dealer sent an assassin to murder the witness and there was a shoot-out. Kate killed the assassin, but there were casualties and the powers-that-be decided that Kate would be the scapegoat.

Even though Kate left the force under a cloud, she still had friends, like Billie Brewster, who knew the truth about what the press had termed "the Holiday Massacre." Kate had called a friend who had been with the bureau far longer than anyone else she knew and got the name of the detective in Internal Affairs who had investigated Reginald Kiner.

Neil Denton was living in an assisted living facility in Clackamas County. Denton's caregiver had placed his wheelchair in a sunny corner of a spacious lounge next to a picture window that looked out on a rolling river. A stroke had left the retired detective partially paralyzed, but the doctor she'd spoken to at the facility had assured her that Denton's mind was still razor-sharp.

"Thanks for seeing me, Detective," Kate said as she sat in a comfortable chair across from Denton.

"Thanks for providing me with a little excitement. When they told me you wanted to talk to me about an old case, it made my day. I usually spend my time watching television or playing checkers."

"Jack Nunez sends his regards. He wanted me to tell you that he still expects you to pay him the ten bucks you owe him and he plans to come out soon to collect."

Denton laughed. "Did he tell you why he thinks I owe him the money?"

Kate smiled. "No, he said it wasn't something fit for the ears of a member of my delicate sex."

Denton laughed again. "He's got that right. So, why are you visiting an old crippled retiree?"

"When you did a stint in Internal Affairs, you investigated a detective in Drugs and Vice named Reginald Kiner."

Denton stopped smiling.

"If you're willing to talk about his case, I'd like to know everything I can about him."

"Why?"

"Have you read about the murders of two of the partners at the Masterson, Hamilton law firm?"

"I thought Masterson's son confessed to killing his father and a crazy veteran murdered the woman."

"Amanda Jaffe is representing both defendants. I'm her investigator. We think both of our clients are innocent, and we have reason to believe that Kiner is involved in the murders."

"What makes you think that?" Denton asked.

Kate explained that there were certain aspects of the case she couldn't talk about. Then she filled in the retired detective on the links between RENCO, Masterson, Hamilton, and the murders of Dale Masterson and Christine Larson. After Kate finished, Denton stared out at the river. A motorboat was cruising by and a man in a shell was straining against the current. Kate let Denton think.

After a while, Denton turned his eyes back to Kate. "Kiner is scum, someone who should never have been allowed to become a cop. I could never prove it, but I'm sure he was paid by a Mexican cartel to kill a dealer who was going to cut a deal with the DA and I'm pretty certain he made a key witness in another case disappear, and those were just the most serious of his felonies."

"Why wasn't he prosecuted?"

"Funny things happened with the evidence and the witnesses."

"Funny how?"

"They kept disappearing. For instance, there were disparities in the money defendants claimed Kiner confiscated in raids and the money logged into the evidence room. When we started to look at the situation, the evidence and the logs disappeared. Then there was the witness I was going to talk to who OD'd."

Denton shrugged. "It was like a magic act. He was always one step ahead of us. We never figured out the trick by the time he quit and went to RENCO Oil. I tried to make a case for a while after he left. I would have loved to find enough for an indictment, but I never got there."

"Did you ever have a theory about how he was able to avoid prosecution?"

Denton nodded. "I'm certain he had help, someone who was working with him. He had to, because we had him under surveillance on a few occasions when he wormed out of trouble."

"So you have no idea who was working with him?"

"I had ideas but never any proof, and if you're thinking of asking me for names, don't. I'm not going to ruin someone's career when all I've got is gossip."

"But you had more than gossip when it came to Kiner?"

"Kiner was dirty. I knew it in my heart. I just couldn't prove it."

Chapter 43

There was a crisis in Nigeria. Some members of Kiner's security force had gotten into a fight in a bar in Lagos and there had been civilian casualties. The press was calling with questions Kiner had no intention of answering, and his bosses were bombarding him with questions he couldn't answer yet.

Kiner's secure cell rang.

"We have a problem," the voice on the other end said.

"I'm in the middle of something at work. Can this wait?"

"No. We need to meet right away. There's an abandoned construction site by the waterfront. No surveillance cameras and no night watchman. We met there when we talked about that problem."

"Okay. I'll be there at eight, but it will have to be quick. I'm in the middle of something and I'll probably have to be in my office all night."

Kiner parked his car near a high-rise several blocks from the construction site. This area had been an industrial wasteland until developers got a hold of it. Suddenly condominiums started sprouting like mushrooms, until the boom busted. Kiner's destination was a wide-open field that was supposed to have been an apartment complex but had stalled at the concept.

Kiner walked by one apartment building before the streetlights became scarce and the area gave way to shadow. He was upset about the meet because he needed to be at the office near his phone, but there was no way he could refuse. Kiner was almost at the lot when he heard a car approaching. His hand went to the gun in the holster on his belt and he made a half turn. The car slowed, and Kiner tensed. Then he relaxed when he recognized the driver. The car stopped even with Kiner. He took a step toward the car and leaned down until he was flush with the window.

"What's so important?" he asked when the window lowered.

The driver smiled reassuringly just before he shot Kiner between the eyes.

Billie Brewster swore silently as she did a knee bend to get closer to the corpse. It was two in the morning, but the lights the lab techs had set up illuminated Reggie Kiner's body and the blood-encrusted hole in his head.

"You know what's bothering me?" Billie asked Alan Hotchkiss.

"No, but I'm guessing you're going to tell me."

"What's bothering me is that the head of security for RENCO Oil is lying on a sidewalk with a bullet in his head in the middle of nowhere. Look around you. There's not a store, a bar, or a residence for blocks. And where is his car?"

"Obviously, Kiner was meeting someone and they didn't want to be seen so they chose this empty lot," Hotchkiss said.

"You know what I find interesting?" Billie said. "A few weeks ago I'd never heard of Reginald Kiner. Then his name started to pop up all over the place. RENCO is a client of Masterson, Hamilton. Then there are the two guys in the trunk. They worked security for RENCO and at least one of them bled in Tom Beatty's house. And there are the bodies in the park who are linked to Dale Masterson and Tom Beatty through the pokeweed berries. They also provided security services for RENCO. And Greg Nowicki tells me Kiner knew Carol White. So we have connections between Kiner and Tom Beatty, Dale Masterson, and Christine Larson, and it looks like we've got our killer. But now we're back to square one."

"He still may be our killer," Hotchkiss said. "The new question is who killed him?"

"When I learned who the victim was I spoke with some people at RENCO," Billie told her partner. "There was a shooting in Lagos, Nigeria, involving members of RENCO's security force. From what they told me, this is a real hot potato. No one knows why Kiner would leave his office in the middle of a high-profile crisis but he must have believed the meeting was very important."

"It seems to me that we have two possible killers," Hotchkiss said. "Tom Beatty would want revenge if Kiner and the partners at Masterson, Hamilton killed Christine Larson and framed him for the murder."

"Who is killer number two?" Billie asked.

"Mark Hamilton. He knows he's a suspect, so he would have every reason to get rid of a witness who could link him to multiple murders."

Chapter 44

An hour later, Brewster and Hotchkiss parked next to the front door of Mark Hamilton's house. It was pitch-black in the countryside, but lights illuminated the grounds around Hamilton's mansion. An armed man had checked the detectives' ID at the bottom of the driveway and radioed ahead to the bodyguard, who was now waiting for them at the door. He was thickset and broad-shouldered, and he carried an automatic weapon.

"Mr. Hamilton says he doesn't want to talk to you," the man said.

Hotchkiss stared into the bodyguard's eyes. "We don't give a fuck what Mark Hamilton wants. Go inside and tell your boss that Reggie Kiner was murdered tonight, and he'll talk to us now or in an interrogation room downtown."

The bodyguard turned pale. "Mr. Kiner is dead?"

"Yeah," Billie answered. "Someone shot him right between the eyes."

The man thought for a moment. Then he made a decision.

"Wait here. I'll tell Mr. Hamilton."

"Before you go," Billie said, "were you with Mr. Hamilton all day?"

"No. We're here at night. Then we drive him to work and pick him up when he's ready to go home."

"When did you pick him up tonight?"

"He worked late. We got him at nine thirty."

As soon as the man disappeared, Hotchkiss turned to his partner. "The people at RENCO say that Kiner left their headquarters at seven forty."

"We need to check the surveillance cameras at Masterson, Hamilton and talk with anyone who was in the office tonight."

Ten minutes later, the bodyguard returned.

"He'll see you. I'll take you in."

Hamilton was waiting in the den, and he looked worse than he had a few hours ago when they'd talked to him in his office. He had thrown on a warm-up suit. Salt-and-pepper stubble covered his cheeks, and his eyes, red-rimmed and still dull from sleep, wouldn't meet the detectives'.

"Did your security guard tell you why we're here?"

"Yeah, but I don't know what it has to do with me."

"Where were you tonight between seven thirty and nine thirty?"

"I don't want to talk to you two," Hamilton said. There was a tremor when he spoke.

"That's your right, Mr. Hamilton," Billie said, "but it's going to go really bad for you if you can't prove where you were during those two hours."

"I want to talk to a lawyer. You told me to do that."

"We did, but you can take your name off our list of suspects in Mr. Kiner's death if you can prove your whereabouts during those two hours."

"Lawyer," Hamilton repeated stubbornly.

"While you're lawyering up, Mark, we're going to do a little detecting, just like Sherlock Holmes," Hotchkiss said. "We're going to look at tapes from security cameras and talk to witnesses, and if you killed Reginald Kiner we'll get you, and your lawyer will get on TV when he escorts you past the cameras while we perp-walk your ass into a police car."

"I think Hamilton's in this up to his eyeballs," Hotchkiss said, "but with Masterson and Kiner dead there's no one left to implicate him."

"I just thought of another person who might be involved," Billie said.

"Who is that?"

"Veronica Masterson would have a motive to have her husband killed. She's going to be a very rich woman when Dale Masterson's will is probated. I've done some checking: There's a prenup but it only cut her out of the estate if there was a divorce. And there's scuttlebutt that she was having an affair with Mark Hamilton."

"Interesting, but there's no way she beat hubby to death," Hotchkiss said.

"No, but what if Mark and Veronica decide that Dale has to go. Then Larson is beaten to death, Beatty is framed, and he takes off. So they get the bright idea of getting Kiner to have someone create a copy-cat murder so they can blame Beatty for committing a revenge killing."

"Then Hamilton kills Kiner to get rid of the only person who knows he and Veronica were behind Dale's murder," Hotchkiss said.

"Or Veronica kills Kiner," Billie said.

"Now that is an interesting thought," Hotchkiss said.

Chapter 45

Amanda had a court appearance in Washington County in the afternoon and needed her car, so she drove to work at seven that morning. It was pitch-black when she left her garage and started to walk to her office. Suddenly the caws of hundreds of crows echoed through the canyon of high-rise buildings that lined the street. The eerie cacophony set her nerves on edge, and she looked around for the source of the unearthly sound.

Tall trees had been planted on both sides of Sixth Avenue. Amanda looked up and shuddered. Hundreds of crows perched on the highest tree limbs. The death-black birds radiated menace, and their call grated on her. They seemed to be waiting for the order to attack, like the predatory birds in the Hitchcock horror film. Amanda walked faster, and her heartbeat didn't slow down until she was in the lobby of the Stockman Building, with solid walls between her and the crows.

She gave one last look through the glass doors and noticed a woman standing across the street. She was wearing a business suit and had short black hair, and something about her looked familiar. It wasn't the suit or the haircut—it was her build! She had the same build as the heavyset blonde who had ridden up to her floor in the parking garage when Tom Beatty had been waiting for her. Amanda stared at the woman, but a bus drove by and blocked her view. When the bus had passed, the woman was nowhere to be seen. Amanda shook her head. It couldn't be the same woman. They were dressed differently and their hair color and styles were completely different. Amanda decided that she was still unnerved by the crows and that her fear was playing tricks with her imagination.

Amanda took the elevator to her floor and had just turned on her computer when Kate Ross burst into her office and dropped the morning paper on her desk.

"Have you seen this?" Kate asked, pointing at the headline.

Amanda swore as she read the lead article about Reginald Kiner's murder.

"When Tom told me he thought Reginald Kiner was involved in this mess, Kiner's name rang a bell but I couldn't remember where I'd heard it before. Then I remembered. You told me that Greg Nowicki used Carol White as an informant about ten years ago to bust a mid-level drug dealer."

"Kiner was Nowicki's partner! He knew Carol White!"

"Exactly. He knew Nowicki used White as an informant, so he could set up Tom by paying White to go to Nowicki with her bullshit story about Tom selling drugs."

"I just interviewed Neil Denton," Kate said. "He was IA when Kiner was with PPB. He was investigating Kiner."

"Why?"

Kate told her boss what she'd learned from Denton.

"Damn," Amanda said when Kate finished. "Kiner had to be involved in this. He might have been our best chance of clearing Tom and Brandon. Now he's dead."

Amanda sounded more dejected than Kate could ever remember.

"He's not our only chance," the investigator said. "We still have Hamilton."

"Yeah, but he can stonewall now that Kiner's dead and can't hurt him," Amanda said.

"He'll still be scared of what Tom can do to him."

Amanda let her chin sink to her chest and sighed. "Okay, let's see if we can bluff Hamilton."

A dangerous-looking man holding an automatic weapon signaled Amanda to stop as soon as she turned into the drive that led to Mark Hamilton's house. As the man approached the driver's window, he spoke into a radio.

"Can I help you?" the man asked.

"Yes, we'd like to talk to Mr. Hamilton."

"Is he expecting you?"

"No, but why don't you tell him that Amanda Jaffe and Kate Ross, friends of Tom Beatty, would like to chat."

The guard tensed when Amanda spoke Beatty's name. Then he backed away and talked into the radio so low that Amanda couldn't hear what he was saying. A short time later, he told Amanda to drive to the end of the road and park.

A fire-engine-red Porsche was positioned near the front door of Hamilton's house. While Amanda was parking, another guard walked up to her window.

"Please step out of the car," he commanded. "I've got to search you before you can go inside."

"No problem," Amanda said.

After the man did a professional pat-down the women were escorted into the house, where another bodyguard was waiting.

"Wow," Amanda thought, "something really shook up Hamilton."

She wondered if it was Kiner's murder, the fact that Tom Beatty was still at large, or both of the above.

Hamilton was waiting for them in his den, dressed in a warm-up suit and T-shirt. He was unshaven, his hair was in disarray, and he looked like a train had run over his face. Angela Forsythe, a Waspy, blonde beach girl with a UCLA law degree, was sitting next to him. Angela was a formidable defense attorney whom new DAs frequently underestimated because of her airhead-blond looks.

"Angela," Amanda said with a nod.

"Amanda," Angela answered.

"Are those your wheels parked by the front door?"

"You bet," Angela answered with a smile.

"Are you going to pay them off with the fee you get for representing Mr. Hamilton?"

Angela laughed. "I guess you didn't take the class in tact at charm school. But, yes, Mr. Hamilton has retained me. So, what can we do for you?"

Amanda stared directly at Hamilton, who wouldn't meet her eye.

"Kate and I have a confidential matter we'd like to discuss with your client that concerns a client of ours."

Angela started to speak, but Hamilton waved her off. Though it was early in the morning, he was holding a glass half filled with liquor. When he spoke, his speech was slurred, and Amanda deduced that this was not his first drink of the day.

"Why don't you wait outside," Hamilton told his lawyer. "I don't think we'll be long, and I can call you in if I think it's necessary."

"I don't know if that's such a good idea," Angela said.

"Well, I do. So please step out."

Angela colored, but she picked up her attaché case and left the room. While she was leaving, Amanda studied Hamilton's face.

"You don't look so good," she said.

"Your psycho client did this," Hamilton answered angrily, pointing to the stitches on his cheek and the tip of his ear.

"Is that why you have all the firepower guarding you?"

"What do you want?" Hamilton asked, ignoring Amanda's question.

"I'm sorry Mr. Beatty hurt you, but he did have some provocation. Murdering his friend Christine

Larson, then trying to frame him by putting her body in his bedroom . . . Well, anyone would be a tad upset if that happened to them."

"I had nothing to do with that," Hamilton insisted. "That's what I told him, but he still broke my nose and cut off part of my ear."

"Have you filed a complaint with the police?"

"That's none of your business."

"So you haven't told the authorities that Dale Masterson hired Reginald Kiner to murder Miss Larson?"

"That's not true. Anything I told Beatty I said to stop him from cutting me. I was scared to death, so I fed him what he wanted to hear to get him out of my house."

"You know Mr. Kiner was murdered last night, right?"

"The cops were already here. Did Beatty kill him?"

"I have no idea who shot Mr. Kiner, but if I were you I would worry if it was Mr. Beatty."

"What do you mean?" he asked, his voice panicky.

"With Kiner dead, you're the only person who can tell the police Mr. Beatty didn't kill Christine or your law partner."

"Why would I do that? I think the man's a lunatic who is perfectly capable of beating Christine and Dale to death."

"But you know he didn't, because you know Kiner and Masterson were involved."

"I know no such thing."

Amanda stood up. "If that's your position, I guess there's no reason for me to stay."

"Wait—do you know how to get in touch with Beatty? Can you assure him I had nothing to do with Christine Larson's murder or the attempt to frame him?"

"Mr. Hamilton, I have no idea where Tom Beatty is hiding and no way to get in touch with him, but—if I did—why would I tell him you're an innocent party?"

"Because he might kill me if you don't."

"You have all these bodyguards to protect you. I'm certain you'll be fine, especially if you're innocent."

"Get out."

"We'll go, but you should think about something: Once Tom's name is cleared, he won't have any reason to come after you."

Angela was waiting in the hall outside the den.

"He's all yours," Amanda said as they passed her on their way to the car.

"How come Angela drives a Porsche and you're driving a ten-year-old Volvo?" Kate asked as they drove away.

"I don't have self-esteem issues," Amanda said.

Kate smiled. Then she got serious. "If Hamilton doesn't crack, we're at a dead end."

"It looks that way," Amanda answered with a sigh.

The two women drove in silence for a while, both working mentally on a way to unknot the problem Kiner's murder had created.

"What do we know about our killer?" Amanda asked.

"He's got a connection with Kiner, but that could be for one of two reasons. If Kiner was arranging hits for money for Masterson and Hamilton, he has probably done the same thing for other people. And then there's his job, which involves dealing with dangerous people in trouble spots all over the world. So he could have been killed because of something he was doing that had no connection with our cases."

"What's possibility number two?" Amanda asked.

"If the person who killed Kiner was involved in Larson's and Masterson's murders and the attempts on Tom Beatty's life, Kiner was probably killed to keep him from talking."

"Mark Hamilton is the obvious suspect."

"It could also be someone else we don't know about."

Amanda swore. "I was starting to think I had a handle on this case. Now I have no idea what's going on."

Chapter 46

Moments after Billie Brewster rang Veronica Masterson's doorbell, a brown-skinned maid in a crisp white uniform opened the door. Billie flashed her badge and told her that they wanted to speak to the lady of the house. While they waited, Billie looked around the Masterson property. She spotted three gardeners. One was pruning hedges, one was mowing the lawn, and one was on his knees, working in a flower garden. Billie thought about the tiny cottage where she and Sherman had grown up. The lawn was a small brown patch overrun by weeds and surrounded by a rusted chain-link fence. If flowers ever grew in it, Billie had never seen them.

"Senorita Masterson is by the pool," the maid said when she returned. "This way, please."

Any evidence that the Masterson house had been a crime scene had disappeared, and there was a notable absence of the stench of death when they passed the den. The maid led the detectives through a massive living room and out a set of French windows that opened onto a wide flagstone patio. A narrow strip of lawn separated the patio from a large pool. Veronica Masterson was stretched out on a lounge chair, clothed—if you could call it that—in a skimpy, yellow string bikini that was unlike any widow's weeds Billie had ever seen. Veronica's eyes were hidden behind a pair of designer sunglasses.

"Good afternoon, Mrs. Masterson," Billie said.

"Have you caught Dale's killer?" Veronica asked without turning her head.

"Not yet, but we're getting close. That's why we're here. We have a few questions we'd like to ask you."

"Okay."

"You seem to be handling your grief well," Billie said.

"Life goes on," Veronica answered with a brief shrug. "Dale and I weren't married that long. I mean I miss him, you know, but . . ." She shrugged again.

"Yeah," Billie said. "I get it. So, we heard you made out pretty well."

Veronica turned her head toward Billie. "What's that supposed to mean?"

"The will—we heard you got this house and a lot of dough. Not a bad return for such a short investment."

"Why do you care?"

"When a person is murdered we always ask who had a motive," Billie said.

"Are you suggesting what I think you're suggesting? That I might have . . ."

She paused, her mouth agape, giving the impression that she was speechless. Then she laughed.

"Did you ever meet Dale? Do you know how much bigger than me he was? You try telling a jury that I beat him to death and they'll fall over laughing."

"Oh, we never thought for a moment that you could do the deed, but you or your boyfriend could have hired someone to do it for you."

"What boyfriend?" Veronica asked, and Billie thought she sounded nervous.

"There are rumors about you and Mark Hamilton. Are they true?"

"I don't like where this conversation is going. I think you should leave."

"One more question, then we will: Where were you between seven thirty and nine thirty last night?" Billie asked.

"Why? What happened last night?"

"The prime suspect in your husband's murder was shot to death," Billie said, staring hard at Veronica to catch her reaction.

"Who was he?"

"A man named Reginald Kiner. Ever heard of him?"

"No, and if you think I shot him . . ."

Before she could complete the sentence, a muscular, bare-chested man in a black swimsuit walked across the lawn. Billie put him in his mid-thirties. He had wavy black hair and clean features. In a TV movie he would be the club tennis pro who was screwing the rich widow. Billie wondered if life might be imitating art.

"Any problems, babe?" the man asked as he looked back and forth between the detectives.

"None whatsoever." Veronica smiled. "Derrick, can you tell these nice detectives where we were last night between seven thirty and nine thirty?"

Derrick blushed. "Where we were *exactly?*"

"No need to be shy. We're all adults," Veronica answered.

"Uh, in Veronica's bedroom."

"The whole time?" Billie asked, knowing what he'd answer but asking just the same.

Derrick nodded.

"Satisfied?" Veronica asked.

"For now," Billie answered. She started to leave, but halted and turned to Derrick.

"You aren't a tennis pro by any chance, are you?"

Derrick looked confused. "No, I'm an electrical engineer, why?"

"Just an idea I had," Billie said before she turned her back on the lovebirds ands led Hotchkiss back to their car.

Chapter 47

Amanda had the Sunday *New York Times* delivered to her condo. After breakfast, she would take a cup of coffee into her living room and curl up on the couch with the crossword puzzle. She liked the Sunday puzzle because it usually had a theme or a gimmick. Once you figured out the trick, you could fill in a lot of the words and the puzzle was easy to solve.

While Amanda was working on her puzzle, Mike was studying a variation of the Petroff Defense on a walnut chess table with beautiful inlaid squares he had brought over from his apartment. The Sunday puzzle was getting the best of Amanda and Mike's concentration was constantly being interrupted by swearing. Then Amanda barked out a victorious laugh.

"I assume you've finally figured out the big clue," he said.

"I'm so stupid," Amanda answered. "The title of the puzzle is 'Reverse Engineering.' You're supposed to fill in some of the words from right to left instead of left to right."

"Great. Now that you've got that solved, is there a possibility that I'll be able to work on my chess opening in peace and quiet?"

"Sorry," Amanda apologized meekly.

"I love you," Mike said with a big smile, "even if you're not too bright."

Amanda gave Mike the finger and started filling in some of the answers that had stumped her. She was working on the bottom right corner of the puzzle when she paused and stared into space. Then her mouth opened.

"You're right. I am an idiot," Amanda said.

Mike sighed and looked up. "What is it now?" he asked.

"This case—Kiner's murder and all the rest of it. I've been looking at it the wrong way, just like I looked at the puzzle."

Amanda pulled out her cell phone and walked into her home office so she wouldn't bother Mike. Then she speed-dialed Kate Ross.

"I've got two jobs for you," Amanda said when Kate answered the phone. "First, I want you to find every newspaper article, TV news story, and mention on the Internet about Tom Beatty's assault case."

"That should be easy," Kate said. "What's task number two?"

Amanda gave Kate a name. "I want a complete net worth: every bank account and investment account, real estate holdings, jewelry, art, cars, boats . . . everything. And I don't care how you get the information as long as you don't get caught."

"Can you tell me why I'm going to spend my day of rest working overtime while risking a stay in a federal penitentiary?"

"Yes, I can."

Amanda explained what she expected Kate to find and what they would do with the information if Kate's search panned out the way Amanda thought it would.

Chapter 48

Amanda walked into Jaffe, Katz, Lehane and Brindisi a little after seven on Monday morning. Before she went to her office she checked to see if Kate Ross was in. When she didn't find her in her office Amanda left a note for the receptionist to have Kate come to where she worked as soon as she walked in the door. Then she went to her office and tried to concentrate on a brief she was writing.

Kate knocked on Amanda's doorjamb at one-thirty. Amanda told her to come in and close the door.

"So?" she asked when Kate was seated.

"First, as far as I can tell, there were no stories about Tom's arrest or the fight at the Lookout, but that's not surprising. A bar fight usually isn't newsworthy unless someone dies."

"Okay, what about your other assignment?" Amanda asked.

"You were right. The problem is you won't be able to use anything I found because I broke several state and federal laws finding it."

"That's okay. I just wanted to know if I was right. Now we have to get Billie Brewster on board, because she can legally get ahold of the information we need to nail the person who murdered Reginald Kiner. All we have to do is point her in the right direction."

"These are the ground rules," Billie said when the three women were gathered in a booth at the back of Juniors Cafe. "One, this meeting never happened."

"That works for me," Amanda said.

"Two, we put all our cards on the table. No attorney-client bullshit."

"I'm bound by the attorney-client privilege, Billie; you know that. But I could speak hypothetically about things a client might have told me if I knew you wouldn't subpoena me to a grand jury."

Brewster shook her head. "I am so glad I didn't go to law school. You must have gotten an A plus in obfuscation and doublespeak."

Amanda cocked her head to one side, raised an eyebrow, and remained mute.

Billie sighed and said, "Okay, I'll let you play your games if it helps nail the person who's behind all these killings. So why don't you start."

"Here's what we think," Amanda said. "It all began with Masterson, Hamilton's attempt to land Global Mining as a client. The firm was in financial trouble. I'm pretty certain that Dale Masterson and Mark Hamilton worked on their books to make it look like their financial position was better than it was."

"Do you know if any of the other members of the firm were involved?" Billie asked.

"I have a source who told me that Dale Masterson and Mark Hamilton ran the law firm, and the rest of the partners were just along for the ride. You can probably get the partnership agreements and see if any other partners were in the inner circle."

"I'll do that. Go ahead."

"I'm positive that Christine Larson found out about the cooked books and threatened to spill the beans to the people at Global. Dale Masterson and/or Mark Hamilton panicked and got in touch with Reginald Kiner. It was probably Dale Masterson."

"What makes you think that?" Billie asked.

"Hamilton told someone who told me," Amanda said.

"Who is this confidant?"

"A little bird, and that's all I can say."

"Did this little bird cut off the tip of Mark Hamilton's ear?"

Amanda just stared at the detective. After a few seconds, Billie shook her head and told Amanda to continue.

"We believe that the firm used Kiner in the past to deal with situations like this," Amanda said.

"You mean to kill people?" Billie asked.

"Or something similar: threats, coercion. I don't have details about crimes unconnected with the current cases, but I am very certain that the men who were found in the car trunk went to Tom Beatty's house on the evening he was released from jail and tried to kill him. I am equally certain that Tom Beatty killed both men in self-defense and would be found not guilty if a jury knew all of the facts."

"What about the men we found at the campsite in Forest Park?" Billie asked.

Amanda flashed on the violence she'd witnessed in the park and had to take a deep breath to calm down. She was subdued when she answered the detective's question.

"I was there when that happened, Billie. Those men followed me to Tom's camp. They were going to torture me. Tom rescued me. He saved my life."

Billie lost her hard edge. "Why haven't you said something?"

"I didn't know if you'd find Tom's camp and the bodies." She looked down at the tabletop. "I couldn't get him in more trouble after he saved me."

"There's something else," Kate said. "Amanda realized that she must have been under surveillance, so she asked me to sweep her condo and her office and check her phones and her car. I found state-of-the-art, very expensive bugs in her office and home, taps on her phones, and a tracking device on her car—the type of equipment an outfit like RENCO could get their hands on."

"Interesting," Billie said. "What about Dale Masterson? Did your client kill him?"

"So you think Brandon is innocent?" Amanda asked.

"Since we're off the record, I can tell you that I have very serious doubts that Brandon Masterson killed his father."

"Why haven't you dismissed the charges?"

"I said that I had doubts. Alan isn't as open-minded as I am."

"If it helps, Brandon told me that his father was dead when he found him. He confessed to get a platform to spout his views about the environment and to tell the world what a shit his father was. Now he deeply regrets that lamebrain decision."

"You still didn't answer my question. Did Beatty kill Masterson?"

"He swears that he didn't. He was in Masterson's den but he says Masterson was dead when he found him. I'm pretty certain that was also Kiner's work."

"Did your boy pop Kiner?" Billie asked.

"No, but I'm pretty certain I know who did. Only I'll need your help to prove it. Kate talked to a retired PPB detective who was investigating Kiner when he was on the force. He said Kiner was a bad cop. Can you tell us anything more about him?"

"When Kiner's name started coming up I did get curious, and I talked to Greg Nowicki—Kiner was Greg's partner just before he left to work for RENCO. Nowicki didn't have anything good to say about him. Alan Hotchkiss knew him too. Alan told me that everyone thought Kiner was dirty. He was suspected of killing a drug dealer, stealing drug money he'd confiscated in other cases, and making a witness disappear, but they could never get enough evidence to go to a grand jury.

"And there's something else that could be important. Kiner was partnered with Nowicki when Carol White started informing for Greg. Greg says that Kiner knew her. So Masterson or Hamilton or both could have gotten Kiner to send men to murder Christine. Then Kiner could have paid White to go to Nowicki so he'd get a warrant for Tom's house. After that, all they had to do was lure Tom to the law office. That would give Kiner's men the time they needed to plant the body and the heroin in Tom's house."

"Have you checked on Mark Hamilton's whereabouts during the time Kiner was murdered?" Amanda asked.

"We're taking a hard look at Mr. Hamilton," Billie assured her. "He says he was at his office from seven thirty at night until his bodyguards got him two hours later. Most of the employees were gone by seven-thirty, and no one we talked to can say he was or wasn't there during the crucial times. We checked the law firm's security cameras and there are blind spots, so he could have left and come back."

"Do you have any other suspects?" Amanda asked.

"Veronica Masterson is going to be a very rich woman when the will is probated. She signed a prenup, but it cut her out of Dale's estate only if they divorced."

"Does she have an alibi for the time Dale was murdered?"

"She told us she was shopping all day, and we've talked to salesclerks who back up her story for some of the day, but there are some times she can't account for during which she would have been able to drive home, kill Masterson, and go back to shop. Two girlfriends cover her from five to seven thirty. They had dinner at the Westmont before she drove home."

"What about Kiner? Does she have an alibi for the time of his murder?" Kate asked.

Billie told them what Veronica's hunk had told her and Hotchkiss.

"Do you have any other suspects in Kiner's murder besides Veronica Masterson and Mark Hamilton?" Amanda asked.

"I thought you wanted to meet me so you could tell me whodunit," Billie said.

"All I have is a theory," Amanda answered. "What we need is hard evidence. And that's where you come in."

The women talked a little longer before driving off in their separate cars. Amanda was lost in thought during the return to Portland, but part of her brain had been on high alert ever since Kate had told her that she was being spied on.

On the way to Juniors she'd thought that a dark green Chevy had followed her into Washington. Then the car had taken the exit before the one that led to Juniors and she'd written off her suspicions as paranoia. Now, as she crossed the border into Oregon, she thought she saw the Chevy several cars behind her, but it was too far back for her to be certain. Before she drove to her condo, Amanda took several fast turns and circled through back streets until she was convinced that she had lost any tail that might be following her.

Chapter 49

Mike was watching a movie when Amanda got back to the apartment. She sat next to him on the sofa and tried to lose herself in the film, but her mind wandered as she tried to twist and turn the facts in the Masterson and Larson cases this way and that, with the same lack of success she'd always had when she tried to solve a Rubik's Cube or a Chinese box puzzle. She was pretty certain she knew who had killed Kiner, but she wasn't in a position to prove it until Billie found the hard evidence the case was lacking.

The movie ended, and Mike wanted to make love. Amanda was distracted, but she didn't want to disappoint him, and she hoped sex might take her mind off murder. It didn't. When Mike fell asleep, she was still wide awake, and what little sleep she got after that was fretful.

The next morning, Amanda crawled out of bed, more tired than she'd been when she went to sleep the night before. She had no appetite, so she ate a piece of toast and drank a cup of tea before heading to the gym in hopes that a vigorous workout would clear the cobwebs that were wrapped around her brain.

During the first ten laps Amanda's mind wandered to the questions posed by Reginald Kiner's murder, but she went all out in every set, and the harder she swam, the less energy she had for anything but survival. When she hauled herself out of the pool, she was thoroughly exhausted and it took everything she had left to shower and dress.

Amanda didn't have any court appearances or client conferences on her calendar, so she decided to carboload with a hearty pancake breakfast before going into the office. She was walking to her car, thinking how great it would be to polish off a stack of blueberry pancakes and a side of thick-sliced bacon drenched in maple syrup, when she saw a car racing toward her. She'd started to turn when she was tackled into a space between two cars. Before she could defend herself she heard a gunshot and a car window just above her head exploded, showering her with glass.

"Stay down," a voice shouted in her ear. Then the weight that had pressed her to the asphalt lifted.

Amanda rolled onto her side and saw a woman in a shooter's stance. The car sped out of sight and the woman straightened up, dropping the hand holding a .45 automatic to her side. Amanda struggled to her feet. The fabric at her knee was ripped and the knee was bleeding. Her elbow throbbed where it had smashed against the asphalt.

The woman turned. She was dressed in a warm-up suit and she had mid-length red hair, but she was definitely the same heavyset blonde from the parking garage, and Amanda was willing to bet she was also the woman with dark hair in the business suit who had been watching her on the morning she'd been unnerved by the crows.

"Are you okay?" the woman asked.

"What just happened?" Amanda asked.

"Someone tried to shoot you."

Amanda tried to process what she'd just been told. It was hard to believe, but the glass fragments that covered her and the ground around her were pretty good evidence that the woman was telling the truth. Until this moment Amanda had been in shock, but now she started to shake.

"Who are you?"

"Jenny Harwell," the woman answered. "But, many moons ago, I used to strip as Candy Delight."

"You're a stripper?!?" Amanda asked as her addled brain tried to fit this fact into what she'd just seen.

Harwell laughed. "*Ex*-stripper. Now I do this and that for Martin Breach. After you told him about the guys who tried to kill you in Forest Park, Marty asked me to keep an eye on you."

"Jesus," Amanda swore as she leaned against the trunk of a car for support.

"Yeah, well, you needed more than divine intervention to save your ass just now. Someone wanted you very dead."

"Did you see the driver?"

Harwell shook her head. "I was too busy getting you out of harm's way. By the time I got to my feet, all I could see was a blur through the car's rear window."

"Man or woman?" Amanda asked.

"I have no idea." Harwell shook her head. "You sure pissed somebody off."

"And I have an idea who," Amanda replied. "Have you noticed anyone following me since you've started being my shadow?"

"I thought a green Chevy followed you to Juniors last night. It turned off the exit before the cafe, but I spotted it parked down the road just before you left. It was hiding on a side street; that's why I didn't see it earlier. It followed you back to Portland and I tried to get a license number but the driver had caked mud on the plate. I went after the car when you went home. He must have spotted me, because he sped past your condo, then lost me later on."

"When you see Martin, tell him thanks."

Harwell smiled. "He really likes you, kid. That's why I moved so fast. He'd never have forgiven me if something happened to you. I'll keep watching, and I may even call in some backup now that I know this guy means business. But you better stay on your toes and carry your gun. Popping you was a desperation move, and someone that desperate is going to try again.

"Now go back inside the gym and call the cops. Then have someone patch up your knee. Oh, one more thing: I was never here."

Amanda returned to the athletic club lobby after calling 911 and Billie Brewster on her cell phone. She was in a small office placing a large bandage over the cut on her knee when Billie arrived. As Amanda limped down to the parking lot, she told Billie an edited version of the attempt on her life, one that did not include an ex-stripper. In Amanda's version, she dove between the cars just before the shot was fired, then leaped up in time to see the car with her assailant drive out of sight. A uniformed police officer had taped off the area around the car with the shattered window and was keeping onlookers away as they waited for the team from the crime lab to arrive.

"You think the shooter was in the same car that followed you from Juniors?" Billie asked as she took in the crime scene.

"I can't be certain because I never got a license number, but both cars were dull green and Chevys."

"That's not enough to go on."

"True, but I'd bet on it. And the attempt on my life is good news."

"How do you figure that?"

"I was the first one to get to Juniors last night. If the shooter was the same person who followed me last night, he would have seen you arrive. I think he tried to kill me because we've got him spooked. If he's figured out that someone has been looking into his finances, he must be scared to death."

"I'm relieved that you're so thrilled that someone tried to shoot you. If it was me, I'd be scared to death."

"Yes, there is that, isn't there," Amanda said, suddenly subdued. "Oh, and, Billie, I did some thinking before you got here, and I have a suggestion. When you find the bullet that was meant for me, why don't you compare it with the bullet that killed Reginald Kiner."

Chapter 50

"Gee, two times in one month," Martin Breach said with a grin. "You ain't looking for a job here, are you, Amanda?"

"I'm a lousy dancer, Martin. I'm here to thank you. Jenny Harwell saved my life."

Martin nodded. "She told me, but something else tells me that's not the only reason you're here."

"No, it isn't. I need another favor."

Breach leaned back and folded his hands across his stomach. "I'm listening."

"I need to talk to a member of the Desperados motorcycle gang, someone who's been a member for at least ten years and maybe longer."

"Is this for a case?"

Amanda nodded. "The one that almost got me killed just now."

Breach thought for a while, and Amanda waited. Finally the gangster sat up.

"There's a guy in the pen, he's in his sixties, doing hard time, only now I hear he's got cancer, some bad kind, the kind they can't cure. He might talk to you if he had the right kind of incentive and if what he told you wouldn't come back on another Desperado."

"The person I'm after isn't a gang member, and I might be able to arrange compassionate leave if he's terminal and helps solve my case."

"Yeah, compassion is nice, but you've been in your business a long time. This guy has a wife and kids."

Amanda sighed. "If things work out, Tom Beatty's case will be dismissed. He gave me a healthy retainer. Would twenty-five thousand be persuasive?"

"It might. I think ten would work, too."

"Only I can't pay him directly. It would look like I bribed him."

"Understood. I can take care of the arrangements. I'll have Arty talk to his wife. She can ask him to talk to you when she visits, and she can tell him why he should."

"Thanks, Martin."

"Don't mention it."

Amanda had a determined look on her face when she walked out of the stygian darkness of the Jungle Club into the glare of a blinding sun. As she headed to her car she pulled out the cell phone Tom Beatty had given her and told him they had to meet. Beatty told her where he would meet her, and Amanda drove to Tryon Creek Park, a large forested area with many hiking trails located behind the Lewis and Clark Law School. After parking in the lot, Amanda walked down one of the trails and waited for Tom to show up. She had been waiting for a half hour when her client materialized beside her. Amanda jumped.

"Sorry," Beatty said. He was wearing jeans and a sweatshirt with a hoodie that concealed his face. "I've been watching to make sure you weren't followed. Why are we meeting?"

"Judge Chang said he'd hold a bail hearing if you turned yourself in."

"I told you before that going into a jail would be a death sentence."

"I don't plan on you going to jail," Amanda said. Then she told him what she was going to do.

"What happens if this doesn't work?" Beatty asked.

"Then we have a problem."

"No, Amanda, *I* have a problem."

"But I'm pretty certain it will work, and I'll know for sure after I talk to a member of the Desperado motorcycle gang and I hear back from Billie Brewster. If they say what I think they will, I'll tell Larry Frederick, the DA in charge of your case, what I know. If I can get him on board, you'll walk. What do you say?"

"Your plan makes sense, but I won't turn myself in until you nail everything down."

Chapter 51

M ark Hamilton slumped in a chair on his patio and stared into space. Before him, a plate of congealed eggs and cold buttered toast sat uneaten next to a cup of tepid coffee. It was eight in the morning, two hours later than the time he was normally downtown at his desk, but he couldn't bring himself to go to his office anymore. It was too depressing. The once bustling three stories that housed the law firm of Masterson, Hamilton, Rickman and Thomas had become a ghost town. Global Mining, RENCO Oil, and many of the firm's other clients had taken their business elsewhere, several of the partners had left to form a new firm, and the associates and support staff were planning to abandon the sinking ship as soon as they found another job. Soon, Hamilton mused dejectedly, the newly arrived agents of the IRS, FBI, and other alphabet agencies of the state and federal government would outnumber the employees.

The door to the patio opened and Hamilton heard footsteps crossing the terrace, but he didn't have the energy to turn toward his guests. Moments later, Angela Forsythe and Larry Frederick blotted out the sun and cast his uneaten breakfast in shadow.

"Good morning, Mr. Hamilton," the prosecutor said.

"What's good about it?" Hamilton said.

"Possibly a lot, Mark," Angela answered.

"May we?" Frederick asked, indicating the chairs that ringed the circular table.

Hamilton nodded and the lawyers sat down.

"Angela and I have been discussing your future. You are at a crossroads in your life and you have to make a choice. Regardless of which path you choose, your future won't be great, but your decision will make it either terrible or bearable."

Hamilton raised his head and looked at Frederick. The prosecutor could see that he was talking to a beaten man.

"Cut to the chase," Hamilton said. "What do you want me to do and what's in it for me if I take your deal?"

"We're pretty sure we know who killed Reginald Kiner and what happened to Christine Larson and Dale Masterson, but we need someone to fill in the blanks. Right now I consider you an accomplice to several murders and attempted murders, as well as financial fraud. If you turn down our plea offer, I will try my hardest to send you to prison for life, and I may seek the death penalty. The Feds are also very interested in the creative accounting you used to lure Global Mining to hire your firm. They will pursue you in federal court. One or both of us will get you, and you will definitely spend the rest of your life in a cell."

"You don't have to scare me—I'm scared already. So what do you want me to do and what do I get if I cooperate?"

Angela leaned across the table. "Larry needs you to be totally honest about everything. He needs to know what you know about the murders of Christine Larson, Dale Masterson, and Reginald Kiner and the attempts to frame and kill Tom Beatty."

Hamilton sat up. He no longer looked tired. He did look terrified.

"Did you get Beatty?" He pointed at his face. "He did this to me. He's a maniac."

Frederick looked Hamilton in the eye. "One side benefit of cooperating with us will be that you will no longer have to be afraid of Tom Beatty. I can guarantee that."

Hamilton closed his eyes and took a deep breath. "Tell me what you want me to do," he said.

Chapter 52

Someone had tipped off the press, and the corridor in front of David Chang's courtroom was a mob scene. Kate Ross ran interference for Amanda and Tom Beatty as Amanda called out "No comment" over and over until they were inside. Larry Frederick and Alan Hotchkiss were sitting at the table closest to the jury box and Billie Brewster and Greg Nowicki were seated in the spectator row directly behind them. Amanda took her place at the other counsel table, with Kate on one side of her and Tom on the other. They had just gotten settled when the bailiff smacked the gavel and Judge Chang took his place on the dais.

"Good morning, Your Honor," Larry Frederick said. "We're here for a bail hearing in *State v. Beatty.*

I'm representing the State, and the defendant, Mr. Beatty, is present with his attorney, Amanda Jaffe."

"Very well," Judge Chang said. "Miss Jaffe, I revoked Mr. Beatty's bail at a previous hearing because he failed to comply with several of the conditions I set when I released him on bail after granting your motion to suppress. I also remember telling you I would reconsider the matter after your client was in custody. Is he in custody now?"

"No, Your Honor. I spoke with Mr. Frederick, and he promised that he would not have Mr. Beatty arrested until this hearing was concluded if Mr. Beatty voluntarily appeared in your court. I'm confident that you will let him remain on bail when you've heard why he did not comply with the conditions you set."

"Very well. Are you going to present evidence?"

"I am, and I'd like to start by calling Mr. Beatty to the stand."

Beatty was showered and shaved and dressed in a dark suit, white shirt, and conservative blue tie. As he took the oath, Amanda marveled at the contrast between the way he looked now and the Stone Age savage who had killed two men in Forest Park with a spear and a rock.

"Mr. Beatty, are you accused of killing Christine Larson?" Amanda asked.

"Yes."

"I'm going to ask you several questions and I'd like you to answer yes or no to them."

Amanda picked up a sheet of paper and began to read from it.

"To your knowledge, did you ever meet a woman named Carol White?"

"No."

"Did you ever sell heroin to Carol White or any other person?"

"No."

"Did you ever knowingly have heroin in your home?"

"No."

"Did you kill Christine Larson?"

"No."

"Your Honor, before Mr. Beatty came to court, we met with Mr. Frederick at the headquarters of the Oregon State Police, where Mr. Beatty waived his Fifth Amendment right to remain silent and was asked these questions and others by a polygrapher chosen by Mr. Frederick. With regard to the questions I just asked, the polygrapher concluded that Mr. Beatty was being truthful."

"Is that right, Mr. Frederick?" Judge Chang asked the district attorney.

"Yes, sir," the DA replied.

"Mr. Beatty," Amanda continued, "a condition of your release on bail was that you stay in contact with Parole and Probation. Did you do that?"

"No."

"Please tell Judge Chang why you violated this condition?"

Beatty turned to Judge Chang. "Miss Jaffe's investigator, Kate Ross, drove me home from the jail after you granted my release. I noticed a car following us. There was an armed man in my home. I decided to confront him and try to learn who had killed my friend, Christine Larson. While I was attempting to subdue this man, the person in the car came in. There was a fight, during which the man in the car shot his companion and I killed him while trying to disarm him."

There was a stir in the courtroom, and the judge rapped his gavel to silence it.

"Did you place these men in the trunk of their car and drive to a location far from your home?"

"Yes."

"Why didn't you call the police?"

"I should have, but the men struck me as well trained and I had no idea if they had backup. I fled because I was in fear for my life."

"Was that fear justified?"

"Yes. I established a camp in a remote section of Forest Park. You figured out where I was living and came to the camp. Two men followed you."

"Were they armed with guns and knives?"

"Yes."

"Did you hear these men threaten to torture me?" Amanda asked.

There were more gasps and whispers in the spectator section. This time Judge Chang did not rap his gavel, because his attention was riveted on the witness.

"I did."

"Did you rescue me?"

"Yes."

"In the course of rescuing me, did you kill my assailants?" Amanda asked.

"Yes."

"Your Honor," Amanda said, "both Mr. Beatty and I were polygraphed concerning the Forest Park incident and Mr. Beatty was polygraphed concerning the incident in his home. The polygrapher concluded that we were telling the truth about these incidents."

"This is very disturbing," Judge Chang said.

"I agree, Your Honor," Larry Frederick said.

"Why did you remain in hiding until I contacted you about turning yourself in?"

"I was concerned that there would be another attempt on my life if I was confined in jail."

"I have no more questions of Mr. Beatty," Amanda said.

"No questions," the DA said.

"Do you have any more witnesses?" the judge asked Amanda.

"I do. I call Mark Hamilton to the stand."

Larry Frederick stood up. "Mr. Hamilton has negotiated a plea with my office and the United States Attorney's Office. I'm handing a copy of the plea agreement to the court. As part of the plea deal, Mr. Hamilton is required to testify truthfully about any matter brought up in this hearing."

Moments later, a chastened Mark Hamilton was led into court from a holding area for prisoners and took the stand. He was dressed in a suit and looked like a lawyer, but his shoulders slumped, his eyes were downcast, and he avoided looking at Tom Beatty.

"Mr. Hamilton, what was the condition of your law firm earlier this year before Global Mining hired you?" Amanda asked after some preliminary questions.

"We were in bad shape and on the verge of bankruptcy."

"Did you do anything illegal to entice Global to hire your firm?"

"Yes. Dale Masterson and I created a false set of books that made our financial condition appear far better than it was."

"Did a junior partner, Christine Larson, threaten to tell Global what you had done?"

"She told Dale Masterson. I wasn't there. I learned about the threat later from Dale."

"What did you decide to do about Miss Larson?"

"I didn't decide anything. I was out of town on business. When Dale couldn't reach me, he panicked and called Reginald Kiner."

"Who was Mr. Kiner?"

"He was the head of security for RENCO Oil."

"Why did Mr. Masterson call him?"

Hamilton looked down, and his voice dropped low enough for the judge to tell him to speak up.

"Mr. Kiner had helped us when we needed him in the past."

"Did Mr. Kiner use intimidation and violence when he assisted you?"

"Not personally, but he used mercenaries to protect pipelines and oil fields overseas, and he would hire these men to do the . . . dirty work."

"Where was Mr. Kiner when Mr. Masterson called him?"

"He was in Iraq."

"What did Mr. Kiner do when Mr. Masterson told him about Miss Larson's threat to tell Global Mining about the doctored books?"

"Dale told me he promised to take care of Miss Larson."

"Meaning, he was going to kill her?"

"I . . . I didn't ask and Dale didn't say."

"Was part of Mr. Masterson's plan to have Mr. Beatty framed for Miss Larson's murder?"

"I learned that after Miss Larson was killed and Mr. Beatty was arrested."

"Will you tell the judge whether Mr. Beatty had anything to do with Christine Larson's murder?"

"No, Your Honor, he's completely innocent. He was set up."

"Thank you. Now let's turn to Dale Masterson. Who killed him?"

"I don't know for sure, but Dale was panicky after he learned that Carol White had been murdered and Beatty was on the loose. We met with Kiner, and he made several comments to me when Dale was out of the room that led me to believe he was worried that Dale would panic and go to the police. Kiner may have sent more of his men to kill Dale and make it look identical to Christine's murder so everyone would think Beatty killed him, but I'm just guessing."

"One more question: Who killed Reginald Kiner?"

"I have no idea. It wasn't me."

"No further questions, Your Honor," Amanda said.

"I have no questions of the witness," Larry Frederick said.

Mark Hamilton left the stand and two deputies took him away.

"Any more witnesses, Miss Jaffe?" the judge asked.

"We call Greg Nowicki to the stand."

Nowicki looked confused, and he whispered something to the DA. Frederick whispered back. Moments later, Nowicki took the oath.

"Detective Nowicki," Amanda asked, "did the case against Mr. Beatty start when you entered his home pursuant to a search warrant and found the dead body of Christine Larson in Mr. Beatty's bedroom and heroin in his house?"

"Yes."

"Why were you able to get a search warrant for Mr. Beatty's home?

"Carol White, an informant, contacted me and said she'd purchased heroin from Mr. Beatty on several occasions and had made one purchase outside his house after he confided that he had more heroin in his home."

"And she said she'd read that he was arrested for an assault at the Lookout tavern?"

"Yes."

"I had my investigator look for stories about the fight at the Lookout. Will you take my word for it if I tell you that the fight was so unimportant that there was no mention of it on the Internet, in any newspaper, or on any television news program?"

"Okay, if you say so."

"We know that Miss White lied about buying heroin from Mr. Beatty, don't we?"

"Yes."

"And there is a strong possibility that she never met him. Tom Beatty swore to that and passed a polygraph."

"Okay."

"If Carol White never met Tom Beatty and the incident at the tavern was not reported in the media, someone must have told her about him."

"It looks that way."

"Would you agree that the blood spatter patterns indicate that Miss Larson was probably killed elsewhere and her body was placed in Mr. Beatty's bedroom after he was lured away from his home?"

"I think that's a reasonable conclusion."

"And Mr. Beatty's fingerprints were not found on the heroin you discovered in his house?"

"Yes."

"Would you agree that there is also a lot of evidence that supports Mr. Beatty's contention that he was set up?"

"I'm beginning to think that is what happened," Nowicki answered.

"But this whole chain of events began when Miss White approached you?"

"Yes."

"Can you agree that the person who developed this plot to frame Mr. Beatty must have known that you would trust Carol White?"

"Yes."

"Miss Larson was killed approximately twenty-four hours before your search. When did Miss White come to you?"

"Earlier on the day of the search."

"So within hours of Miss Larson's murder?"

"I guess so."

"So the killer had to know how to get in touch with Miss White on a moment's notice?"

"Uh, yes. That sounds right."

"You knew Reginald Kiner, the head of security at RENCO Oil who was murdered a few days ago, didn't you?"

"He was my partner about ten years ago before he went private."

"We have information that Mr. Kiner sent the mercenaries who killed Christine Larson and tried to kill Mr. Beatty. Did Mr. Kiner know Carol White?"

"Yes. We used her as an informant shortly before he left the force."

"Mr. Kiner had been working in the private sector for a decade, dealing with security in places like Nigeria and the Middle East and was far removed from low-level junkies, wasn't he?"

"I really don't know what contact Mr. Kiner did or didn't have with Carol White. We hadn't spoken for years."

"Is that because Mr. Kiner left the police under a cloud?"

"Yes."

"He was investigated by Internal Affairs for several crimes ranging from theft to murder, was he not?"

"Yes, he was a bad cop."

"But he was never prosecuted, was he?"

"No."

"And that's because evidence that would have implicated him in crimes disappeared."

"I didn't know that."

"Getting back to Miss White, you kept in touch with her over the years, didn't you?"

"I didn't keep in touch. She would call me."

"Well, you knew she'd been arrested shortly before she approached you?"

"Uh, yes. I knew that."

Amanda carried a police report to the witness. "This is an account of Miss White's most recent arrest. It has her address, doesn't it?"

Nowicki studied the report, then agreed.

"Since there were no reports about the fight at the Lookout in the media, Miss White could only have learned about the fight if she was told about it by someone who knew about the fight, needed an informant for the search warrant affidavit, and knew where Miss White was staying. Someone like you."

"Kiner could have tracked her down and sent her to me."

"Actually, he couldn't. You just heard Mr. Hamilton testify that Mr. Kiner was in Iraq when Dale Masterson asked him to solve his problem with Miss Larson, didn't you?"

"Yes."

"Would you agree that it would have been highly unlikely that Mr. Kiner, who hadn't dealt with Miss White in ten years and was in Iraq on the day Miss White allegedly came to you, could have found a junkie in Portland on a moment's notice?"

Nowicki glared at Amanda. "What are you suggesting?"

"I'm suggesting that you and Reginald Kiner were always friends. You were the person who made the evidence that could convict him disappear when he was a detective. And you continued to work with him over the years.

"I'm suggesting that Kiner called you after Dale Masterson hired him to kill Christine Larson and frame Mr. Beatty. You had to act fast. You knew that Tom Beatty worked with Christine Larson and had been arrested for assault, because Detective Hotchkiss complained to you when he was investigating Mr. Beatty's assault case. You came up with the scheme to put Christine's body in Mr. Beatty's house and falsify a search warrant affidavit that would let the police find her. But you needed someone who would be your informant, and you knew Carol White would do anything for the money to buy heroin.

"I'm also suggesting that you learned that the murder investigation was starting to focus on Mr. Kiner and you decided to get rid of the only person who could connect you to the murder of Christine Larson."

"This is ridiculous," Nowicki said. His face had reddened with anger and a pulse beat in his temple.

"Can you explain how, on a detective's salary, you are able to afford a condo and a sailboat in the Cayman Islands and bank accounts totaling three million dollars?"

"What . . . what are you talking about?"

"We can present the judge with details about your secret accounts and the condo you own that was bought by a shell company. It took us only a very short time to find that evidence. What would we find with more time?"

Nowicki didn't answer. He just glared at Amanda.

"You've been crooked since your early days riding with the Desperados motorcycle gang. You were supposed to be gathering evidence against the gang, but you were taking money from them to smuggle heroin and kill people, weren't you?"

Nowicki stood up. "I've had enough of this." He turned toward Larry Frederick. "Why aren't you objecting to this bullshit?"

The DA stared hard at the witness. "I'm not objecting because I've seen the evidence of your secret accounts and talked to a member of the motorcycle gang who supports all of Miss Jaffe's allegations. But you can prove her wrong by taking a lie detector test like Mr. Beatty did."

"Your Honor, I move to have all the charges against Mr. Beatty dismissed," Larry Frederick said as soon as the deputies escorted a handcuffed Greg Nowicki out of the courtroom.

"Motion granted," Judge Chang said with a smile.

Tom Beatty sagged in his chair, too stunned to speak.

"Are you okay?" Amanda asked.

"Yeah, it's just . . . Even after you told me what to expect, I didn't believe it would happen."

Amanda smiled. "Well, it did, and you're a free man."

Beatty turned to her. "I don't know how to thank you," he said.

"I think saving my life is thanks enough."

Tom blushed.

Kate and Amanda stood up. "I'm going out to face the lions," Amanda said. "The reporters will have questions for you, too. I advise you to just say you're happy the system worked, then get away as fast as you can, and have Kate drive you home."

"That sounds good."

Tom turned and saw Brittney Vandervelden standing in front of the gate in the low fence that divided the spectators from those having business before the court. She smiled at him.

"I'm so glad you're free," she said. "I never once thought you'd hurt Christine."

"Thanks," Tom answered, suddenly shy.

"Look, this is awkward and I'll understand if you don't want to, but you've got to eat and I'd like to treat you to a meal that's not jail food or something you foraged in Forest Park."

Tom broke into a grin. Then he laughed. "That sounds great, but I don't think I'd make good company tonight. I'm too wound up, and I haven't had a good night's sleep for some time. But I'd love a rain check."

"Sure," Brittney said. "Here's my number. And don't call me at Masterson, Hamilton, because I'm no longer there."

Chapter 53

The day all charges against Tom Beatty were dropped, Larry Frederick also dismissed Brandon Masterson's case. Brandon had recovered sufficiently to be sent back to jail, but Larry Frederick had asked for an order from Judge Chastain that kept Brandon out of danger in the hospital after Amanda and Billie Brewster told Frederick about the evidence against Greg Nowicki.

Amanda was waiting for Brandon in the corridor outside the secure wing. He was clean-shaven, his hair was combed, his face was relatively unmarked, he was dressed in a set of clothes his mother had bought for him, and the bravado that had been present during their early meetings was missing. Brandon stopped when he saw Amanda. Then he crossed the distance between them and embraced her.

"Thank you for everything," he said. "I was such an asshole."

Amanda laughed and gently disengaged. "You certainly were, but I was pretty certain you were innocent so I didn't let that bother me."

Brandon followed Amanda into the elevator. When the doors opened, Sarah Hartmann was waiting for them. Brandon didn't see her right away. He walked out of the elevator, stopped in mid-stride, and stared at his mother. Sarah stared back, nervous, unsure how her son would react to seeing her.

Brandon rushed over and embraced her. "Forgive me, Mom," he said.

Sarah squeezed him to her. "There's nothing to forgive. You're my son and I love you."

Amanda stayed out of the way and watched the reunion with a huge smile on her face.

"If it isn't the amazing Miss Jaffe," Mike Greene said with a wide smile when Amanda let herself into the condo. "Two death cases dismissed in one day. That's got to be a record."

"You heard?" Amanda said, blushing.

"It's the only thing anyone was talking about at the courthouse. Congratulations."

"It has been a very good day. Tom and Brandon are free men, and Brandon and his mother have reconciled."

"And you earned two fat retainers without having to go to trial."

"True, but no amount of money could match the feeling of seeing Tom walk out of the courtroom, Brandon hugging his mother, and Greg Nowicki being marched out of court in handcuffs."

"What's Tom Beatty going to do?"

Amanda's smile vanished. "That's a good question. He's got PTSD, and he killed four men and tortured another. That's been a huge burden for him to bear, even if everything he did was justified. He's talking with Dr. Fisher, and I hope that helps. I told him I would help him get another job when he's ready."

"You hungry?" Mike asked.

"Always," Amanda replied.

"I thought you might like to celebrate, so I made a reservation at your favorite restaurant."

Amanda placed her palm on Mike's cheek. "Why are you so nice to me?"

"I guess I'm just a sucker for bossy, irritating women."

Dinner was fabulous, the sex that night was great, and it should have been one of the best days of her life. But it wasn't, because Amanda woke up in the middle of the night and remembered where she'd first seen Brandon Masterson before she'd met him in the county jail.

Chapter 54

Amanda swam hard. She swam until each stroke was agony and each breath an ordeal. She swam so hard that all she could think about was survival. She pushed herself to the limit so she wouldn't have to think about her talk with Dr. William Cameron, a former state medical examiner. And swimming hard worked until she stopped. Then she couldn't stop thinking about what Dr. Cameron had said.

Amanda was desperate to talk to someone about her suspicions. While she showered and dressed she ran down the short list of people in whom she could confide. She couldn't use Mike as a sounding board because he would have a duty to reopen Brandon's case if she told him what she suspected. Kate was too involved in Brandon's case to be objective. What she needed was someone who knew very little about *State v. Masterson* and could look at it with fresh eyes. And there was one obvious choice.

When Amanda's mother had died in childbirth, Frank Jaffe was totally unprepared to raise a little girl, but he'd put every ounce of energy he had into the job. Amanda's mother, Samantha, had done all the cooking while they were married, so one thing Frank had to learn was how to cook so he could feed himself and his daughter. For most of her life, Amanda accepted the fact that her dad was a barely adequate chef. Nevertheless, since returning to Portland, she'd made a point of having dinner with her father several times each month. Starting roughly a year ago, Frank, inspired by the Food Channel, had started experimenting. As luck would have it, her father had invited her to his house this evening for an Italian dinner.

Amanda parked in the driveway of her father's green, steep-roofed Eastlake Victorian a little after six thirty. Dinner was almost ready, so she sipped a glass of Chianti while Frank finished setting the table. Frank's minestrone soup and spaghetti carbonara were excellent, and Amanda stuck to small talk while she ate. The night was balmy, so they carried their coffee onto the back porch.

"I've got a serious problem, Dad," Amanda said.

"What's wrong?"

"I think Brandon Masterson may have killed his father."

"What?"

Amanda spent the next half hour telling Frank about the evidence in Dale Masterson's homicide. Then she told him what was worrying her.

"When I read the autopsy report in Dale Masterson's case, I was struck by the similarity between the way he was beaten to death and the way Christine Larson was murdered. I was so struck by the similarities that I reread Christine's autopsy report. I thought that Masterson's killer must have had access to Christine's autopsy report. Then I remembered there was another opportunity for the killer to have learned about Christine's injuries. Larry Frederick showed Judge Chang a graphic picture of Christine's face and read pertinent parts of the autopsy when he argued against bail."

"What does that have to do with Brandon Masterson?"

"The first time I met Brandon, I thought I'd seen him before. Last night, I remembered where. There was a heavily bearded man sitting in the back of the courtroom during the hearing on the motions in Tom's case. I didn't give any thought to him while I was in court, but yesterday I realized that Brandon was that man. After seeing Christine's photograph and hearing the details of her beating, he would have known how to duplicate the injuries Christine suffered when he killed his father."

"Why would he come to the motions?"

"The only theory I've been able to come up with is that Christine's murder gave him the idea of killing his father and setting it up to look like Christine's killer was responsible."

"That's a stretch."

"I know, but Brandon is smart. Maybe way smarter than anyone thinks."

"Didn't you tell me that everyone concluded that Brandon would never be able to defeat his father in a fight?" Frank said.

"That's true, if the fight was fair. I scanned Masterson's autopsy report and his crime scene pictures to Bill Cameron. There was a depressed skull fracture on the back of Masterson's head. It was just above the knot of bone above his neck. Bill told me that a person like Brandon could knock out someone like his father if he struck a hard enough blow to the back of the head with a blunt object. The victim would be stunned or unconscious, and the killer would have no trouble finishing him off."

"But what about the blood spatter and lack of marks on Brandon's knuckles?" Frank asked.

"If Brandon planned the murder, he would bring gloves. Let's say he lets himself in with his key. Maybe he catches his father by surprise. Maybe they argue and Dale turns his back on Brandon. Brandon strikes and Dale goes down. Brandon uses a blunt object—a paperweight, a rock. Then he beats Dale to death with his gloved hands. There's some blood spatter, so Brandon covers it with more of his father's blood to make it look like it was smeared on and not the result of spatter. Then he kneels in the blood, knowing a forensic expert will conclude that the blood on his pants was inconsistent with spatter from a wound."

"That's an awful lot of maybes. And why would he confess?"

"The den looks out at the front of the house. What if he saw Veronica driving up and knew she'd see him. So he confesses, but does his crazy act and hopes he'll get a lawyer smart enough to have a forensic expert examine the blood if the state's expert doesn't draw the conclusion that the blood on his clothes wasn't the result of blood that spattered while his father was being beaten to death.

"His plan was perfect. As soon as anyone heard that Dale had been beaten to death, they looked at Brandon with his string-bean arms and sunken chest and thought, 'No way could he have defeated an ex-wrestler and football player in a fight.'"

"I don't know, Amanda. Brandon's plan hinged on Tom's being set free."

"Which became a real possibility when he heard the judge's reaction to my motion to suppress."

Frank thought over what Amanda had said. Then he looked at his daughter.

"What are you going to do with this? He's your client. You can't tell the cops."

"I know. And it is just guesswork. But no one else confessed to killing Dale. Veronica Masterson and Mark Hamilton deny they had anything to do with it. Hamilton told Larry Frederick that he thought Reginald Kiner was behind the murder, but he also said that Kiner never told him he was involved. Tom was polygraphed, and we know he's innocent."

"Let's assume you're right," Frank said. "Dale Masterson arranged to have Christine killed and he and Mark Hamilton used Kiner to commit other crimes. Dale was a very bad person."

"So you're saying I should forget this?"

Frank shrugged. "You really don't have a choice. But you can look at it this way: Is letting Brandon walk any different from winning an acquittal for a client you know is guilty?"

Amanda was quiet. Then she sighed. "You're right. I have to let this go. It's just . . ."

"You *think* you want to know if you're right, but you really don't. Let it drop. Enjoy your victories. Tom is innocent and he's free and Brandon . . ." Frank shrugged. "If he's guilty, justice was served when Masterson died. If he's innocent, you saved him. You're never going to know unless you confront Brandon, and you have no reason—other than curiosity—to do that. Let sleeping dogs lie. There's no reason to wake them up."

Frank and Amanda dropped the subject and turned the conversation to more pleasant topics. Amanda put up a good front, but she brooded all the way home. In the end, she decided that her father was right. Dale Masterson was evil and Brandon might very well be innocent. And he was her client, so the only purpose that would be served by pursuing this question would be the satisfaction of her curiosity.

After a fitful night, Amanda drove to the office and worked on a brief that she was filing in an assault case. Then she read the investigative reports in a rape case. Later that day a new client hired her and provided her with another distraction. By the time she went home, she had forgotten about Brandon Masterson—almost.

Acknowledgments

I could not have written *Violent Crimes* without help from experts in several fields. Attorney Ryan Scott told me about the Shadow Challenge; Kip Nordstrom solved my plant problem by explaining about pokeweed; my son-in-law, Andy Rome, taught me how to commit financial fraud; and once again Dr. Karen Gunson told me how to kill someone. Thanks also to Dr. Thomas Dodson, Brianna Borders and Jay W. Pscheidt, and my excellent assistant, Robin Haggard.

I can't say enough about my fabulous agents, Jean Naggar and Jennifer Weltz, or the crew at HarperCollins: Claire Wachtel and Caroline Upcher, my excellent editors, and the intrepid Heather Drucker and Hannah Wood.

I appreciate the support of my daughter, Ami Margolin Rome; my son, Daniel, and his new bride, Amanda; and my special friend Melanie Nelson.

And, finally, I thank my muse, Doreen, who is always in my heart.

About the Author

Phillip Margolin has written nineteen novels, many of them *New York Times* bestsellers, including his latest novels *Woman with a Gun, Worthy Brown's Daughter, Sleight of Hand,* and the Washington trilogy. Each displays a unique, compelling insider's view of criminal behavior, which comes from his long background as a criminal defense attorney who has handled thirty murder cases. Winner of the Distinguished Northwest Writer Award, he lives in Portland, Oregon.

www.phillipmargolin.com